Heather Rose is the author of two novels – *White Heart* and *The Butterfly Man*. *The Butterfly Man* won the 2006 Davitt Award for the Crime Fiction Novel of the Year. It was shortlisted for the Nita B Kibble Award and was longlisted for the 2007 IMPAC Awards in Ireland. In 2006 it was voted by Tasmanians as their favourite book. Heather was born in Tasmania and continues to live and write on her island home. She is married with three children and is the 2006 recipient of the Eleanor Dark Fellowship.

www.heatherrose.com.au

Also by Heather Rose

White Heart

THE
BUTTERFLY
MAN

HEATHER ROSE

First published 2005 by University of Queensland Press
PO Box 6042, St Lucia, Queensland 4067 Australia
Reprinted 2005
This edition, 2007

www.uqp.uq.edu.au

Typeset in 11.5/14.5 pt Bembo by Post Pre-press Group, Brisbane
Printed in Australia by McPherson's Printing Group

Australian Government

This project has been assisted by the Commonwealth
Government through the Australia Council, its arts
funding and advisory body.

Queensland Government
Arts Queensland

Sponsored by the Queensland Office of Arts and
Cultural Development

Cataloguing-in-Publication Data
National Library of Australia

Rose, Heather, 1964-.
The butterfly man.

I. Title.

A 823.3

ISBN 978 0 7022 3636 5.

For Rowan

*A single event can awaken within us
a stranger totally unknown to us.*

Antoine de Saint-Exupéry

IT WAS THE WINTER WHEN I was so ill that I first heard him. Sweet and terrible stories he told me as I lay sedated. I did not believe him, yet still I listened, for the sound of his lovely voice turned the hours gently. And then, one morning, when I was well again, I opened the newspaper at the breakfast table and found his picture. A photograph taken when he was a young man. It was an article about his disappearance more than twenty years before. His name was Lord Lucan.

I knew it was impossible. But a chill ran up my spine.

I cannot say if somewhere in the strange frequencies that travel between life and death there is a shred of truth to what you will read here. I only know that when I asked him if he was that man, he sighed and said his time was short. Over the following months he peeled away the layers of story he had clothed himself in. What he told me, you will read here. If any of it is true, it is pure coincidence. But what is true is that it is only a fortunate few of us who make peace with those we have loved, and those we have hurt, before we die.

Heather Rose

SEPTEMBER 1995

I WAKE TO FIND A young woman sitting beside me. She is Asian. Japanese. Chinese. I don't know.

'Hello, Henry,' she says, smiling and taking my hand.

I try to take it back but it doesn't respond.

'It's Suki, Henry.'

She has on a red shirt. She has earrings too. Large Indian earrings that move and sparkle.

'I'm sorry, young lady, but I am not Henry.'

She rubs the back of my hand. Mine looks awfully white and I can't feel anything.

I can see she is determined to be kind.

'Where the dash am I?' I ask, too tired to put much bite into it.

'You're at home in your own bed, Henry,' the girl says.

Rain splatters across the windows. Trails of water bead and run down the glass. I don't know the view. The sea is far away beyond a sort of forest. Clearly not England. Over the trees half a rainbow appears. The rain is easing. My mouth is parched and my lips are cracked. My teeth feel big in my mouth.

She helps me swallow a few mouthfuls of water from a glass. It's awkward and she has to hold my head.

She says, 'Now, how about a gin?'

'Splendid,' I reply. 'Pink.'

She leans forward and whispers, 'You've got ten minutes to go.'

She speaks like a colonial. Must be an Australian. Don't know any Australians.

We both observe the bedside clock. 10:50.

'Ah, yes,' I concur. Never before eleven.

The girl reaches over and adjusts the buttons on the clock. She turns it to face me. Now it says 11:03.

'My how time flies . . . ' she remarks. 'You're a funny one. Lili says you never drank gin before.'

'Before what?' I ask but she is already gone. I can hear her footsteps descending a wooden stairway. I close my eyes. There is a bad ache coming on in my head. Can't seem to keep my eyes open.

The girl has returned with a glass. Not crystal but a decent tumbler nevertheless. She has mixed it well. The colour of the drink matches the two tablets she shows me.

'You're an addict,' she says.

'What's this?' I ask.

'For the pain in your head, Henry. Here, I brought you a straw.'

She puts the tablets on my tongue. She slips the straw into my mouth. I gulp and swallow the tablets down. They are big and I nearly empty the tumbler.

4

The sharp rush of effervescence is exquisite. It's Gilbey's. I'd bet my life on it. A black and white bird glides past very close to the glass. Its feathers are shining as if it has been cleaned and buffed.

'Magpie,' says Suki.

I look about me. There is a cream couch in the window. On my left there is a large wooden cabinet and a chest of drawers. A blue blanket is folded at the foot of the bed over a pale cream bedspread. I glimpse a bathroom beyond the bedroom.

'Where am I?' I say to the girl.

'You're home, Henry,' she says. 'In your own bed. We moved you back upstairs last weekend, just the way you wanted.'

'Do I know you?' I ask.

'Of course you do. I'm Suki,' she says. 'Lili's daughter.'

'Lili?' I say.

'Lili,' she says.

'Who is Lili?'

'You live here with her.'

She goes over and opens the cupboard. She fiddles with a stereo. Chopin fills the room. Nocturne in E. A rush of pictures come with it. A woman with the same black hair as this girl, tomatoes growing on vines in a garden, a yacht half built, this girl getting out of a car with a child by her side, a small boy with curly hair.

Something about the image gives me a sudden sharp pain.

'What the dash is this?' I ask.

'I'm sorry. You usually love me to play it. Don't be upset.'

'Where am I? What on earth has happened to me?'

She walks over to me, leans forward and kisses me on the forehead. I can see she's upset, but she smiles at me.

'You had a bad turn last week. A stroke actually. You haven't been yourself since then.'

I gaze at her dark eyes. She reminds me of someone but I can't think whom.

'Close your eyes. Just rest . . . '

And I do. Whatever she has given me has taken all the kick out of me. I feel it numbing the pain in my head. My arms, my legs, everything seems to be so heavy. I close my eyes and fall slowly like a feather on the wind.

I wake. A bedside clock says 3:17.

'Hello?' I call. My voice sounds feeble.

There are footsteps coming up a stairway. It's a girl in a red shirt. She's Asian. Japanese. Chinese. I don't know.

She says, 'Hello, Henry' as if we are old friends. She looks very young. Twenty-one. She offers me water through a straw.

'Damn thirsty all right,' I say. 'Most kind.'

'Did you sleep well?' she asks.

'I'm afraid I've forgotten your name,' I say.

'Suki.'

'Really? That's most unusual. Are your parents foreign?'

'Yes, Henry.'

We both stare out the window at the river far below.

'It's come out lovely now,' she says. 'You'd never know it. Not a cloud in the sky all the way down to the peninsula.

Could almost see the surfers on Roaring Beach.'

'Roaring Beach?'

'Yes. That one way away in the distance.' She turns and smiles at me, rearranges the tissues beside the bed and refills the water from a glass jug.

'Lili will be back soon, Henry. She's just picking up Charlie from school.'

'I'm not Henry, you know.'

'What makes you say that?' the girl asks, straightening the covers and refolding a blue blanket at the foot of the bed.

I do not reply.

'Pretty certain you are Henry Kennedy. You certainly look like him and you're in his bed, just like you were yesterday and the day before that. You've lived up here for years. You even built this house.'

'That's preposterous! Don't know the first thing about building. Look at these hands!'

I try to lift them up but only the left one will move. To my surprise it has calluses and scars and looks like a labourer's hand, not my hand at all.

'It's okay,' says Suki. 'You've just forgotten. Sort of forgotten who you are.'

'Oh no, I know exactly who I am, I can assure you. Been a frightful bother having to keep it to myself.'

She sits down beside me.

'What's your name, young lady?'

'Suki.'

'Suki. It's a nice name once you get used to it.'

7

A wave of nausea runs through me and I go suddenly cold. A terrible ache is coming on in my head.

She reaches for a packet on the bedside table and flips two pink tablets from it.

'What's this then, eh?'

'Morphine.'

'I say, do I need it?'

'Yes, you do. Doctor's orders.' And then she adds, 'You're very ill, Henry. You had a stroke nine days ago.'

'Ah.'

She holds the cup and straw while I swallow down the tablets. I rest back into the pillows. She begins straightening the covers.

'Is anyone about, Suki?'

'No, we're quite alone.'

'They're still looking for me. They'll never stop.'

She smiles and sighs. 'You're very safe, Henry.'

'Never safe. Must be vigilant. Never safe.'

'Come then, who's really lying in your bed? Not a criminal, I hope? Royalty? I always wanted to know someone famous.'

'Not famous, dear girl. Notorious.'

'Really? You? Why?'

'I am Lord Lucan,' I whisper desperately. 'Yes, Lord Lucan! All these years. But they've never found me. You must make sure they don't, Suki. You must keep watch.'

'I will, Henry.'

Pulling a tissue from a box the girl wipes my mouth. She does not appear surprised.

'Have I told you this before, young lady?'

'Yes, Henry,' she says, leaning forward and smoothing the sheet across me, 'you tell me every afternoon.'

ONE YEAR EARLIER

LILI WOULD BE ON HER way home. Soon her car would appear up the driveway. When she walked towards the house the afternoon light would catch her face, her beautiful oriental face. Normally I'd meet her at the door. I'd kiss her and help her carry her books and papers to the kitchen. We'd make tea or open a bottle of wine. If the weather was fine we often went out on the balcony. Sometimes we walked in the garden and our words blew away in the wind. And sometimes we made love and rose late in the evening to share supper and catch the nine o'clock news.

But today I had become dangerous. I wanted to confess. I wanted to tell her stories I had held back all these years. I wanted at last to be free of the seventh of November, 1974. And I wanted to be free of today. As if in the telling there would be a cure. But I also knew nothing I could say now would change this last fate of fates. Nothing I could give, or do, or say. I had played all my cards. My kitty was empty. And the die had rolled against me.

It would hurt her. All of it. I knew that. I must pull myself together. She must not be harmed. Not Lili. She must be kept safe.

I took a mark upon the horizon and watched the clouds moving east. A dour wind forged on the slopes above us had buffeted the house since early morning. Sharp moments of bright blue sky fractured the heavy, grey cloudbanks. Jack Frost weather. The wattles were in bloom, festooned in iridescent yellow, their fragile blossoms scattering in bright yellow gusts when the wind broke through the forest, rushing across the paddock, over the forested hills and down to the river.

I'd thought lately of chopping the wattles down. They were a fire hazard, and a falling hazard, too, being so close to the house. Jimmy said they only lasted thirty years or so – nature's way of making sure the baby gum trees got shade to grow strong. Lili liked the wattles. Said they were pretty. Loved the carpet they made after a wind. I imagined Lili naked on the carpet of yellow petals. Lili in my arms with the wind blowing down upon us and one of the trees falling and crushing us. Not Lee-Lee but Lily. The fragrant Lili Birch.

I remembered suddenly I was meant to make dinner. Lili was bringing someone home. She'd rung at lunchtime, before my appointment. Who had she said? Someone, a woman from work? Yes, perhaps that was it. I'd call and see if we could cancel. Tell her I'd had a hard day, forgot all about picking up provisions for dinner.

Walking back though the open balcony doors to the phone, I dialled Lili's mobile.

'Hello,' she said, almost before it rang.

'You driving?' I asked.

'Almost home.'

I heard her car beyond in the trees as it came up the road.

'Are we still having people over for tea?'

'They're right here with me,' said Lili.

'Ah.'

'What's the matter?'

'Nothing. So who is it?'

'It's a surprise, Henry. It's a big surprise.'

She did not sound excited. It was hard to tell sometimes with Lili. Her television presenter's voice remained evenly modulated, expressive yet impenetrable.

I opened the door and walked out onto the stone entrance-way. I watched as her Karmann Ghia came into the clearing. Instead of parking in the garage, she pulled up on the gravel. She opened the door and stepped out, pulling her bag behind her. A young woman emerged from the other side of the car. The wind blew her hair across her face.

Lili said, 'Henry, I'd like you to meet my daughter Suki.'

She looked at me and I looked at her and I'd never known Lili was a mother. My Lili.

Suki closed the door, looked around and then back at me and said, 'Howdy.'

Dark-haired like Lili, wearing a thin shirt and a suntan, her face a curious version of her mother's. Behind her the seat was pushed forward and out leapt a small boy with a head full of sandy curls. He looked like neither Suki nor Lili.

He grinned and said, 'Cool, smell that.'

Lili walked around the back of the car and stood beside him.

'Charlie, this is Henry. Henry, this is my grandson Charlie.'

I breathed. I walked. I shook hands. I kissed Lili's cheek. I put her car away. I carried bags. I maintained eye contact. I tried to forget the appointment I'd had this afternoon and the letter in my pocket.

'It helps,' Geraldine Holloway had said as she handed me the envelope, 'to have it all written down later, when you're thinking about it, trying to explain to loved ones.'

It was unlikely I was going to forget the words of Doctor Geraldine Holloway, FRACP. 'It's not good, Henry,' she had said. 'I'm very sorry.'

'They got me, then,' I said.

'Who?' she asked. The CT scans on the light box illuminated the outline of my head and the grey shape of brain. Within the brain were dark marks revealing the swelling where tumours no larger than small coins were growing and multiplying.

'The odds,' I said. 'The odds that I would get to be an old man.'

I took off my jacket and hung it by the back door, leaving the letter in my pocket. It would have to wait. The diversion caused by these sudden visitors would allow me time to gather my thoughts. I had been unsettled, unnerved. I had considered some kind of confession. It was the rash sort of thing only an amateur would do. Fool! Henry Kennedy did not confess. Henry Kennedy had nothing to confess. It was Lili Birch who had a confession to make.

Suki had her mother's straight-backed walk. She had Lil's ivory skin and the same sleek, Asian hair, but she was taller than Lili, much taller. She wore hipster pants swirled with green and blue. Lili's delicate features were larger and more awkward on her face. She had silver rings on her fingers and in her bellybutton. Her heels were cracked above the flat leather of her sandals. She watched me like an animal afraid of being taken in an unexpected attack. Her son, if indeed he was her son, was nothing like her. The boy never stopped chattering like an overexcited monkey. And where had he got that hair?

Lili and I prepared dinner. She had brought home a roast of beef. My favourite.

'I clean forgot to go to the shop,' I said.

'I had a feeling you'd forget.'

'Would I normally be forgetting?'

Lili looked at me. 'Are you okay?'

'Well, would I?'

'Well, lately, yes. Sometimes.'

I wanted to say, What? What have I not remembered? I wanted to shake her and say, What have you noticed? And what about yourself? Did you just forget to tell me you had a child? And a grandchild? Did it just slip your mind?

Instead I said very calmly, 'Where have you been hiding her all these years?'

Lili glanced briefly at Suki. The girl was on the rug in front of the open fire. She could not have heard my question but she looked over at us.

'It's a long story,' Lili said.

'And the boy's father? Do I get to meet him too?'

Lili shook her head. 'Later,' she whispered in a hushed tone.

She did not say, I'm sorry Henry. I lied to you. She did not say, My whole life is a sham. She continued cutting carrots into thin strips. I continued peeling potatoes. We stood there together at the bench with the sky a wash of pink out over the trees. The wind had dropped as it often did at dusk, as if half-time had been called. The evening songs of birds rang in the gum trees behind us. Suki sat hunched up on the hearth as though she was freezing, and I wanted to tell her to put on a pullover if she was cold. The boy had been run a bath and we could hear him in there talking to himself, the door a little ajar. Every now and again he made a loud explosion as if the bathroom was a battle zone. Clearly he was making a terrible mess. If it had been my child, I would have put a stop to it. But these women did nothing. They did not speak, at least not to each other.

This is not my life, I thought. I did not have children in my house. They did not walk barefoot from the bathroom, leaving wet footprints, with nothing but a towel wrapped around them. They did not stand on the rug by my fire. I did not have young women in my house I didn't know. I knew everyone in my life and there was nothing I did not know about them. Until now, I thought. How had I not suspected? I have been a fool, I thought.

We watched the news as the meal cooked and the boy hummed. Now dressed in pyjamas, he produced a box of Lego, which he proceeded to spread across the floor.

'I think there's a dragon on this mountain,' he said.

Lili looked at him and said, 'We live on the dragon's back, but Henry doesn't mind. He's strong enough for the dragon.'

She gave me a small smile, testing my friendliness. I smiled back. She was not my enemy. She was the woman I loved. She had betrayed my trust, but I did not hate her. It was the first time I had considered hating Lili. But I couldn't. I looked at her and I wanted nothing more than to be alone with her and lay my head in her hands.

'Does it breathe fire?' the boy asked.

'Not since 1967,' I replied.

'What happened?' the boy asked.

'The whole mountain caught fire. I wasn't here then but people still talk about it.'

Suki said, 'He's a metal dragon.'

'A what?' I asked.

'It's his birth sign. I think it's why he's mad about them.'

Lili looked at Suki. I wondered if it was surprise she was trying to suppress. Or curiosity.

We sat down to eat. I carved the beef. It was dark and crusted on the outside and pink at its core, seeping fine, red juice.

'I'm a vegetarian,' said Suki. 'So's Charlie.'

I looked at her. The smell had been wafting from the kitchen for an hour or more. She'd not said a word.

'I like meat,' said Charlie, eyeing the roast.

Lili looked at Suki.

'I guess he can have it if he wants,' sighed Suki. 'He probably won't eat it anyway.'

'Well, there's vegetables and salad,' said Lili.

'Can someone cut it up for me?' asked Charlie.

Suki took her knife and fork and cut the boy's meal into small squares. She wiped the knife carefully on her napkin before returning it to the side of her plate.

'Is there tomato sauce?' asked Charlie.

'No,' said Suki.

'There's some in the fridge,' said Lili.

'He doesn't need it,' said Suki.

'I'll get it,' said Lili, standing up.

'That bath is really big,' said Charlie. His hair was a mass of unruly ringlets. 'Can I have another one tomorrow? Is this a new house? It smells like a new house.'

'Yes, we just finished building it,' I said.

'Henry built it himself,' Lili said as she returned with the sauce. 'That's what he does. He builds houses. And other things too. There's a boat out the back he's building as well.'

'I'm scared of boats,' said Charlie.

'We had a rough crossing,' Suki said. 'He'd never been on one before.'

'That's a ship,' I said, 'not a boat, lad. Ships are nothing like boats.'

'They both go on the water,' Charlie said.

I wanted to slap him like a mosquito. He was so happy. So talkative. But it would set Lili at ease if I befriended the boy. And that would help me. His mother would be a harder case.

Suki said nothing. She picked at her meal, moving salad around her plate. Cutting a roast potato into tiny pieces. Charlie popped a cherry tomato into his mouth. It burst as he bit it and squirted across the table.

The boy dissolved into peals of laughter.

'It went off like a water pistol,' he said. He looked at his mother who was staring at the arc of green seeds and juice on the tablecloth.

'Sorry,' she said.

'No harm,' I replied, dismissing the incident with a wave of my hand. 'So Suki, you've not seen your mother for quite some time?'

'Please, let's not start this now,' said Lili. 'It's dinnertime.'

'No,' Suki said.

Lili said, 'She ran away.'

Suki was still staring at the tablecloth and then she lifted her head and stared right at me.

'She didn't tell you, did she? Fifteen wasn't I, Mum? The first time. Fifteen?'

Lili shook her head.

Suki said, 'Well, here I am.'

She didn't look at Lili. She had her chin up as if daring her mother to say anything.

'Where have you been?' I asked.

'Up the coast. Spent some time in Darwin, too, didn't we Charlie?'

How old was she? Maybe twenty? Twenty-two? I don't know. Girls looked younger every year at my age. Anyway it was all wrong because Lil was only forty-two and the boy must be five.

I wanted to say, Your mother hasn't mentioned you. Not once in three years. And I can see why. But instead I said, 'And Charlie's dad? Will he be joining you?' She wore no wedding ring. I had no reason to suppose she was married.

'Hardly,' said Suki.

Charlie looked at her and said nothing.

Lili was cutting her meat in bite-size proportions.

Was I the only one wanting answers? How long would Suki be here? What were her plans? Where was Charlie's father?

Lili said, 'I thought, Henry, that they could have . . .' She indicated the bedroom at the end of the hall.

'Aye, of course.'

Suki's shoulders dropped a little. The girl was as tense as her mother.

Lili said, 'Our bathroom is upstairs.'

I went for broke. 'Maybe we should be drinking champagne,' I said. 'I mean, really it's a celebration. A family reunion. I think there's a bottle in the fridge.'

Champagne wasn't normally my drink. I'd been given some by a client a few weeks earlier. Opening the fridge I plucked the bottle from the shelf and held it up like a trophy.

'So how did you two find each other again?' I asked as I

peeled back the foil, worked the cork, slowly feeling the pressure, easing it up.

'I saw her on TV one night. Thought I'd call,' said Suki.

Why now? I wanted to ask. Why now and why did you have to come today?

The cork ejected and it sounded like a gun going off. I imagined Suki dead on the floor. Bullet wound to the temple.

The froth rose up and spilled over the neck of the bottle. I scooped three glasses from the shelf and half filled them. I grabbed a tumbler for Charlie and poured a smidgen. Taking the glasses to the table I said to him, 'There laddie, 'tis not every day you get the finest grandmother in the world.'

Lili was watching me and I saw in the way she moved her mouth that she didn't know whether to laugh or cry.

'Why now, Lil?' I asked, as we prepared for bed.

She slid between the sheets and pulled the covers up over us. I held out my arm and she moved close, resting her face upon my chest.

'I don't know,' she whispered. 'She was just there at work. I didn't know what to do. So I thought I'd bring them home . . .'

'And the boy? Did you know?'

'I had wondered.'

'Are you sure . . . I mean he hardly looks . . ?'

'I'm sure. You only have to see him laugh . . . but it's a surprise to see him so fair. As if there's hardly any Vietnamese in him at all.'

20

She paused, and then said, 'You know, I thought I'd never see her again. And somehow it was easier after a while to pretend I'd never had a daughter.'

I lay back and stared at the strip of moonlight between the curtains. She turned onto her side away from me and I put my arms about her. She held one of my hands and rubbed the skin between my thumb and finger.

'It's been seven years.'

'You should have told me. I would have liked to know.'

'I'm a grandmother,' she said. 'She's all grown up and I hardly recognise her.'

She sighed and rubbed her nose with my hand. 'I've been so . . . secretive. I thought if I could pretend she didn't exist it would stop hurting. And it did. It was so easy somehow once I'd started.' She sighed and reached her hand behind her to caress my cheek. 'I saw her standing in the lobby at work today and it all came back. This awful guilt.'

I held her close and slowly I caressed her arms, her belly, and I grew hard. She said nothing but dropped her hand and slid my cock against her, rubbing me back and forth as she grew wet and then pushed herself against me and gasped. She was a mother. She had birthed a child and I had not known. Her body had revealed none of her secrets. I wanted to tear her then, to bloody her, scar her, so I knew I had made my mark. That somewhere I registered on her flesh. I remembered the words of Doctor Geraldine Holloway. Six months if you're lucky, Henry. I saw Suki and her breasts through her shirt and her tight floral pants and I wanted to screw Lili so hard that whatever happened she would never forget me. Never pretend I had not been in her life. I wanted this day and all its confusion rubbed away. But I was tired and my head ached and I came quickly, too quickly.

'It's okay,' Lil said. 'We're both tired.'

'It's all new to me, Lil.'

'I know.'

'I'll get used to it,' I said.

In the morning I said, 'Lil,' and it sounded gentle enough. 'There's something . . .'

'I can't say,' she said. 'Maybe a week. Could you bear a week?'

'Fine, they can stay, but I need to talk to you.'

'Not now. I'm running late. Tonight?'

She kissed me and slipped from the bed. It was not a conversation I wanted to force upon her. It needed its own time and place.

After she was done in the bathroom, I showered. I soaped, rinsed. I held my face to the showerhead and the water pulsed against my eyelids. Slowly I turned the water up, little by little, harder and harder. Then I killed the heat and only the mountain rush of pure cold bombarded me. I stood in its force counting down from ten, compelling myself to breathe. Forcing myself not to utter a sound.

Rituals reassured me. Leave no trace, that was what had

saved me again and again. I had made a friend of the unknown but I prepared myself each day. Suppressing the urge to speak or shout or make any motion that might surprise or shock or give too much away. Compressing the highs and lows of life into a steady stream of evenness that had me appear a man of measure and restraint.

After my shower I shaved. The blade running over stubble and the unchanging white line of scar tissue the length of my right cheek. I placed my feet into slippers, a lingering vestige of Englishness. I combed back my hair. The tarnished silver that matched my whiskers. I inspected my hands looking for new splinters which had risen to the surface. Noted the ingrained dust in the quicks and lines, the healing cuts, the contours and ridges of old wounds. I trimmed my nails, folding the debris into tissue paper and deposited it in the swing-top bin beside the shower.

When I emerged into the kitchen, Lili had made coffee but she was collecting her keys.

'I'll finish early,' she said. 'They're still sleeping.'

I held her to me and wished I'd told her last night. Or this morning.

Lili reached up and stroked my face with her hand. 'You look so tired. Bad dreams again?'

'I don't remember.'

'I don't like you looking so pale,' she said. 'Weren't you going to see Nick Powell?'

'Aye.'

'Monday, please. Make an appointment. You're not yourself.'

And then she looked embarrassed, as if struck by the ridiculousness of that after yesterday's events.

She kissed me briefly but tenderly and said, 'I'm sorry Henry. I should have told you before.' Then she kissed me again and was out the door.

I heard her cross to the garage. The engine started up and the car reversed and pulled away. I walked outside and watched her disappear between the trees.

She had lied to me and I never even suspected. Suddenly she was unknown. Unpredictable. I had slipped of late. I saw that. I had let myself get comfortable. I was guilty of that most dangerous of human traits. Assumption. I had assumed I was safe. That life was as it seemed.

I didn't want to push Lil away. Once I would hardly have got through the morning without needing to hear her voice. After three years nothing had changed. She was still the only woman I'd ever really loved.

DISCARDED SKINS

As I WENT BACK INTO the house I saw the shoes. The boy's red runners beside my work boots at the back door. How easy it was, when all was said and done, to find myself back twenty years. Small shoes and children's socks. Three pairs of socks.

And there was that other pair of shoes. The neat black shoes draped in red hair. Sandra Rivett's feet beside her pretty face. As if she was a contortionist, Sandra Rivett, dead but still warm. Dead in my kitchen with her shoes still on.

I stood in the silence of the house which housed now a mother and a child I did not know, and watched a sharp finger of light descend upon South Arm illuminating the distant stretch of white sand as if epiphanies were possible to retiree, dog or early morning jogger. And then the light was gone. God's moment faded as fast as it had come and the entire limb of land receded back into greyness. For one rare moment, there was not a single boat upon the great expanse of river below, no vessel dragging south or north, leaving, coming home.

The day would be without rain. A restless day of cloud shadow and sudden chill breeze which would blow ash about in the fireplace. I suspected we'd had the last of the snow.

Weather. It was the erratic metronome by which we lived our lives on this island. It was the beginning of almost every conversation. Spring was here at last and the mountain had come alive with water. Creeks rose and overflowed onto paths and gardens. Every walking track was wet underfoot. Toadstools pushed up in any warm spot. Fungi sprouted on tree trunks. Higher up, the snowfall from last night would be dissolving on the mountain's pinnacle. At any moment, the thick, green stalks in the garden would erupt with snowdrops. Soon yellow and white daffodils would bloom in the front paddock.

I was drawn from my thoughts by the sound of the boy coming out of the guestroom, sounding for all the world like a Boeing 747.

'Morning there,' I said.

'We're on the top of a mountain.'

'Almost.'

Charlie said, 'Do you have pancakes?'

'That depends.'

'I love pancakes, I could eat twenty-seven-hundred pancakes.'

'Can ye cook?' I asked.

'No, I'm too little. Are there koalas here?'

'No.'

'Tigers?'

26

'No.'

'Lions?'

'No.'

He looked disgruntled.

I reached into the cupboard for cornflakes, sugar. In the fridge I grabbed milk. I put a bowl and spoon on the table in front of him. I heard him pour the cereal as I found bread for toast. Then I heard, 'Whoops. Too much milk.'

I turned to see a small eruption of cereal overflowing from the bowl and running onto the floor.

'Mum never lets me do it myself,' he said.

'Lord Almighty, I can see why. Stay right there; dinna move a muscle,' I said, my temper flaring.

I picked up the bowl and laid down a tea towel. Under the table, on my hands and knees, I saw his naked feet sticking out of his pyjamas, dangling at least a year or two's growth above the floor. My anger dissolved quick as it came. Something in the bare ankles and the blue stripes of the pyjamas took it right out of me without me having to push it down.

I wiped the floor then got back up slowly. He was looking at me and looking away. His hair was all sticking up at the back from where his head had rested on the pillow. His hands were working at the spoon as if he'd bend it if he could.

I looked at the clock. 8:10. It was Saturday but I'd promised to meet Stan in the office at nine. It was a maximum twenty minutes from kitchen to desk.

I said, 'Are you up to a few pancakes then?' I picked up the phone and rang Stan, perfecting a nasty cough as he answered.

'Bug got you too?' he asked.

'Aye. Seems like it.'

'It's a tough one. Echinacea's what you need. And garlic. You don't want to get worse.'

'I think, Stan, a wee dram will do the trick just as well.'

He laughed. 'It's your body. So what's going to happen this afternoon? You going to make it down?'

In the upheaval of yesterday, I had clean forgotten about today.

'There's not much point,' I said. 'The Eagles will win.'

'Negativity has no place in my day.'

'You've no chance.'

'Ah, God is on our side, mate. And Brownless is back.'

Stan was a Cats supporter and today was the day they were going to win the Australian Rules Grand Final with the unassailable help of the football god Garry Ablett.

'Hey, what about the Howroyds?' continued Stan. Stan had a voice that sounded either ebullient or crestfallen, which were his two moods. He was transparent as an open window.

'I can speak to them Monday.'

'Nah, we can't. She'll have made a sponge cake. I could go see them, I suppose. What time was it?'

'Eleven. And the sponge is always good.'

'Bugger. I have to pick up the beers. Sharon's got people coming at twelve. Oh well, no avoiding it. Where're the plans?'

'On my desk.'

'Hang on while I look.'

He put me on hold and I watched the boy put his hands up

to his eye to make a telescope and stare about the room, taking in the exposed beams and skylights, the long view out to the river.

The day was bright and sunny but I knew outside it was cold enough for several layers and a jacket. It was one of the things I was proud of with the house. It was warm. I'd been living on the land for years before building. I knew how cold it got. So I'd insulated every inch of the house, put in under-floor heating and double-glazing and it was warm as toast. People here had no idea how to build for the conditions, but this house was proof that you could cocoon yourself even through the harshest winters.

Stan came back on the line.

'It's a pigsty in here and I can't find it.'

'The blue folder. Bottom in-tray.'

'No. Yeah. Got it.'

'Enjoy the cake. And tell them it's going to cost another $1000. Tell them the price went up on the stone and there's nothing I can do about it.'

'Henry.'

'Just do it, they'll pay. And good luck for the game.'

'You're a rogue and I won't. Okay, see ya. We are going to lick their feathery arses.'

We'd been in business together eleven years come December, Stan Campbell and I. He was the architect, I was his project manager. Stan had a kind of integrity that was hard to ignore.

He never broke the law, did not, to my knowledge, cheat on his wife, didn't drink to excess, and was always there in a fix. I knew he'd call me later and tell me the Howroyds were fine and it was all signed off. His girls would have decorated the balcony in blue and white streamers. Half the street he lived in would come over to watch the game. That's how it was. Stan had that sort of life. Except Stan's spinal cord had been partially severed in a car accident a few years back. He could get about on crutches, but mostly he was confined to a wheelchair. It had given us a unique relationship. We were essential to each other, though Stan did not understand that quite the way I did.

'Charlie,' I said, putting down the phone, 'you are the perfect excuse to avoid the client.' And the Grand Final, I thought.

It wasn't that I didn't like the game. It was the crowds I didn't like. Even loungeroom crowds. Crowds were not safe places. And a crowd combined with distraction was always tricky. People got worked up, they yelled and cheered and all their pretence at civility dropped away. The bare mask of them showed through. I did not have that luxury. For a while, after I came here, I'd go and hit a round at the golf course. But people started inviting me for drinks at the club, wanting me to go on trips up north to play other clubs. I quit going. I missed it. But then I missed a lot of things.

I had worked hard to be the man I'd created. I had not become Henry Kennedy by the coercion of a wife, nor the desires of a parent. I had not become him to cure an addiction to alcohol or sex. I was not forged by hard labour, prison sentence, nor political service. I was carved from the school of survival. I had shed the past to become, I liked to think, something new.

Occasionally memories rose up in me and snagged me; the face of a child in the street; yet another article in the newspaper; a car following me; a man glancing across at me in a café. At first these things disarmed me; the bright fear of discovery, the passing taste of regret, a tremor of panic. But as the years slipped by, and I was still safe, I chose to remember little else but my life as Henry Kennedy here on this island. Builder, neighbour, partner, friend.

I remembered Ranson, the detective assigned to the case, crowing in *The Times* that he had Lucan's passport. Did he not have any idea how easy a passport is to come by when you have friends with the right connections?

I had been a month short of forty. Newspaper photos show an unremarkable face, perhaps distinguished but a little bland. I was six foot one inch tall, with dark swept-back hair, dark eyes and a square chin, a pale English complexion. But it was the moustache that said it all. The moustache belonged to the dilettante, the gambler, the vapid and arrogant fool I had become. I had frittered away my early inheritance over the baize of the backgammon board, at chemin de fer, poker, bridge.

After Sandra Rivett died, people thought I'd drowned in the Channel. But no. I took flight like a confused migrating bird seeking not warm weather but a suitable place to hide. One by one my connections slipped away. It was better to pretend I was really dead, and they were certainly as good as dead to me.

By the time I settled here, even I was surprised at the old photos of me that appeared from time to time in the press, on television shows. 'Could it have been me?' I'd ask the man who looked back at me from the mirror. 'C'thart 've bin I?' I'd ask in my new Scottish brogue.

It is a lovely thing the Scottish tongue. A masterstroke, I thought, for a story such as mine. It lacked the unreliability of character inherent in the Irish accent. It had a solid, rigorous honesty that never failed to put people at their ease, and yet it had romance too. Like all good lies, my Scottish story was not so very far from the truth. As a young man I spent a good deal of time hunting grouse and rabbits in the Highlands. I was never a student of any merit, but the accent had been surprisingly easy to acquire. Sometimes I forgot I had ever sounded any different. And as the years went by the burr had softened and the Australian accent filtered in. I now saved the extremes of the Scottish tongue for dramatic effect or to underline a story.

Yes, I was a liar. I stole from the past to make a life in the future. Scotland Yard had not found me. Such things are always possible for a price. The world had been kept at bay by disguise, by false paperwork, by friends in the right places. My dental records had been destroyed, my medical history removed from my old military headquarters.

These past few years, life had been easier than I could ever have imagined. I had become the man I hoped I could be. I lived among people who knew the best of me, and who, through some strange and wondrous generosity, accepted me and even, dare I say, loved me, as I was.

Yet all that was slipping away from me. Disappearing like clouds on a time-lapse camera. For so many years I had viewed the exterior world as the enemy. The place from which my downfall would come. I had never considered a silent enemy might grow inside me. A thief that could steal all I had worked so hard to achieve.

There are times life comes to bear upon us in unimaginable ways. We have no prior warning. No chance to make other plans. No chance to wind back time when the moment is upon us and we have acted not for better but for the worse. I remember the scent of evil. I have never forgotten the grimness of death.

I wanted to fight those growths in my brain and win. But I knew it was over, the game. All I could do was rage at the unfairness of it, but even that seemed ridiculous given my circumstances.

Within minutes there was egg white on the bench, flour on the floor, and Charlie, on a stool, drizzling mixture onto the griddle with the precision of a beginner cook. It used to be Lili's favourite thing – pancakes, bacon and maple syrup with fresh strawberries. I'd heard her say to people that she moved in with me because of my pancakes.

'You're a natural.'

'I'm not a natural,' said Charlie. 'I'm only five.'

'You're still a natural.'

'What's a natural?'

'Someone who's good at something the first time they do it.'

He was quiet, eyes intent upon the bubbles appearing on the pale surface of the batter.

'They need turning now,' I said.

He watched as I did it. 'Can I?'

'That one.'

'Why do you sound funny?'

'Well, I was born a long way from here. A place called Scotland. That's the way, just slide the spatula straight under.'

'Why?' he asked.

'Well, because my mother and father lived there.'

'Are they dead?'

'Aye.'

'Ooops,' he said pulling the pancake half over itself.

'It's fine. Now that one.'

'Did they die a long time ago?'

'My mother died when I was ten. My father when I was grown up.'

'My mum said her mum and dad were dead. But they aren't. Her mum is Lili.'

Standing there on the chair beside me at the stove, his eyes looked into mine.

'Are dead people really alive? Are they alive only we can't see them?'

'No, laddie. Once you're dead you're generally good and gone.'

'My father was eaten by a crocodile.'

'Was he now?'

'He was,' he said.

'Where?'

'In the North.'

'How old were you?'

'Three.'

'A crocodile . . .'

'He didn't get his sword out soon enough.'

'And I guess it was bigger than him.'

'Not bigger,' he said. 'Longer.'

'I'm sorry, Charlie, about your dad.'

'It wasn't your fault.'

Suki appeared as I was clearing the table. She was wearing the same clothes as yesterday. I searched her face for clues about Lili while she took in what Charlie and I had been doing. I knew my kindness to the boy might do two things. She'd be wary I had ulterior motives. Sexual motives. Women worried about that these days. And likely she'd be disarmed by the cook in the kitchen routine. Couldn't tell yet if she'd like it or not. As for me, I was keen to know if the crocodile story was true, but I'd bide my time.

Charlie said, 'I made pancakes and we saved some for you.'

I was on my second coffee and I poured one for her but she said, 'I don't drink it.'

'Neither should I. In fact I'm turning over a new leaf right now,' I said, pouring the rest down the sink. I watched the blackness of it against the stainless steel then said, 'Look, tea's in there, cereal's in the pantry, fruit's in the bowl and there's a stack of pancakes in the oven.'

'You're being nice.' She picked up an apple and polished it against her patterned shirt, her breasts moving as she rubbed. She bit into it, leaning against the bench, and pulled Charlie against her.

'It's because it's Saturday. I'm a right arsehole the rest of the week.'

She didn't laugh. Just like her mother.

Charlie said, 'Have you got any videos?'

'None that'd interest you, lad. But there's a grand mountain out there we can climb if you like.'

'Right now?'

'Ask your mother.'

'I thought you had to work,' she said.

'No, I called in sick.'

'Why?'

'Och, I could do with a day off.'

'Maybe you didn't want strangers in your house nosing about.'

'Maybe,' I said, smiling.

'Are we going?' asked Charlie.

'I don't mind,' she shrugged at the boy. 'I don't suppose he's a paedophile.'

'Ah, thank you for the vote of confidence,' I said.

'So,' she said, looking away out the window, 'how long have you and Lili been together?'

'Three years.'

'When did you come out to Australia?'

'1979.'

'What were you running away from?'

'Not everyone is running away, Suki.'

'So is your family still there?'

'Aye. Some of them.'

'The wife and kids?'

I shrugged and laughed, 'No, Suki. I've never been married and I have no children. So what made you run away?'

And because I had been so forthcoming I knew she would find it harder to avoid talking.

'Just seemed like a good idea.'

'And you couldn't go home again . . . after Charlie . . .'

'Nuh. No way.'

'So why now?'

'Dunno. Just figured it was time.'

'C'mon,' I said, 'if you're only eating an apple, let's all go for a walk.'

She yawned. 'I'll pass.'

'Does the lad have a jacket?' I asked her.

'I'll be fine,' said Charlie.

'You'll need one,' I said.

Suki went and returned with a soft green jacket for the boy. It looked brand-new. Like she'd been planning this trip.

'Good camouflage,' I commented.

'What's camel flush?' Charlie asked as we headed for the door.

'Cheers,' I said to Suki.

She was already heading back towards the bedroom.

It felt awkward leaving the house with her in it. But she would find nothing if she went looking. There were no locked wooden boxes. No signet ring and matching cufflinks, no treasured photos, no old passport. Such things were long destroyed, passed over for cash, discarded as dangerous. The only thing linking me with the past was the filing cabinet in my head and it was locked and the room it stood in was bolted shut.

Charlie and I made our way along the track which was flat and easy going. We passed the round sandstone water catchment where people had been coming to fill bottles and flagons for one hundred and fifty years. People think that's a long time here. History's only two hundred years old in Australia. Since white people came here – that's the generally accepted version. But you wouldn't say that to Jimmy, my neighbour.

Charlie was silent, looking about him. He knelt down to watch the rushing water descend into the pipe which took the spring melt down the hill and under the road. He pressed his face against the wire mesh of the fence and stayed there.

I sat down on the sandstone wall. The foundation stone said 1846. A blue wren with its upright tail bobbed down onto the grass. It pecked about and hopped forward. I sat motionless. Then very slowly I reached into my jacket pocket and pulled out the letter from yesterday. As I drew it out of the envelope the wren shied away.

The letter was neatly typed. Doctor Holloway's beige paper stock had her name and her string of initials centred at the top.

Dear Henry, it said, *further to our discussion this afternoon, it is with regret I confirm in writing that the results of your CT scan have revealed several metastases in the left hemisphere of the brain above the left ear. It is evident comparing the March CT scans from Dr. Feltham that the number and size of the metastases has increased. As we have discussed, these small growths are inoperable due to their proximity to vital structures. Whilst it is always very difficult to offer any kind of time frame, we estimate that untreated within six months you may be experiencing some loss of speech, memory and mobility. Such a prognosis is always difficult because the brain may react in any number of ways. We recommend a course of radiotherapy to slow the growth of the metastases. This will moderate your symptoms and hopefully extend your life. Again there are no assurances and such an initiative must not be seen as a potential cure.*

As we have discussed, I have listed below a number of practitioners who will become part of your health management team. But most importantly, Henry, I urge you to consider what needs you have at this point. Take time to make plans with your loved ones so there are no issues troubling you or causing you undue stress. Also, you must begin to organise alternative transport arrangements and hand in your driver's licence within the month.

I look forward to seeing you next week to discuss your wishes and to plan your radiotherapy and ongoing care. Call me should you need to discuss anything sooner.

Sincere regards,

Geraldine Holloway.

I looked back to see Charlie climbing the fence and leaning far over.

'Eh, down from there,' I said.

'It's not dangerous. I won't fall.'

'How can you be certain?' I asked, folding the letter back into its envelope, sliding it into my jacket pocket. I picked him up under the armpits and dropped him back to the ground. He was heavier than I'd imagined.

'I just won't,' he said.

'If we're going to walk together it means doing what I say.'

'Who made you the boss?'

'I did. I'm bigger and I'm older.'

'Okay,' he said, shrugging his shoulders and looking about him. 'Which way?'

'That way. There's a bridge a wee bit further on.'

I wondered, not for the first time, as I followed the boy down the path if Lili ever suspected my game. Did she ever get an inkling I was not what I seemed? No. I did not think so. Would I ever confide in her? Of course not.

Once, on that night Sandra Rivett lay dead upon my kitchen floor, I had confided in a woman – sitting by a fireside

40

with a whisky in my hand just past midnight. I also related it once in the middle of Africa cutting a track through the hills of Zambia. I have come to realise such stories are never for the listener, only the confessor.

I would have liked to tell Jimmy, my neighbour. I had bitten it back several times. I would have liked him to know who he had for a friend and neighbour. After all these years I thought I could trust Jimmy. But not Lili. Lili was too close. Lili was a journalist. And I'd been right not to trust her. I'd been right never to breathe a word. Should have kept her more at arm's length. Too late now.

Of course, the story had never come out the same way twice. But if I had been misleading, if I had been economical with the facts, if I had been evasive, then it was hardly unusual. Every politician knows the disadvantages of the truth; every teenager discovers the shortcomings of honesty; a husband understands the necessity of manipulating the facts; a wife avoids the pitfall of too many details. It would be a mistake to think of friendship as a confessional. The past is not something erased by the telling.

THE SCENT OF WATER

JIMMY OWENS WAS UP ON the ridge. He lived across the paddock to the north of us. There was a wedge of gums which kept me from seeing his house or him seeing mine, although at night I could glimpse his lights. He had twenty acres of mostly forested land, unlike mine which had been cleared through the front part before I owned it. Jimmy climbed the ridge behind his house every night. Saying goodbye to the sun, he said. The sky was silver, bleeding saffron. Night starlings swooped in close. The days were getting longer again.

Jimmy was a jack of all trades. He was a plumber, a carpenter, a welder, an electrician. There was no better bloke to have next door. But in the local community he was actually known as a poet. He'd had several volumes published. I'd been to a couple of his book launches. Jimmy in a sharp-looking shirt with a whole group of people I'd never seen before. I hardly knew him.

The house he'd built was mud brick with eucalypt poles and ceiling. It had three bedrooms, although only one of those was in regular use these days. There was a long kitchen with a broad open fireplace at one end and a big cast-iron Stanley wood stove at the other. Pearl, Jimmy's wife, had recently bought a microwave but the stove was always warm and the coffee always brewing.

Tuesday night was our regular night. It had started with cards with some of his friends years back. When that fell apart Jimmy and I kept Tuesday night. Some nights we went to the pub. Others we went fishing down on North-West Bay with waders and a spotlight looking for flounder and squid. Some nights we just walked up the mountain or down to his dam.

Pearl had made a habit of taking herself off on Tuesday nights to adult education. Mexican weaving, pottery, basic mechanics. She was pretty handy too, Pearl. Their kids, Toby and Ruth, were on the mainland now. Jimmy and Pearl had been in Melbourne for the weekend with Toby to catch the Grand Final. Toby was a plastic surgeon.

'Don't know where he got it,' Jimmy said about his son's achievements. 'Must have been his mother.'

Ruth was an actor up in Sydney.

'Don't know where she got it,' Jimmy said. 'Must have been the dog.'

Molly Watkins was Jimmy's blue-heeler-cross. Now she was arthritic and barely lifted her body from her rug by the fire-place. But back when I had first met Jimmy and Pearl, Molly Watkins was a wild laughing dog. She'd do cartwheels chasing seagulls. Catch any ball in midair. Arrive home with a rabbit for breakfast. Jimmy devised rubber toe grips for her so she could go surfing on the back of his board. He even made her a go-cart and she'd learned to steer the thing with her teeth. Legend had it she'd beaten them all in a race down the road, but I never saw it myself.

I fondled her head and she closed her eyes and groaned deeply. It was one of my great denials. I never got a dog after England though I would dearly have loved one. I had always had a dog. Since I was eleven. We were sent to America during the war, my brother and sisters and me. I had only been about Charlie's age. The dog I befriended there had saved me from utter loneliness. But though dogs had been important to me, had been some of my favourite companions, I resisted. I didn't want attachments. Henry Kennedy needed nothing and no-one. It's what I liked to think, at any rate.

The coffee was done. Jimmy liked Turkish coffee. He had a special long-handled saucepan for it and he brewed it strong. He said it was as good as any homoeopathic remedy to treat lethargy or depression. Or even halitosis. He reckoned the gritty sediment had the same effect on teeth as sand had on skin. But then Jimmy had also drunk his own urine to cure the flu. Said it was an ancient Indian custom and kept a strange pottery cup with two spouts to administer his body fluids warm to his mouth and nasal passages.

I flicked open the paper on the table. Some military cad had revealed his affair with Princess Diana. I had hunted with her father at one time, poor girl. She'd saved Charles a lot of bother by marrying him and had been on trial ever since, thanks to the wolves of Fleet Street. My dislike for the media was only second to my dislike of the British legal system.

I took the small saucepan off the stove and filled two mugs with the thick fragrant coffee. When Jimmy came in he left the door open and sat at the table.

'Bloody fantastic win,' he said. 'Walked all over them. Lewis didn't lose his temper for once. It was almost a bit sad. One point I found myself wishing Geelong'd play better to make it more of a game.'

Jimmy reached for his coffee and sipped slowly at it.

'I watched the first three quarters, then I gave up.'

'Ablett was useless. Ah, can't help but love the Cats getting walloped. Stan must be in bad shape.'

'Apparently he was like a stunned mullet for the rest of the day. I reckon it'll take him a month to recover.'

Jimmy leaned into the mug, inhaled, looked up. After a moment he dropped my gaze and grinned.

'They canned it then.'

I paused and then said, 'No. No news.'

Stan, Jimmy and I were waiting on the government to approve a land transfer so the Aboriginal community could build a cultural centre down at Oyster Cove. It was a prime spot. It had special significance for Jimmy's people, but the wider community were divided. A few years back the whole land issue had been stymied by the conservatives. Saw it as a Green move and didn't want a bar of it. I'd agreed at the time. But I'd mellowed a bit since then.

'Och, it'll happen all in its own time.'

'I'd like to believe it.'

Jimmy reckoned people still had this notion that these black bastards were going to be running around with spears and stealing their stock all over again. They saw nothing but compensation claims and private land-grabs.

We went around it again. Who'd said what this last week. What had been written in the Mercury. What had been said in Parliament.

'Stan said the Upper House is due to have the special session tomorrow. We'll know soon enough,' I said.

'We will,' he said. 'But you're not convincing me one iota. What's up?'

I stretched my legs and looked into his face. It was an unexpected face for an Aborigine. His hair was pale, receding but long, tied at the back. The blue of his eyes had faded over the years. His face was deeply lined. Two big furrows beside his mouth made room for his smile. It needed room. It was a good smile. The skin on his forehead was marked with a deep crease between his eyes not so much from frowning but squinting into sunlight in search of birds in the sky, fish jumping, breeze on the water, children up to mischief. His father's people had once been Vikings. Centuries later in England, they were continuing the family tradition of pillage when one of them got caught and transported to Van Diemen's Land. Eventually he'd got his ticket-of-leave and settled down with a native woman out on one of the islands and started a clan of half-breeds.

I drained my cup and put it down on the table.

'I'll be giving up coffee, Jimmy.'

Jimmy's blue eyes settled on me.

'I'll be giving up quite a few things actually,' I said. 'Like being able to drive.'

'C'mon,' he said. He took the bottle of scotch from the cupboard above the sink and two enamel cups and we moved outside and wandered across the garden to the log by the dam. We sat and looked out over the water. It had the smell of dam water – nothing like the smell of saltwater. A muddy smell that was part grass and trees, part rain and sky. And the still sound. Waiting. With only the occasional amphibian throat clearing.

'Two black swans flew in,' he said. He unscrewed the lid off the scotch and half-filled our cups in the dark. He handed one to me and I filled my mouth and let the heat of it sink into my cheeks and tongue before I swallowed it.

'I'm dying, Jimmy, that's what.'

Three words. I am dying. Not a figurative, 'I was born and hence I will die.' No, this had a time frame all its own.

I thought of a few things to add. I suppose he did too. And then very quietly, as if he was stretching his legs before bed, he said, 'Time to be making peace then.'

'Peace?'

'With yourself.'

I was silent. He had known me fifteen years.

'Does Lili know?' he said after a time.

'Not yet. Her daughter showed up Friday night.'

'I didn't know . . .'

'You and me both.'

'She never said?'

'No.'

'How long?'

'Six months if I'm lucky. Then it'll be downhill.'

'Shit.'

'It's in my brain, Jimmy.'

'Well that's not news.'

'Aye. I thought you'd not be surprised . . .'

I knew we were both trying to grin, but the only thing I could see was his watch face luminous in the dark.

'So, you haven't told Lil?'

'Not yet.'

'And this daughter. She staying with you?'

'For a wee while. And the boy.'

'A boy?'

'Aye. Charlie. He's five.'

'Lil's grandson?'

'Aye.'

'Blimey, things are changing at a rate of knots.'

'That, they are.'

'So, what are you going to do about it?'

'Well . . . there's radiotherapy, but ultimately it won't stop anything.'

'I don't mean that kind of thing. I mean you.'

'Me?'

'How are you about it?'

'Right bloody pissed off.'

'Yep.'

'Ah, Jimmy.'

'It's a mongrel.'

■

I had worked to perfection my face, my voice, my hand and eye to create the person I had become. I had read other people with the precision of a man with a magnifying glass studying the face on a stamp, the wings of a butterfly, the tiny hairs on a beetle's legs. I had been so busy watching everyone else I had forgotten to watch myself.

I had a plan, Jimmy, I wanted to say to him. Have you ever had the desire to disappear, Jimmy? To move from one world to another and start afresh? To find a little paradise where the war never happened, the mistake, the boredom, the pain, the unfruitful dreams, the disappointment that came like water from the tap, the fall from grace, the gruesome truth, the crime never happened? I did that, Jimmy. I slipped away. But now, despite my best efforts, it's all come to naught.

'There are things we've all been, Henry,' he said. Almost as if he'd heard a whisper of what I had thought. 'Things we wish had been different. It's human.'

'There are things I can never change,' I said.

'You and me both, mate,' said Jimmy. He refilled my cup. 'It's probably the best and the worst of us.'

I heard him unzip his jacket and then he handed me something.

It was the pouch he took with him every night up the mountain at sunset. It was warm from his pocket. I opened it and sniffed. Eucalyptus leaves. Mint and earth.

'You know I don't believe in anything, Jimmy.'

'It doesn't matter whether you do or you don't. It'll still help.'

'I think I used up my help, Jimmy.'

The whisky heat was right through my body now. The cup was warming in my hands. The same blue enamel cups we'd been drinking whisky out of ever since I'd been coming over here to see him and Pearl. Same cups with the kids growing up; Molly Watkins a pup; the road over the years turning into a street with a row of houses, not just a dirt track, leading to my gate and then onto his.

'It's curious,' I said. 'I would have thought by my age it'd be something I was getting used to.'

'Well,' Jimmy said, 'there's death, and then there's your own death.'

Later I headed back along the path between his house and mine. I could see lights on but when I got home no-one was up. I listened at the end of the hall but I heard nothing of my guests. I walked away and then stopped. I heard Suki's bedroom door being closed very gently.

When I got into bed, Lil was fast asleep. I reached out for her and she batted my hand away. She said something in her dreaming voice. It was in Vietnamese and it sounded like, '*Fong ya cha.*'

I could not sleep. A combination of the alcohol, coffee, a pain in my head and my mind turning this way and that. I imagined letters I might write. Photos I could request. But I dared not pull at the thread of the past.

I could not put my affairs in order. I felt the locked door in my mind straining at the bolt. I felt myself sending tentacles to retrieve memories of my children. I could not make my peace with them. Sometimes there are things we do to our children that are unbearable to think of. Things we think we do for love.

Just the year before last they had been in the paper again. No pictures that time, just their names – Frances, Camilla and George. The article had announced that I had been officially presumed deceased on the eleventh of December, 1992. Eighteen years it took. Did it finally curse me, the court ruling that gave my son the right to use the title he'd been born to? Having been presumed dead, was it now simply a matter of my body catching up?

Within six months you will be experiencing considerable loss of speech, memory and mobility. So this was to be my final test. I must somehow maintain my faculties. It was imperative that I keep up my pretence. The pretence which kept at bay the memory of a street lamp spearing the ground floor rooms with a pale beam of light. The dark shape on the floor. A mail sack full, but not with letters. There was something sticking out from it. A face. It was a woman doubled up. Not a person acting dead, but a real person who had been alive only a few minutes before. A woman with her head smashed in.

It was not Veronica, my wife. No, not at all. It was the children's nanny. Blood was sprayed all across the floor and up the cupboards. There was blood dripping from her cheek into a pool on the floor. The pool ended at the toes of my evening shoes. Soon my wife would call for the nanny and come looking for her. She too would be attacked and bludgeoned about the head but she would escape and run to the pub on the corner and scream that there was a murderer in the house. The following day she would tell the police that I had killed the nanny. But by then I had disappeared.

VENUS ON A MOUNTAIN-TOP

I AVOIDED TELLING LILI FOR a whole week. It was Sunday and I was cocooned by lethargy. The house was quiet. Lili had left early for her show. The regular 7am Sunday start. The sheets where she'd lain had cooled. I considered never telling her. I considered asking her and Suki and the boy to leave. Let them go make a life for themselves somewhere else. I hardly needed a family around me.

After all, Lili was not the sort of woman I would ever have imagined for myself. Lucan would never have looked twice at her.

Though we shared a bed, a bathroom, the building of a house, the stocking of the fridge, the choosing of window blinds, I could never get past seeing Lili in all this, first and foremost, as Asian. I expected all things about her to be because of that, or to follow on from that. It had taken me months to get used to the idea she didn't eat rice for every meal. That she actually was more Australian than I would ever be.

Perhaps if she were anyone other than Lili Birch, host of *The*

Sunday Show on SBS, I might have been more troubled by it. But there was no-one here to answer to. There was no-one to be shocked by such a thing, me with a Vietnamese woman. In fact she was the one people noticed in the supermarket. I was in her shadow, rather like Denis Thatcher. Which was fine by me.

For a week I had pursued my flu excuse on the phone to Stan and to clients. I had watched Suki and Lili hover about one another. This way and that their words went, pivoting on Charlie's world. I had watched Lili with the boy. Saw how she looked into his eyes as if she could not believe she had a grandchild. And more than that. As if she wanted to pick him up and cuddle him, but she didn't.

'Can I have jam?' he had asked one morning as Suki buttered his toast.

'Mum, is there any jam?' Suki asked.

'What sort of jam are you after?'

'What sort of jam?' pondered Charlie. 'Do you have banana jam? Only joking,' he laughed. 'What about worm jam?'

'I'm sure we could make some,' said Lili.

'No!' said Charlie. 'We couldn't eat that!'

'What about cockroach jam?' said Suki. 'Nice and crunchy like peanut butter.'

'I hate peanut butter,' he said.

'You better come and have a look in the pantry,' said Lili.

They all went together into the darkness. Lili turned on the light and pointed up.

Charlie's eyes widened. 'I've never seen so much jam in my life! Where did it all come from?'

Lili laughed. 'Pearl and I made it together last summer while the house was being finished. The kitchen was in and, well, Pearl does lots of preserving so she said she'd teach me. The trouble is I'd need an army to eat it all.'

'That's amazing,' said Charlie surveying the reds, bright and dark; the purples, oranges and greens of preserves, chutneys and relishes. He spotted the ladder.

'Can I see?'

From the ladder he peered more closely.

'That one,' he said.

'Good choice,' said Lili. 'Those blackberries grew just down on the other side of the road.'

'Can we pick some today?'

'Not at this time of year,' said Lili. 'Late in summer they start ripening.'

'When the snakes come out on warm afternoons,' I added from my stool in the kitchen where I was perusing the newspaper.

They all swung to look at me, as if they had forgotten I was there.

'Yes,' said Lili, after a moment, 'there are snakes . . .'

'Can we catch one and eat it?' asked Charlie.

'We'll ask Jimmy for a recipe,' I said. 'Come to think of it, we'll ask Jimmy to go and catch one for us. When the weather warms up a bit.'

'We won't be here then,' said Charlie. Suki looked away.

Lili looked at me and I said, 'Och, you never know.'

Maybe I liked the distraction. Maybe, despite my misgivings,

I liked having people about. The week had served me well. I guessed Suki thought my staying home was about them. Perhaps being protective of my home. Maybe they'd really thought me unwell. I'd kept to myself. And I did have a cough. It just wasn't the flu.

'Suki, how long will you be staying?' Lili asked.

'Dunno. You can just kick us out when you're sick of us.'

'Suki . . .'

'It's all right,' I said. 'You can stay as long as you need.'

But it was only the boy who smiled at me.

I drifted in and out of wakefulness, aware as Sunday morning moved on of Charlie's noises downstairs, Suki's voice. Later I heard them leave the house and I lay there soaking up the silence. It had been a lifetime since I'd stayed in bed until 11am. There had been years in London when I was never up before midday. I'd start the day with a pink gin for breakfast, followed by a vodka martini at the St James. I ate a late luncheon at my club where I read the papers and caught up with some chums. I'd play a game of backgammon and then I'd go home to bath and see the children. I was dressed and off to the club each night by nine. My wife, Veronica, would accompany me. We dined in the company of my friends. I ate the same meal each evening. It may sound ridiculous but I did. Smoked salmon and lamb cutlets in the cooler months. Smoked salmon and lamb *en gelee* in the warmer ones. Veronica was usually the only woman at the table. Not the sort of places the wives came generally.

After dinner I went to the tables until two-thirty or three. Some nights I played bridge at the Portland but usually I stayed at the Clermont. There it was backgammon and chemin de fer. Veronica stood behind me and watched. She preferred the Clermont because at least it allowed women. If I went on to St James or White's she went home. Women were not permitted there. People said later on that she was bad luck. But she wasn't. Did she enjoy it? Did she wish to spend the night in a place where no-one cared for her presence or her opinion? She rarely spoke and when she did my friends usually made a point of ignoring her. But for a long time she was part of the ritual.

'You don't think it's too much, the club, John?' she asked in her soft voice which I had once taken for gentility.

'What do you mean?'

'Well, every night . . . '

'It's what I do.'

'Yes. But can we afford it?'

'But I win . . . '

'Really?'

'Veronica, you know, you are there. I'm ahead.'

'Every night?'

'I do not go every night.'

She sat there and pulled at her hair, winding it about her finger.

'What do you want, Veronica? Is all this still not enough?' I waved my arm to indicate our home.

'You don't have to like it. Perhaps you'd prefer I did

something else to pay our expenses. Run a pub like your family?'

I had a lot of trouble sleeping in those days. Often I went to Annabel's on the way home for a nightcap. I'd drift off when the pallid London sun was creeping through the curtains. Upstairs I'd hear the nanny begin rousing the children for school. Much later Veronica would rise and by the time I was dressed she would be in the drawing room on the sofa. She had no interests, so few friends. Taking her out at night at least gave her something beyond the house.

Suddenly I heard footsteps downstairs and Jimmy's voice called up, 'Are you coming or do I have to finish the whole bloody boat on my own?'

Damn it. Sunday. Yes, that was the plan.

'I'll be right there,' I said.

There was a silence and then Jimmy called up, 'You don't have to, mate. If you're not feeling up to it.'

'Great Jimmy. Just great. The sympathetic tone. But you can leave it at the back door, thank you.'

Downstairs I pulled on my boots and we walked together across the yard. The day was blustery but just warm enough not to freeze our fingers off. The cold was one of the hazards of boat building on the mountain. It slowed us down a good three months of the year.

We'd built a rough shelter for her, just four raw timber posts and a roof. Jimmy had flipped off her covers. Now there she was. *Venus* – a traditional Laurent Giles sloop. Thirty feet of celery top with a teak deck, oregon mast and a huon pine interior. Well, the mast was in storage in the shed and the deck was half finished.

As we approached her, the wind blew through the paddock, moving the grass like an ocean waiting to sail her away. I shrugged off the ache in my head and breathed in the mountain air, fresh and fertile on that spring day. A boat, I had discovered, was something altogether different from a house. A house was a matter of shelter and purpose. But *Venus* was a thing that must harness the elements. And that made her a little magical.

Jimmy and I had spent near a decade of weekends seasoning timber, sizing timber for frames and ribs, lugging timber, steaming timber, mulling over the fit of plank against plank, sanding, painting and varnishing timber.

That Sunday we intended caulking the deck. Caulking is a backbreaking task no machine will ever take from us. It wasn't necessary. None of this stuff with wooden boats was necessary. Jimmy often lamented the woes of wood as opposed to fibreglass. He wanted to epoxy everything. I liked to think if I'd let him at a vat of resin and a roll of fibreglass cloth he wouldn't have gone through with it. The truth was, it was too cold up here for glues and epoxies, so there wasn't an ounce of the stuff on her and I was pleased with that.

Jimmy liked having stories to tell people about how I was such a damn perfectionist. How it was no wonder it had taken so long to build her. 'Lucky he's quicker about it with the houses he builds,' he'd say. Yet if anything he was prouder of *Venus* than I was.

We'd laid the deck in a herringbone pattern. I'd had an old-timer from the channel come up to help us out on the hull and give me a few lessons. He'd lent me his caulking mallets and irons and shown me how to lay the caulking cotton. Then we'd primed the deck seams twice over. Now came the sealant. We each had a caulking gun housing a tube of rubber-like compound. We were squeezing it in between the narrow planks of teak to seal the deck against water. Our backsides were in the air and our noses inches from the chemical scent.

'Och, it's a fine sight today, from the decks of herself,' I said, peering at Jimmy's backside where his shorts had slipped about his hips, leaving him somewhat exposed. It was an Australian thing, I'd discovered, this disregard for nudity or even privacy in any of its various forms.

'I'm showing off to the woman of my dreams,' said Jimmy. 'Mind you, she's a lot more work than most women I've known. And a bit broad in the beam for my liking.'

'I like her that way. Something to grab onto.'

'Least she'll have an even keel.'

Such jokes went back and forth, year in, year out. Lili and Pearl had long acquiesced to the other woman in our lives.

We applied the sealant slow and steady. It was an exercise in even pressure and finger strength. It wasn't warm enough to take off the pullover I was wearing though the sky was clear and the sun was warm on our backs through the corrugated perspex of the roof.

'I still can't believe it's gone back to the drawing board,' he said. The Upper House had knocked back the land transfer for the Oyster Bay site. The whole thing had to be redrafted.

'We've formed a working group for the new proposal,' Jimmy continued. 'The Premier and the Legislative Council say they're supportive, so maybe it's just a matter of time. It's due to be re-presented before Christmas.'

'Are you getting the survey done still?'

'Yeah, next week. And soil testing.'

I nodded. We'd thought it only wise that if there was going to be such a fuss over getting the land, we'd better make sure we could actually build on it. No underground lake or anything nasty to set us back.

Jimmy said, 'So have you told Lili?'

'Not yet.'

'Well, you don't have to. You could pass it off as tiredness for a while longer. The old aches and pains of the ageing body.

'I mean,' he went on, 'she's got Suki here now. And young Charlie. She's preoccupied. Won't notice you wasting away in front of her eyes. How long are they staying?'

'Indefinitely, it seems. They don't appear to have anywhere else to go.'

'You're not obliged to tell people anything.'

'No,' I said, working the glue.

'Friends do,' he said. 'Tell each other things. I guess it could be about trust.'

'I can trust Lil,' I said mildly.

'Oh, it's not Lil I'm thinking of.'

A crow alighted on the woodpile and barked at us.

'See,' said Jimmy, 'he knows.'

I laughed and said, 'It's just a bleeding crow, Jimmy. What does it know?'

Jimmy looked at me with his steady blue eyes and the crow looked at me with his small black shining beads and there was not much difference in the gaze.

'That this is your chance.'

'I thought I was dying.'

'Yes, but you know it. The rest of us think it'll go on forever.'

I sat back and leaned myself against the cabin. I wanted to say, What if you knew and Lil knew and everyone knew I had been living past my death for twenty years? That all these years later I was here, alive. Would this death finally be enough?

'Right,' I said. 'I'll tell her. I'll tell her tonight.'

'I'll go get us a beer,' said Jimmy.

'I shouldn't,' I said.

'Ah,' said Jimmy. 'So you're going to fight it.'

'It's just off the list.'

'Tea?'

'You're a right bastard.'

'That's better,' he said.

He climbed down the ladder and disappeared into the house. I looked out over *Venus* to the workshop. When I'd first arrived on the island I could have rented a place to live but escape was still fresh in my mind. Longing for somewhere I could go unseen and unnoticed, I moved up here. The workshop in those days was an unpainted vertical-board shed weathered almost white. In the space of a few weeks I'd laid a floor and lined the walls.

I'd learned a number of surprising skills since departing England. I turned the hayloft into a place to sleep. I put in a couple of windows and rigged up hot water from copper pipes that ran behind the wood heater. When I wanted a bath I had it outside in an old clawfoot that had once been a feed trough. I had a gas ring for cooking and no electricity. Truth was, it was luxury compared to where I'd been in the years between London and Tasmania.

It took me ten years living in the shed to work up to the idea of building the house. But *Venus* began within a year or two of moving onto the land. I knew I'd never leave this place by plane if I could help it. Airports were risky places. Strangers on planes were risky people. So perhaps the notion of a boat gave me options for escape. Or maybe it was simply the idea of getting out on the river like everyone else here seemed to do. I'd been a powerboat man, back in England. I could afford no similarities to anything from then. I started reading up on wooden boats, studied designs, subscribed to Wooden Boat magazine. I began collecting the timber for her and slowly she began. And I was lucky to find myself living next door to a man who could turn his hand to any sort of woodwork. Now the old shed was full of timber and boat-building tools, and with the house complete, Jimmy and I were into the final months on *Venus* before we could launch her into the Derwent River.

Next to *Venus* was the vegetable garden I'd put in last spring. It was fenced with chicken wire to keep out the wallabies and possums. The month before two geese had flown in and tried to nest there. I thought they'd likely break their wings trying to take off and land, so I'd made a chicken wire roof as well. It looked strange but it was a concession to living here. And, of course, beside the garden was the house.

It ran north-east along the land. In terms of the southern hemisphere sun it was built the wrong way, but the view was south-east. And the view was special. Forest, meadow, big river. From the first silver light of dawn to the fading red of sunset, the house lived with weather and nature on a grand scale. It was Stan's design with a fair bit of bullying from me. The structural walls were clad in red cedar which had weathered grey like the trunks of gum trees. The non-structural walls were mahogany. The metal roof was powdercoated stone grey. In the west there was a stone chimney built of river rock.

The house was built on concrete piers which made it float a little on the contours of the land. The front of the house was all glass sliding panels framed in teak and mahogany with a broad deck along the entire lower floor and steps running down into the paddock. Out of the wind adjacent to the kitchen at the rear was another deck for dining and reading on the long summer evenings. Up here, with fifteen acres all about me, I didn't have to work at privacy.

There was a long driveway and no-one could see the house from the road. And next door was Jimmy. All these years I'd lived two lives with him. The life I lived now and that life was good. And the life I hid inside myself and that life was a dark place. Jimmy would not have liked that man.

'Jimmy,' I said, when he returned from the kitchen with two mugs and a packet of ginger biscuits. 'There's something . . . I did look death in the eye once before. A long time ago.'

'What did you see?'

'I ran away.'

'Where to?'

'Here.'

'So is there something back there you need to sort out?'

'No, God no. I can't.'

'Ah,' he said. He tore open the packet of biscuits and offered them to me before dipping one in his tea and then sucking it.

'See, to me, Henry, the past's like a movie. Some days it's a comedy and other days it's a bleeding tragedy. And the future's the same. It all depends on your thinking,' he said, shrugging. 'You decide if you're a winner or a loser. No-one else.'

'I'm not who people think I am.'

'What, you're not Henry Kennedy, adequate house builder? Paltry boat builder? A terrible drunk? A man with no poetry upon his shelves? A beautiful woman in his bed and a black man for a friend?'

'You're the whitest black man I ever saw.'

'And you're Henry Kennedy. That's who I see.'

'And if . . .'

'What is it, Henry? Are you going to tell me you killed a man?'

I shook my head.

'It's a long time ago,' he continued, softer. 'Whatever happened. If you can't make it better, let it rest.' He looked at me. 'Every new day is really a kind of miracle. Keep your mind on that.'

Collins would have said the same. The man who had saved me from capture. There in Africa he had lamented that I would never truly understand what it is to be alive.

'What you lack is a romantic soul,' he had said. 'Bred out of you, no doubt. Whipped out of you at school. You need a story to help people warm to you. Compassion. It needs to grow in you. Ah, compassion. How do I teach you that?'

He took me into the nearest town, a four-hour drive from his estate to the squalid shanties where twelve people might live and cook and sleep in one tiny room. He took me to the copper mines where a white man earned ten times the wage of a black man for the same day's work. He took me to a village where almost everyone, children and adults alike, had leprosy.

'There is no place crueller than Africa,' he said. 'Yet people are friendly, smiling, laughing, generous. Oh yes, they can steal, they can kill you soon as look at you if you threaten them, but they have nothing. Nothing but the day they find themselves in. No possibility for their children save for the goodness the gods bestow upon them. No relief for themselves. Yet for the most part they know what to be happy about.'

'Do you know what to be happy about, John?' he had asked.

'It's a foolish question. There is precious little to be happy about in my situation.'

'I have no son. No-one I can share all this with,' he tapped his head with his forefinger. 'I am an old man, far older than you think. My wife died many years ago now. My daughters have grandchildren themselves. This may be my last dry season. I may never know another day, let alone another month, so I understand what it is to know that I will lose this life. But you, you've never been alive enough to know you are already quite dead.'

'That's a rugged thing to say,' I said.

He rested his fingers against his chest. 'When this wakes up, then you will know you are alive.'

But it had woken up. Africa and all I endured there woke me. Now that I am dying, I wanted to ask, what do I do with all this life I feel?

INDELIBLE STAINS

JIMMY RANG MIDWEEK. HIS VOICE sounded taut and harsh.

'You are not going to believe what we found today.'

'What?'

'Murder.'

'Murder?' I asked. People use the word very loosely. But not Jimmy.

'Well, maybe it won't come as any surprise to you.'

Now I was unsettled. What the hell was he talking about?

'A woman,' he went on.

'What woman?' My mind was racing. I thought about the words we'd exchanged on *Venus*. My admission that I had run from something. What had Jimmy found out? Had he found a newspaper article? It worried me how much information was coming out these days with DNA testing.

'You don't want to know about it and neither do I.'

The familiar prickle of unease crawled up my back. I breathed slowly.

'You're not making sense, Jimmy.'

'A child too.'

'No, not a child.'

'Yeah, a baby really.'

'I don't understand . . . '

'It'll be all over the paper,' he said. 'Three years all down the gurgler.'

The baby didn't make sense. What baby was he talking about?

'The soil testing. Dug down six feet and there they were.'

I breathed out long and slow.

'A bullet in each skull. The university's been down there all day. They're calling in some experts from the mainland too. The soil's somehow preserved them.'

'Aboriginal people?'

'They don't know for sure but it looks like it. The guess is early 1800s. There may be more buried around them.'

'Ah, Jimmy.'

'It's over. It'll never get up now. Not there.'

'You can't be sure.'

'You know what'll get up? A bloody memorial. Great! Another bloody memorial. Not some future. Only the indisputably ugly past.'

'Come over.'

'I can't. Got to speak to some people. Tomorrow.'

'I'm sorry, Jimmy. We can still fight for the centre. Maybe it makes it even more important.'

'What possessed them just to shoot people like that? I don't know,' he sighed. 'I don't know if people will want it there any more.'

'You always knew people lived there. Even died there.'

'Yeah, but not murdered. Stains a place, that kind of thing. It's like houses. Never feels right after something terrible's happened.'

I was silent. Veronica and my children had gone on living in the house. Day after day they had gone up and down the stairs, night after night they had walked across the kitchen floor. Other nannies must have been employed. Sandra Rivett's blood had been washed away but did the memory of her linger on? It had not been something I had dwelled upon.

Home is such a fragile thing. So warm and comforting when it is good. So easily ruined.

When did we ruin it, Veronica and I?

We started out well enough. I had not thought much about marrying before I met her. Marriage hadn't interested me. There were plenty of suitable young women, parties full of them. I was considered a catch, but that made it all the less attractive. When I met Veronica she seemed to take no interest in any of that. She wasn't our sort at all. Still, she spoke quite well. She was canny, even cruel in her assessments of people and this made me laugh. She had a pretty chin and wide blue eyes. She was tiny. Hands, feet, ankles. Her sister was a vivacious creature newly married to my friend James, and they seemed terribly happy.

But I was wrong about Veronica. She cared very much about my title. And what I had taken for a meticulous nature that would always ensure a tidy home, an ordered life, were simply the precursors to much worse conditions of paranoia and obsession. Almost immediately after we were married, my father died. Suddenly she was the Countess of Lucan, and it changed her. She fretted at the least thing. How the table was to be set when my mother came to tea; what jewellery to wear; what food to serve; how to address my friends.

'Should it be Baron? Or Your Lordship? Or is it My Lord?'

'For God's sake, just call him Freddie.'

'Are you sure?'

'Or don't speak to him at all.'

She was very low after Frances was born. I organised nannies, made her see the doctor, but there was nothing that lifted her spirits. And when she did begin to get well again it was as if she resented the life I had. She became jealous. While I was at the club, or off with friends, who had I seen? Where had I been exactly?

'Come with me. Get yourself dressed and come with me and you will see that all we do is play. It's ridiculous for you to have these worries.'

'You don't love me.'

'You are being ridiculous.'

We went on. George was born. I was delighted to have a son and I thought she would be delighted too, but her depression worsened.

'It's all very well for you. You have something that makes you happy.'

'For god's sake, pull yourself together. Veronica, just name it and I will bring it to you. You never see the children. You spend all day in bed or here on the sofa. It has to stop.'

'You are ashamed of me. You're all ashamed of me. That's why no-one will talk to me.'

This went on for some time and then she did pick herself up. I insisted on her coming to the club. I didn't want her at home feeling lonely, or fearing my fidelity. I wanted her to see there was nothing to concern her. I thought she might enjoy it. Soon it was almost the only time she left the house. I began to think she was in need of far greater care than the few tablets she was prescribed by her doctor.

After Camilla was born she rarely rose from her bed for almost a year. She wept at the smallest thing. She took no interest in the children for days on end and then, when she did, it was a mad, bright eagerness that was wonderful while it lasted. But all too soon she would tire of us and slip back to her room. She took to cleaning at odd hours. She didn't have to clean. We had a maid. She would change her outfit a dozen times and then be in tears when I said I had to go without her. One night, after I had left her alone, I came home to find she had cut up all her dresses.

I didn't take it well, her illness, for illness it was.

I remember one day Frances was reading aloud to me. Veronica came into the room and Frances stopped.

'Well, go on,' she said, smiling her tight smile at us.

Frances began then stumbled and stopped. Veronica got up and left the room. When the door was closed, Frances leaned against me and whispered, 'I don't think Mummy is angry. She has just forgotten how to be happy.'

THE IDEA OF HOME

AFTER YEARS OF LIVING IN the shed I had grown weary of the relentless cold through winter, stopping up drafts, of waiting for the pipes to thaw. I was weary of keeping out bush rats and possums, happy to never hear the drone of a warm-evening mosquito again. Dirt was ingrained in the floorboards, spiders lived in every corner. The roof needed constant attention throughout winter with the wind blowing up the tin and sending snowdrifts down upon me as I shivered in my bed. Though I'd eventually had power connected at Stan's insistence, I had no electric hot-water system. I longed for a proper bathroom. I imagined a kitchen bench that did not have flies all over it. I was tired of my books and music being stored in boxes to keep them safe from heat and moths. I wasn't getting any younger. After building so many homes for other people, I found myself impatient for a little comfort for myself.

The idea of my own house seemed an incredible luxury. The funds I had kept safe since 1974 were largely intact and I wanted them for retirement. But the business had done well for Stan and me. I had, in fact, been able to accumulate a substantial amount, enough not to have to trouble a bank for a housing loan, which is not easy when you have no credit history.

The main bedroom was upstairs. I'd always envisaged the bed and the view. Just those two things. Simple, unimpeded. And me here alone.

The house did not suit lingering guests. The downstairs living space was all open-plan. The kitchen, dining and living room were each defined by bearing walls every five metres. There were no doors. Each opening was progressively wider so when you stood in the kitchen and looked through to the fireplace at the west end of the house there was a gentle telescope effect. There were no separate living rooms. The extra bedrooms were more about resale than people. Stan had encouraged it. He'd said you never know, that people changed their minds all the time about houses. About places.

In the years I had been on the island, I had only left it once. And that was the time I met Lili. Our firm had been nominated for a national architectural award for a waterfront home we'd designed and built. Stan had been thrilled. He was so keen for me to go with him. And, of course, it's not easy for him to get about. I told him I had a terrible fear of flying. In the end I agreed to go because it seemed churlish not to. We drove up, taking the car on the ferry.

Lili was on our table at the awards dinner. In fact she sat next to me most of the evening. She'd just given up her career as a foreign correspondent and SBS had hired her for their

Sunday arts show. Stan and I didn't win but Lili and I went for a walk along the harbour after dinner. I didn't like to imagine it meant anything to her. I didn't call her and she didn't call me. She came down and did a piece on the waterfront house and Stan invited her to dinner and we met again. It was a slow thing. She liked Hobart and found stories here for her show. I was just getting started on the house. I found myself looking forward to her visits to Hobart. I was naturally cautious, even suspicious of her interest. But Lili never asked me about my past, never pried for details. She would sit on the sand pile and read while she waited for me to finish a particular job on the house.

Lili Birch was curious to me. In the past my affairs with women had made few demands on me. Mostly they'd been brief, haphazard things, the women married. Married women were so much easier. They had no desire for a man to take them to dinner, to movies or Sunday barbecues. They had one of those already. Married women, I had discovered, had more particular activities in mind. They liked the rediscovery of the fragile muscle of their heart. The delight in the phone call, the long conversation. The holding of hands as we sat in the car on the dark edge of river or forest, secluded from prying eyes; her adrift from her routine of job, shopping, children and cooking. Wanting only to rediscover the breathless giddy rush of sensuality washed too clean by family life.

Intimacy, not only because of the inherent dangers of my past, was not a comfortable thing for me. I shied from it. And so, it appeared, did Lili. But I couldn't deny how attracted I was to her. She gave very little indication of her feelings. Once she let me hold her hand on a long drive up the channel, but only for a few minutes. She released my hand gently and placed it back on my leg, but the brush of her hand against my thigh lingered long after she'd flown away again.

I didn't imagine she'd stay in my life. I found myself waking up and not minding she was there. It was as if I had taken some sort of mildly euphoric sedative. I liked her. I never tired of her face, her expressive mouth. She was perhaps the most knowledgeable person I'd met. She was both a woman of words and also of long silences. She could speak eloquently on politics and then be purely irrational over a misunderstanding between us. It is a misconception that Asian women are subservient. Lili would argue with me and berate me. My lack of punctuality; my calling at the last minute to say I couldn't meet her; my occasional insomnia which woke her at strange hours when she was due early at work, would elicit fiery remarks and stubborn withdrawals of affection. Still she stayed and I was glad.

What did she see in me? Lili was eighteen years younger than I was.

'You've surprised me,' I said when it became evident she was spiralling slowly into my life, like an orbiting satellite on an inbound trajectory.

'Why?'

'Because I didn't think you'd be interested . . .'

'Why not?'

'I don't know . . .'

'You feel familiar,' she said. 'Sometimes when you walk away I look back and there you are, looking like you must to the rest of the world. But you don't look that way to me.'

'What do I look like to you?'

'Maybe it's a past life thing. Besides, it's never about age . . . or how someone looks.'

'What is it about then? You're making me feel so confident.'

'I don't know,' she said. 'I know so little about love.'

'Maybe she just likes the fact you're a bloke,' said Pearl when I asked her about it one day. 'Women like that. A man who's good with a hammer is usually good with other things,' she laughed. She and Lil had clicked as soon as they'd met. The way women can without any effort, though they were as different as seasons. Pearl's family had been living on the east coast of Tasmania for generations. As Jimmy said, she was as good as Aboriginal. Her silver hair was tied back from her broad face in a long braid and her hands were always busy with something she was cooking or crafting. She knitted beautiful pullovers, could bake, weave and sew. Lili, however, was an impractical creature, absorbed in economics, history, current affairs. Weekends Lil consumed newspapers and magazines. There was a stack of books beside the bed. Rainy days were for reading on the couch. Sunny days were for reading outside. Her cooking was reluctant, her gardening skills confined to the odd bit of advice like 'Tomatoes would be nice on the wall by the shed.'

She was lovely and I felt out of my depth with her. It wasn't just that she was much younger. It was cultural. I wanted to ask her things like, 'Did you wear one of those bamboo hats? Was your father with the Viet Cong?' I was incompetent with her. And physically I was certain I could never please her. We first slept together on a warm summer night under a mosquito net in the beginnings of the house. The air in the shed had been too close and stuffy, still smelling of the fish we had eaten. Lili's skin was soft. Not just her skin but her body. I laid beside her and traced every part of her and we were not awkward, we were not uncomfortable. It was as if we knew each other. As if I had been waiting all these years to make love to her, and she to me.

It was that night I realised I never wanted to be without her.

Our early relationship was largely conducted in hotel rooms when she flew in to Hobart. Aside from the normal debris of lovers meeting sporadically – bathrobes, room-service trays, gift-wrapping – the only hint I had about Lili was her hotel bathroom and that told me very little. A particular fragrance; skin-care jars and creams; her toothbrush placed in a glass – no untidiness at all. I never suspected her habit of taking off her clothes and dropping them to the floor was anything but a lover's ploy.

Lili's heritage was not evident in her choice of clothes. She dressed very simply. No Chinese collars or satin dresses. A gold chain at her neck. Her hands adorned with a single gold ring on her wedding finger. Nor was her background obvious in how she lived. Perhaps I had expected Asian wall hangings and brass figurines. But there was none of that.

I had never visited her in Sydney. I never saw her flat, the life she had accumulated. When she moved here, all her things arrived in a removal truck. Two cream armchairs, a cream sofa, a dozen large and small cushions, an antique chest of drawers, a yellow and cream carpet, a Wedgwood dinner set, a large lamp with a swirling blue and gold glaze, several crates of French wine, her CD collection, and boxes and boxes of books.

I had told Lil the house had been designed to make the view so striking it would completely overwhelm any need for human clutter. The bookshelves I had created ran low around the lounge room so as not to distract the eye. Simple worked well, I said, but not for Lili it seemed. Lil had a way of cluttering up a place. The small alcove I had allowed for clothes beside our bedroom had been insufficient and she had insisted on her chest of drawers coming upstairs. A few weeks ago Lil had installed a long couch in our bedroom where she liked to read with the view at her feet. Her office had taken over one of the bedrooms downstairs. Piles of paperwork and manila folders were stacked on the desk and the floor. And because there was no more room in the living areas, the walls were hidden by books.

Flowers in vases I understood. But the magazines on table-tops, the cushions and rugs and ornaments, the pantry stocked with food enough for three snowed-in winters, I did not. I had to firmly resist fish and a canary. It was as if simplicity scared her and she ran to cover it up.

I was irritable about this accumulation of things. I did not want to be encumbered. I had wanted to feel like I was making a fresh start. A clean slate. If this was to be my life then I wanted it to stay uncomplicated. Did I really need a pet? Did Lil and I need another rug on the floor? Another bookshelf? A television cabinet? A video player?

Lil and I did not share our finances. She could buy what she liked whenever she liked. So homewares came into the house and I did not say, Take them back. It's too much. I did not say, Lili, you need servants because you are utterly untidy.

I lived with Lili and saw that she had settled into our life and I would not disturb her happiness for anything.

The guest bedroom where Suki and Charlie were staying had become increasingly littered with clothes, toy cars and wet towels. I avoided looking into it as much as I could. The refrigerator was cluttered with small yoghurts with cartoon characters on the lids. There were plastic toys in the sand pile and the kitchen floor was always in need of sweeping.

Simplicity had disappeared.

CAUGHT STEALING

SUKI PROWLED THE HOUSE AFTER the boy was in bed. It was Sunday night. Lil was reading. I was silently flicking through the television channels.

'What can we get you?' Lili said, still in her work clothes.

'I need to go see someone. Can I take your car?'

Lil's Karmann Ghia was a '58 convertible, deep metallic green. It was ridiculously impractical for the winter roads up here but she loved it. She covered it every night and uncovered it every morning, even though it was always kept in the garage. It was one of the only ones in Australia and Lil didn't like even me driving it. She appeared to have not heard Suki but I guessed she was simply avoiding the question.

She said, 'Anyone I know? I don't suppose so.'

'Well can I?' asked Suki.

'Take mine. The keys are by the door,' I said.

Mine was a rust-bucket Land Rover parked under the big gum out the back. It rattled a bit, had 240 000 miles on the clock but was generally indestructible.

'It's a bit rough on the clutch but you'll get used to it.'

'Thanks,' Suki said.

She disappeared back to the bedroom then re-emerged closing the door on the sleeping boy, a long black jacket over her arm; picked up the keys and departed. The engine noise was quickly gone, and Lil picked up her book again and curled her feet beneath her.

'That was good of you,' she said.

'Lil.'

She looked at me. Then she put down her book and slipped off the couch and came over to my chair.

She brought with her a large cushion and placed it on the rug, then sat on it and laid her head on my leg.

'I'll tell her they can't stay,' she said.

I slid her hair aside and caressed the back of her neck.

'It's impossible.'

'No, it's not.'

'They were not invited.'

'I know.'

'I didn't ask her to come back.'

'No.'

'She'll bring trouble.'

'Suki?'

'She always does.'

'Maybe she's changed,' I said.

'I doubt it. She is what she is.' Her voice was defeated.

'He's a good lad. Where do you suppose his father is?' I asked mildly.

'She says he's in Byron Bay but how can one believe

anything she says?'

'Charlie told me he was killed by a crocodile up north.'

'Really?'

'I keep meaning to ask her if it's true.'

Lili shrugged. 'He should be in school.'

'So, what are we going to do then?'

'It makes it somehow more permanent,' she replied. 'If he starts here.'

'Do you think they might never leave?'

She shuddered. 'God help me. I wish she'd go.'

'Have you tried talking to her?'

'Do you think it would make one finger of difference? Whatever she wants from me, I don't have it. I know that.'

I never imagined her as a mother. But I would have expected her to be softer. Kinder.

'How old is she?'

'Twenty-four.'

'Are you going to tell me about it?'

She took my hand. 'Come and have a bath with me?' she asked.

I climbed the stairs with her and as the bath was running I undid the buttons on her blouse, a dark blue blouse, silk maybe. Her bra was blue lace. Her shoes low, black slip-ons, her pants black. Blue lace knickers. Knee-length stockings. She was slender but not thin. Her stomach a gentle curve. Her breasts a small heavy handful with deep rose-coloured nipples. Her skin was very smooth and faintly amber. I had imagined when I first breathed against her that she would smell of tropical heat and Lapsang Souchong tea, but instead she had the scent of some kind of English cologne which made me think of talcum powder and green leaves.

I ran a finger over her belly, slipping around the edges of her navel, tracing the line from hip to hip. 'She's twenty-four. So you were eighteen.'

'Something like that.'

As we stepped into the water, Lili said in an almost offhand way, 'There was a message on the phone. Geraldine Holloway. Why was she calling, Henry?'

So it was here. The moment I had been avoiding since I first went to see Nick Powell, my GP, and he made an appointment with Feltham and Feltham in turn sent me to Geraldine Holloway. Why hadn't I said anything? I had become so good at keeping secrets, I had no idea how to tell the truth.

Now it was as if I had to own up to having an affair. As if I was a schoolboy caught red-handed with stolen fruit, graffiti under my desk. But I could not justify this. I had no excuse for it. I had nothing to offer to make it better. To say, 'But it's you I love. I'm sorry. I didn't mean to. It was an accident.'

I wanted to take her hand and say, Lil there is something I must tell you. That future we planned, the one that goes with this house and the boat and the raspberry canes and growing old together. That future where I look after you for the rest of my days and we hold each other every night. The one where the garden grows ever more plentiful, the one where you tell me everything about you. That one, Lil. The dream that has lived in my heart ever since I first made love to you, it's dead.

But no words came to me. It was as if I had been rendered immobile.

'So,' she said. 'My suspicions are true.'

I looked into her eyes. Her dark-as-midnight-water eyes.

'How long?' she said, looking away. 'How long do you have?'

She looked at me and still I was without speech.

'For God's sake, Henry. When were you going to tell me? I know very well who Geraldine Holloway is. I was at a lunch with her for the hospital last month. I know how you have looked these past months.'

'I wanted to tell you.'

'How long?'

'They don't know. They don't know. Maybe . . . maybe six months . . . before I really go downhill.'

'Where is it?'

'It started,' I said, taking a deep breath and trying to settle my thumping heart, 'in my lung. That's what the cough's been. But it's in my head now. Metastases. Little offshoots from the lung.'

'They can't operate?'

'No.'

'Chemo?'

'They can do radiotherapy. But I don't think I want it.'

'Henry,' she said.

The name hung in the air above the soap bubbles. Gum leaves made rattling landings on the roof.

'Why?' she said. 'Why now?'

'I didn't plan it, Lil.'

'Are you in pain?'

'Aye, sometimes.'

'Where?'

'It comes and goes. Mostly my head; my right arm gets heavy. My leg.'

I reached out under the water and found her feet. I put them on my legs and massaged her toes absent-mindedly. Lili closed her eyes and slowly she slipped around the spa until her body was curled into mine.

After the bath, when we made love, I found myself wanting to fall into her softness and never leave it. In the darkness she asked me was I okay. I squeezed her in my arms and said, 'Just tired.' She orgasmed several times, rippling orgasms that arched her back beneath me. She kissed me with an urgency I had not known of her this past year.

At first when we were new to each other our lovemaking was slow, tender. I am not a young man and I did not pretend to have a young man's vigour. But once we became more familiar with each other our lovemaking became more urgent and I threw off my illusions of age and found myself with her on the bare floorboards as we built the house and on the summer grass in the field below. Slowly that time abated and a gentle passion for each other had settled on us and had not left us. There was no-one I had loved more slowly than Lili.

'What will I do without you?' she said.

I fought back the tears that came to my eyes. I kissed her mouth again and said, 'You've got a wee while with me yet.'

'I feel like I should stay awake with you and talk but I'm so tired.'

'There'll be time for talking.'

She lay in my arms and closed her eyes. Images danced in my head and would not let me rest.

'Damn it,' I said.

'What?'

'It's raining again, is all,' I said. 'And I didn't cover the boat.'

'I'm sorry I have to go to Sydney tomorrow.'

Lili sat up and retrieved her nightshirt from under the pillow. She pulled it on over her head.

'Are you sure you'll be all right with them here?' she asked.

'It's fine.'

'Can we talk about it when I come back?'

'Surely.'

'You are so kind to me.'

'I wonder why?' I asked her.

She smiled and settled again in my arms. 'Can you still run me to the airport?'

'I can indeed.' I did not want to mention that soon enough she would be the one driving me. Every three weeks or so Lil went to Sydney for her show. She was away a week researching, interviewing, pre-recording. I wondered what we would do when I could no longer drive. There was an ache in the left side of my head which would not go away. Nausea was becoming tidal in me, ebbing and flowing through the days.

'I have to go check the boat,' I said to her.

'It'll be fine.'

'I'll only be a moment. Go to sleep.'

I put on my pants and pullover and grabbed my jacket from beside the back door. I crossed the side garden to *Venus* and shone the flashlight on the uncovered deck. The open-air shed meant that rain could easily blow in about her if the wind came up and I liked her protected. Dragging the tarpaulins from under the keel, I hauled them up the ladder. I clambered across the wet deck pulling canvas behind me, spreading it out, pinning it down with bricks from beneath the boat, tying it off on the cradle, going up and down the ladder and round the boat until the thing was done.

As soon as I had finished, the rain stopped quick as it had started. I sighed and looked about me. I was wide-awake with no sleep in me for hours. It was a beautiful night, not windy but still and starlit with a coin of moon hanging over the river. Black patches of cloud moved away east. I unfolded a deckchair beside *Venus* and sat down.

I imagined myself flying up there in the soft infinite darkness. *Venus* suddenly freed from her cradle, her sails unfurling and her keel slipping effortlessly down the paddock, the boat lifting up and up. Me at the helm guiding her over the tree-tops, over the house, over the mountain. Over this island and due west. A flight right across the Indian Ocean then north until we crossed the Channel and came low above London's W1. On Lower Belgrave Street the houses are almost identical white four-storey town houses with black wrought-iron fences. We hovered above number 46.

I lowered a rope ladder and stepped onto the pavement. I went up the steps. Using my key I opened the front door. A small dark-haired boy came running towards me. Two girls, one eleven, one only four, in matching dressing gowns, emerged from a doorway. 'Father! Father! You're home!' they cried. And there they are frozen. They never reach my arms. I have forgotten the smell of them, the softness of their cheeks, the grip of their arms about my neck. They are like a jigsaw puzzle left incomplete in the hope that the last missing piece will mysteriously reappear.

I sat in the dark until my hands were numb with cold and a strip of blue phosphorous slid along the horizon. Back in the house the quiet of dreams lingered in the air. Upstairs Lil slept, her leg above the covers and her skin sepia in the half-light.

I reached out very slowly and rested the edge of my fingers against her hand.

Dear Lili, I said without breathing a word, have I told you how I love you? I cannot imagine how I would survive if I lost you. Yet you may not want to see me through this illness and it would be the harder death if you were not here. Don't leave me. Please Lil, through all of this stay with me. I want you to be the last person I say goodbye to. I want you to be holding my hand when I die. Is it too much to ask? Thank you for never knowing and never having to. Thank you for letting me hide my life away in yours.

And if I cried, the tears were gone by the time she awoke.

The curse of growing older is that we must live not only with what we have become but also with what we will never be.

SELF-INFLICTED WOUNDS

THE FOLLOWING MORNING I FOUND Suki asleep at the kitchen sink. The water was running but she was asleep. At least I thought she was. Her hands were under the water and her eyes were closed. She was swaying a little as if she'd just stepped off a boat after a week at sea.

It was nearly midday. I had been up for hours. I'd taken Lili to the airport early. I'd had a dizzy spell when I arrived home and had a brief lie-down on the bed. I'd called in sick and Stan had a panic.

'Not another week,' he said. 'What kind of flu is this?'

'I'll be in touch tomorrow.'

'I really need you to look at some contracts. Can I courier them up?'

'That's fine. I'll be here.'

After I'd spoken to Stan, I'd fixed the chicken wire over the veggie garden which had blown awry in the winds that had come through at dawn. I'd also collected a whole stack of kindling with Charlie who was banging about the house asking to watch a video. It seemed as if every loose shred of bark and twig had blown into the yard. I'd left the boy out there raking the path and come in to make him a sandwich.

Suki opened her eyes and saw me standing there. 'Haven't you got anything better to do?' she asked.

'It is my house, remember.'

'Yeah, right.'

I offered her tea. Filled the jug. Turned off the tap.

Suki's arms were trembling.

'Are you okay?' I asked.

Suki snapped her head round and slid onto a chair at the table where the newspaper was waiting for me.

'He's a funny kid, young Charlie. Full of stories,' I said, putting on the jug.

'Imagine being on that boat,' said Suki. 'Imagine being on that boat.'

She was talking about the big catamaran that had gone up on the rocks in the river. The headline across the front of the paper read *HIGH AND DRY*.

'He could have killed them all.'

'What is it you did last night?' I asked.

'You think someone's in control. In charge. And they run you up on some great rock,' she said. 'What if it had sunk? And there you were, thinking you were just out for a cruise.'

I glanced at her and she met my gaze. Her eyes were dark marbles and I did not want to know the worlds inside her.

'You look tired, Suki,' I said.

'Men. Fucking men,' she said.

'That's a little harsh.'

'You make the rules and this is how you treat people.'

She rubbed at her arm.

'Did you hurt yourself?' I asked.

She pulled up her sleeve to reveal a large, vivid bruise.

'Lord, Suki, what happened?'

She looked at me with her marble eyes, her face stained white. Then she giggled.

'I missed.'

'Missed?'

'I missed my vein. Couldn't . . . '

She didn't finish. She bent forward and vomited on the table. She slumped off the chair onto the floor and banged her head hard on the tiles.

I leapt to help her. She made no attempt to get up. Blood was seeping from her forehead where she'd cracked it open on the slate.

'Suki, you've hurt your head.'

'Don't touch me . . .'

'Suki, what the hell's going on?'

'You go ask that whore you live with . . . you go ask her what the matter is . . . '

I reached down and lifted her. She didn't struggle and she was heavy as a dead weight. I carried her along the hall and into her room. It was dark in the curtained light. I flipped the switch with my elbow and her stuff was all over the floor.

I lowered her onto the unmade bed and as I scooped up her legs to lay them out I saw the scars. Slice after slice – her shins and calves were marked by long white slashes, the healed effects of what I could only assume were knife marks. I looked at her hand lying limp beside her hip. On the underside of her wrist was a tattoo I'd glimpsed before but there, too, were fine white lines. Slice after slice across her arms. The arm scars were pale and thin. But the leg marks were deeper. And there were round marks that looked like cigarette burns. Her eyes were open and staring at me but she was not seeing me. Her face was grey. And the cold awful possibility hit me.

I ran for the phone.

'Lil,' I said, 'Suki's collapsed in the kitchen. You've got to get her some help.'

'I'll call Nick Powell. He'll know what to do.'

'I think she needs a hospital, not a GP. I think an ambulance.'

'Let me call him first.'

'Lil, what's going on?'

'I don't know. And I can't help. I'm in Sydney and she's going to have to manage without me.'

'There are scars all over her legs like she's cut herself over and over.'

There was a long silence. She said, 'Expect a house call,' and hung up.

'Would that include a house call from her mother, Lil?' I said to the air.

I turned and stared again at the table and the kitchen floor. I grabbed a cloth and wiped up the vomit. It reeked of some awful smell and made me sick to my stomach. I rinsed out the cloth and wiped the tiles again and again. There was no body there. There was no pool of blood. No trace of blood at all. I ran back to the bedroom.

'You're going to get up,' I said to Suki. She was limp as a fish and she did not respond.

I scooped her off the bed and ran down the hall and out through the back door. I yelled to Charlie. He was on the sand-pile.

'For God's sake, laddie, get in the car.'

I heaved her into the Land Rover and dumped her on the back seat. I made Charlie sit in the front.

'I want to bring the rake.'

'You can't bring the rake.'

'Why?'

'You just can't. Your mother needs a hospital.'

I drove fast down the mountain, the curves of the winding road rolling her from side to side.

Charlie said, 'Mum! Mum!'

'She can't hear you, Charlie. She's sick. We're taking her to a hospital.'

'Oh, not again,' he said.

'How many times has this happened, lad?'

'Her head's bleeding,' he said, weeping.

'It'll be all right. She fell over.'

'Is she going to die?'

'No, she's not going to die.'

When I reached the first traffic lights I saw her head had fallen off the seat. The cut was insignificant but a nasty bump had come up on her temple. Her face was beaded with sweat. I grabbed at her wrist and felt for her pulse but found nothing.

I heard myself yelling, 'Suki, Suki, wake up. Wake up.'

Charlie began yelling with me, 'Wake up, Mum! Wake up!'

He looked desperately at me. 'What if she never wakes up?'

He started kneading her limp hand which stuck awkwardly between our seats.

'Turn around,' I said.

'She's going to die.'

'Turn around.'

'She's going to die!' he wailed.

'No, she's not, Charlie. She's not going to die.'

He held fast to her hand, tears running down his face.

I staggered into the emergency department with her in my arms. Charlie ran beside me holding onto her as best he could. They ran a trolley bed out and I dropped her onto it. Nurses and doctors flocked about, questions were asked over and over, charts were filled, drips were going in and curtains were drawn around her cubicle.

Only when an hour had passed and she had shown the first sign of coming round, only when the doctors had once again assured me she would live, only when Charlie said, 'I'm hungry, is it lunchtime?' did I calm myself and know that for today I would not have to explain another young woman dead on my floor.

A LESSON IN DECEPTION

SANDRA RIVETT. AH, MRS RIVETT with her thick red hair and her lovely eyes. Two things had been rare about Mrs Rivett. That the children liked her, and that she had lasted a full month. There had been almost as many nannies through 46 Lower Belgrave as there were buses through Marble Arch. Mostly they were a dull lot, bland, overweight and poorly educated. The more intelligent ones were worse in some ways. They figured out the rot quick smart.

The less intelligent ones accepted her Ladyship's darkened room, her tantrums and tears, her rigid schedules for the children's bath-times and meals, the lack of conversation between the mother and her children. Some of the nannies she even tried to befriend, but still they didn't stay. Some lasted a week. Two Spanish girls lasted several months until their English improved and they discerned the nature of what was being said to them. Nor was it simply a matter of looking after the children either, as the position was advertised. It was a matter of running the house.

Of course there was the kind Lord Lucan, the estranged

husband. He no longer lived in the house (poor man, who could tolerate a creature such as his wife?) but had a flat nearby and would drop in to visit the children before going off to his club in the evenings. Lord Lucan who bought chocolate toffees, who asked how the accommodation was, who ensured the staff got paid on time – so very thoughtful, Lord Lucan. And there was her Ladyship, who would plead with his Lordship for money every time he visited. She would wave the household bills in front of his eyes. 'See, see, we cannot live on air. This, all this, John,' she'd say, indicating the hallway, the furnished rooms, the children, 'it all takes money.'

Lord Lucan would laugh affably and say, 'Do calm down, Veronica. There is no need to upset yourself, the children or the servants. Why, you have such a healthy allowance,' and here he'd wink at the new domestic help, 'that I'm sure now dear Mary (or Olivia, or Jane or Rosita) is here to help, you'll manage the home much more efficiently.'

And Lord Lucan would disappear into the night and seek a fortune upon the green baize to lift the dread of financial ruin from his shoulders. But no luck accompanied him. No great win allayed his fears, and the more he lost, the more he borrowed, and the more he borrowed the further he went in search of ready cash and the deeper he descended into the underworld of London, becoming acquainted with the low-life who have always ridden on the coat-tails of the rich. And the more he frequented the drab rooms of the East End moneylenders, the more he lamented the ruination of all that mattered to him. Time and again he spoke ill of his estranged wife. Told all manner of stories to paint her in a poor light. Taped his phone calls to her and her hysterics when he had goaded her into a fight. He said to his friends that if only Veronica were not in his life, if only he could raise the children himself, all would be well again.

It was this world that Mrs Sandra Rivett stepped into. One month in the employ of the Earl and Countess of Lucan. Twenty-nine years old and already a divorcee. She was an attractive young woman, nicely presented. She had a natural vivacity which was infectious. She had, on the fateful day, come down with a nasty cold that kept her in when it should, by rights, have been her night off. She had a boyfriend. A young Australian lad who had been seen waiting for her outside the house. Perhaps the job was her means of saving to be married again. Perhaps they planned to settle in Australia. He was referred to in the press as her fiancé.

At the inquest the following year they hardly mentioned her. Even in the newspapers the photos were all of Veronica, our set and myself. I read that when her family came to pick up Sandra's belongings, some weeks after the tragedy, Veronica just handed them over at the door. A few clothes and other personal items in a paper bag. No cup of tea. No fruitcake and small talk. No whispered apology. No wax-sealed envelope enclosing a carefully worded letter expressing deep regret, sympathy, a modest cheque for final wages and a little extra to help with things at home. The sort of thing a family might expect when their daughter had been employed by peerage. How they must have hated me. Hated all of us at her inquest.

It wasn't an inquest for her. It was an inquest into my marriage. It was an invasion into the lives of my friends that painted us as characters in some sort of soap opera.

But who lost the most? Veronica? My children? Sandra Rivett? Or was it Sandra Rivett's father who lost his smiling girl? Her mother who waited night after night at the kitchen table for the latch at the back door? In the end the verdict was guilty. Murder by Lord Lucan.

The law was changed after that inquest. No coroner's jury was ever able to name a murderer again because their verdict could have too much impact on any criminal court proceedings.

Who remembers her now? Ironically perhaps it is I who think of her more than anyone else. Whether I like it or not, she was my mistake. There were rumours that I had been having an affair with her. That she knew something I did not want told. If I had wanted a mistress I would hardly have bothered with the nanny living in my wife's house. In fact I cannot recall ever being alone with Sandra Rivett. And sex was never my weakness.

'She's a right case, Suki is,' I said to Jimmy later when he dropped over.

'What did the doctor say?'

'They'll keep her in a couple of days. Of course the police are involved because it's an overdose. And the hospital wants her to go to that clinic on the eastern shore. Dry out for a while. All very quiet, the way Lil wants it. Too small a town and all that. They can't make her go there, though. It's all voluntary.'

'What did she take?'

'They think it's some heroin mix. In my own bloody house.'

'Why would she do that?'

'She's all cut up. She's got scars all over the place. Burns and knife marks.'

'Self-inflicted?'

'The doctors think so. They say addicts do that sometimes. When they're . . . high.'

'I guess it's a kind of initiation.'

I stared at him. 'Initiation into what?'

He shrugged. 'Or maybe it's penance.'

'What sort of people sell that stuff? I mean here, too, in Hobart?'

'Ah, there's always people ready to help you do something illegal.' Jimmy smiled, looking me in the eye. 'I thought you'd know a few for sure, eh Henry.'

Ah, indeed, dear Jimmy, but that's not what you meant, was it? That gaze was not fishing for something. It was seeking reassurance.

'How's that?'

'Well, the building trade . . . you know.'

Jimmy wasn't talking about anything but what he knew of me. And what he knew of me was that I was a builder.

'Ah,' I said. 'The back of a truck is a fine thing. But it's not drugs.'

'No. But where's the line?'

'When it hurts people, I guess. Not just their pocket. Their life.'

'Can't say what might. What mightn't. Don't think it's that simple.'

And he was right. There were always people willing to help. People who had no idea of the contribution they were making. It takes a lot of people to make a successful crime.

Imagine all the preparations which led to that chilly night in November 1974.

A woman in Charing Cross sells the lead piping at the hardware store. She asks if I'll be needing a pair of rubber gloves while I'm at it. To which I reply, 'Thank you, how thoughtful.'

A junk dealer in Portobello Road sells me the US postal bag.

'That big enough for you, Guv'nor?' he asks. 'What you planning – playing Father Christmas?'

There's the friend who lends me his Ford Corsair because the Mercedes has been giving me no end of trouble. And though I do not tell him, I believe it would be much too conspicuous.

I arrange to meet some friends at the club at 10.30pm as an alibi. By 11pm they find themselves dining without me.

The policeman on the beat notices that at 9.15pm the upper lights of 46 Lower Belgrave Street are burning but not the basement lights. A cab driver sees me (or someone very like me) walk from the Ford Corsair to the front steps. 'Just after nine,' he says. 'I'd know his Lordship anywhere. Walks about these parts often.'

In the wings, before any of this happened, there's a judge who won't give me custody of my children. A legal system that won't free up the assets from the family trust. A doctor who prescribes tranquillisers for my estranged wife but does not refer her to a psychiatrist. My wife who'll do anything to prevent me having custody. The nanny who stays in on her regular night out. The children, the eldest awake in her mother's bedroom watching television, the younger two asleep in the nursery on the third floor.

Later there are the cats that pad through the blood and leave a trail across the floor and out into the courtyard even though that door was locked.

Surprisingly there's also a porter at the club who sees me pass. He says it was me at the wheel of my own Mercedes, though he thought the car was still being repaired. Yes, he's sure it was me, at 9pm.

Thankfully, after the deed is done (and done appallingly badly you must admit – the wrong person murdered, the body packaged for transport but left on the floor, the wife stumbling upon the crime and being battered about the head, then fleeing the house screaming murder, the children left alone) there is also a friend who answers the phone. Who opens the door in the dead of night and lets me in. Who offers me the bathroom, fresh clothes, whisky, writing paper. She begs me to do myself no harm, no matter what the events of the night.

I cannot stay. Plied with several drinks and a handful of sedatives, I depart. I have no clue where to go. Overwrought with the shock of wielding a blunt instrument at someone and seeing them fall dead before my eyes; unprepared for the terrible muddle which has me realise I have not only killed someone, but the wrong someone, I drive the borrowed Ford Corsair to Newhaven. There I take a speedboat deep into the Channel. I had registered the boat in a false name in preparation for this dark night. I had fully intended to bring the mailbag and its contents with me, to dispose of it by moonlight in the deep straits before returning posthaste to London by dawn.

Overcome with despair at my wasted life, the utter disgrace I have now brought upon my children, my family, I open the sea cocks and, as water laps about my dress shoes, I lash myself to the driver's seat. Within a few moments all that I have been is a story and I am sinking into the silent blackness of an icy saltwater death. I leave no trace. Save in the bellies of big-eyed deep-water fish who prowl the Channel and feast on my upper-class flesh.

Did John Bingham, the seventh Earl of Lucan, Baron Lucan of Castlebar, Baron Bingham of Melcombe Bingham and a Baronet of Nova Scotia, commit a murder? How could he have mistaken the nanny for his wife? How could he have killed the wrong woman? Was he that kind of man?

Lord Lucan didn't hate his wife. He wanted to be free of her. He needed money. He wanted his children. He didn't hate Veronica. Not by then.

He never would have hurt her. Surely, I never would have hurt her.

'Henry?' Jimmy was asking. 'You're away, mate.'

'Fine. I'm fine.'

'Pigs fly.'

'No time to be anything else. Got Lil gone all week. The boy here. My life's run amok.'

'You know, Stan's got a business to run . . . he can't wait around for you. And you've got more important business now.'

'So who's been talking?'

'Look, we talk . . . and he knows something's up – the least you could do would be to have the guts to tell him.'

'I'm not ready.'

'There's no bloody thing called the right time and you know it. Bloody hell, people depend on you.'

'I'll have Stan take it over,' I said, 'the community centre . . . if you decide to go ahead with it.'

'I don't give a shit about that right now. Look at yourself, Henry. What are you going to do . . . just hang around until you're dead? What about the chemo?'

'Radiotherapy. I don't want it.'

'Why?'

'I don't want to fight it.'

'What about Lil? You're just going to do nothing? You aren't even going to try?'

'If it's got me, it's got me.'

Jimmy sat for a while and stared into his beer. 'I never figured you like that,' he said.

'Sometimes you have to accept what is, I reckon.'

'You try telling that to Lili. You won't take a chance.' He sighed. 'I don't know why I'm getting worked up about it. It's your life.'

We looked at each other and I heard the frailty of those words.

'Just plan things out a bit.'

'Aye, Jimmy. I will.'

'And for God's sake, Henry, tell Stan.'

BEETLES AND OTHER CREATURES OF THE DARK

CHARLIE CAME WITH ME INTO the office.

'What school's he going to?' Stan said.

'He's not at school,' I said.

'What does he do all day then?'

'We've not been sure how long he'd be staying.'

'There's that school right near you.'

'Aye. Though school's a loose description for it.'

Stan grinned. 'Ah, nothing wrong with growing a Greenpeace activist under your roof. The world needs more of them.'

Stan was forty-seven years old with the face of a schoolboy. His cheeks were scarred from teenage acne. He had an awkward nose, a longish chin and bright prominent eyes. Yet he was strangely handsome. Perhaps it was his enthusiasm for everything. He said when I first came to work with him, 'People might take me more seriously with you around. Not because you're walking. Because you're . . .'

'Old?'

'No,' he'd laughed, 'you just have a look – reliable, important.'

He was easy to like. He got the nice vote and the sympathy vote. It was an unbeatable double. He'd had some recognition for a couple of projects he'd done on the Great Ocean Road before he and Sharon moved to Tasmania. After the accident his career hadn't looked too good. A crippled architect. 'What am I going to design,' he'd asked when I first met him, 'a whole lot of ramps?' He'd been looking for a builder to get into a partnership with. I said I'd work with him. I didn't feel sorry for him. And I guessed he'd be loyal. With Stan, I knew I'd never have to worry if I wanted someone to vouch for me.

As it turned out, people wanted to work with him. He was talented. These days he was on several government committees and a couple of boards. Together we'd created some impressive public spaces and private homes. The business employed fifteen people now. He'd become a devotee of new-age thinking a while back. He'd started telling me and anyone else in earshot that life was entirely our creation and money was an expression of how abundantly we could think.

'It's all in the mind, Henry, everything we are.'

'It got you walking yet?' I'd asked.

'In my mind I'm running.'

He and Sharon adopted twin girls from China. They were twelve now, Tilly and Rachel, and as alike as two peas. Save that Tilly wore baseball caps and Rachel had taken to nail polish of late. I liked the girls. They had got themselves into a lot of trouble at school doing practical jokes.

'What's up? You're still not looking too flash. You over it?' said Stan.

'I didn't actually have the flu, Stan. I just needed some time.'

'I wondered. You look like you're about to tell me you're going out on your own.'

'In a manner of speaking but not the way you think,' I said. 'I've got a brain tumour, Stan.'

'Oh,' he said slumping forward in his chair. 'Oh, Henry, that's not right. That's not right at all.'

He looked up, 'You are telling me – '

'Aye, Stan.'

'That's not meant to happen.' He sat silent for a minute and then said, 'How's Lil?'

I shrugged. 'As you'd expect.'

'Oh Henry.'

I watched Charlie out the door talking to Eve, our new graduate. He was waving his arms about and Eve was laughing. Stan followed my gaze and said, 'And the boy? Charlie? Can be very tough on a child that sort of thing. Any kind of loss. We had it with the girls . . .'

I thought of Suki drying out in the clinic. Lil had not jumped on a plane to come home when her daughter had overdosed. She'd kept on working – business as usual in Sydney. I knew Lil had been raised in an orphanage in Vietnam. She'd been married years back. His name had been Keith Birch. He'd been a teacher of hers in Vietnam. He'd married Lil and brought her with him when he returned to Australia. He'd committed suicide a few years later. Gassed himself in his car. Lil hadn't wanted to talk about it. Suki must have only been three or four. She and Lil had been on their own together all those years but something had happened. When had the drugs begun? There were too many questions building up in my mind. Things I had missed.

'I don't think that me dying is the hardest thing Charlie's going to deal with in his life.'

'Ah,' said Stan, eyeing the boy again. 'So what do you need, Henry?'

'I'd like to finish off what we've got on the go as best I can. Some days I feel surprisingly fine. I wouldn't want to be floating round the house with nothing to do.'

'Sure. Of course. Good to keep focused.'

Stan wheeled his chair over to the window and stared out. Our offices looked right over the harbour. The Antarctic ships were in. The big orange *Aurora Australis* and the French *l'Astrolabe* too.

'You might need to find a new partner . . .' I said.

'Not now.' He waved his hand dismissively. There was another prolonged silence. Usually Stan would find some affirmation for a tricky situation, like 'I am an expression of goodness in the world', or 'There is only right action' but he seemed to have run right out of them.

When he turned his chair back from the window I saw it had really hit him, this news of mine.

'It's okay Stan. I'm okay with it.'

'Are you, Henry?' he said with tears in his eyes and his mouth quivering. 'I'm not. It's a real blow.'

———■———

I went back to work and I took Charlie with me.

He liked the building sites and the covered stacks of bricks and roof tiles, the half-laid paths and drying concrete. He'd borrow my hard hat and ask me to lift him up to sit on the parked excavators. He'd wait up on the bank at the nursing home we were building on Macquarie Street watching the trucks and diggers. He'd wave to me when I looked up to see if he was still there. He built Lego tractors and trucks and put them on the sand pile at home. Ellen Howroyd made gingerbread men when she knew he was coming with me to check the landscaping.

At night I'd hear him cry out in his sleep while I watched television. When I went in to check on him he'd be grinding his teeth and calling out as if he was in pain. If I woke him to tell him it was okay, he'd look confused and fall instantly back to sleep.

My life had been kidnapped by the needs of the boy. I had forgotten five year olds know exactly what they like. And this one needed food every two hours. Pearl suggested a trip to the supermarket to let him show me what he preferred. We ate fish and chips, sausages and mashed potatoes, or baked beans on toast for dinner. He liked rice bubbles, bananas and blackcurrant cordial. In one day alone we visited the supermarket, the fruit store, the bakery and then we ran out of toilet paper and I had to make a six o'clock dash to the local store. How could the lad use so much? Suddenly I had to wash and dry things for him. Did he have to get himself dirty every five minutes? It was Pearl who suggested the boy might need another change of clothes.

We went to the bookstore too and found him a new book about trains that came down an old woman's chimney. It was called *An Eye Full of Soot and an Ear Full of Steam* and had lots of food in it. Charlie made me read it over and over. And we read *Thomas the Tank Engine*. He'd brought that one with him. I remember my own son George had loved *Thomas* stories too, although I am not sure I read much to him. There was a nanny for that. I fell asleep on Charlie's bed one night and woke at ten o'clock with a stiff neck from the pillow and the boy snoring away beside me.

He didn't seem to think it strange to have been left with a complete stranger. Neither did he feel strange to me. He was like a warm breeze come back into my life. One afternoon Jimmy took him fishing. The boy had been scared out of his wits, by all accounts, at a fish landing in the boat and had begged to go home. However, when he arrived he marched right in and presented me with a three-inch flathead and proudly announced that he'd caught dinner.

'I'll cook it up for you then,' I said.

'I'm never going to eat it. It's for you.'

'Don't you like fish?' I asked.

'Not any more,' he said. 'Their eyes watch you and they just keep looking at you even though they're dead. It's the saddest thing I ever saw.'

Each day I'd get a call from Lil. She sounded far away and when I tried to tell her the things the lad and I had been doing she seemed very quiet. She did not ask about Suki and when I asked if she had spoken with the clinic she said, 'They have my number.'

'What will happen to her?'

'I have no idea.'

'The scars, Lil. You should see the scars.'

'I saw the first of them. When she was thirteen. I have no desire to see the rest.'

'But why, Lil?'

'Some people are just not normal, Henry. They have parts of themselves they have no way to express. They live with things I don't pretend to understand. I tried. I did what I could and she ran away and I couldn't do any more. And here I am again, the same story. So I'll do what I can for the child, but not for her. She has to do it for herself.'

One morning Charlie held me up getting off to work. I'd sent him back to his room to put his shirt on the right way round, then back to the bathroom to clean his teeth and brush his hair and then he couldn't find the truck he wanted to bring with him. I heard myself yell out in clipped British, 'George! I say, chop chop. Bad form to be late.'

'What?' he yelled from up the hallway.

I shook my head. 'Nothing lad – just get a move on.'

It was the first of my slip-ups but I brushed it aside as confusion, not an indication of decline. I rationalised that having the boy thrust into my life kept my mind off things. I was dead on my feet by the time I got the lad into bed. For that whole week I slept undisturbed. It was good not to have the long stretches at 2am when I found myself awake and thinking.

On the Friday, we picked Lil up from the airport. The time had gone by so fast I could hardly believe she was home again. Pearl and Jimmy came for tea. Jimmy brought fresh flathead and we cooked out on the barbecue. Charlie ate a sausage in bread and went off to play with the Lego Lili had brought him back from Sydney.

We sat around in the golden evening with our jackets on and a lantern on the outdoor table. Lili wanted Charlie to go to the school just along the road from the house. I was dead against it. It was one of those alternative places with no uniforms and all the kids in one class with the same teacher. Only had about twenty students.

'He's only five. Maybe he's too young for school,' Pearl said. 'And they might not be staying anyway and it would – '

'Henry can't be his babysitter while Suki's not around,' said Lili.

'I don't mind,' I said quietly.

'She should be the one making this decision,' Pearl said looking at Lili.

Lil must have listened to a hundred stories about Pearl and Jimmy's kids, but she had never offered a word about her own daughter. I wondered what Pearl made of that. I wondered if they'd talked about it.

'Suki's idea of him being at home is having him sit in front of some TV show. Or dragging him into town day after day,' said Lili.

'It's more like a wildlife park than a school,' I said. I knew the sort of people who sent their kids there. I saw their cars. Their clothes.

Pearl said, 'I might be wrong but I'd say Charlie isn't the sort of kid you'd put in an ordinary school.'

As if to demonstrate this, Charlie emerged from the house whooping and yelling. He leapt up to the table and said to us, 'Come and see this tower I've built . . . you have to see it. It goes all the way up to the sky . . .'

'In a minute, Charlie, we're talking,' said Lili.

'Okay, but don't be long!' he yelled as he ran back inside.

'Henry and I will go in on Monday. We'll take Charlie and have a look. Are we agreed?' asked Lil.

'I don't care where you send the boy. Just don't expect him to learn to read and write while he goes to that place,' I replied.

'It'll be good for him,' said Lili. 'And if it's not, we have the whole of summer to sort it out.'

'He's always welcome at our place,' Pearl said.

'Definitely a fisherman in the making,' Jimmy said, winking at me.

Lili stood up and started to clear the plates. I gave Jimmy a wry smile. Lili the matriarch had emerged. Who would have thought?

Yet having taken on the role of grandmother, Lil seemed unable to remember the role of mother at all. Two weeks had passed and Suki stayed on the eastern shore. The clinic said that visits were not recommended right now so we didn't take the lad to see her, nor did Lili go alone.

'How long do they think she'll be in there?' I asked her one evening as we did the washing-up.

'They said she's doing well. Whatever that means.'

It was a strange time. Lili and I with the care of a child was something we had never anticipated. Our mornings now began with the sound of his feet on the stairs coming up to visit us. He would bring a book with him or his latest drawing. He'd sit up in the middle of us and chat about the wind in the night, the sunrise, the dreams he'd had about dinosaurs.

Over the past year or two I had thought about having a child with Lil. I was acutely aware of how much younger than me she was. I'd wondered if she'd regretted not being a mother, if a child might cement our lives. I seemed to finally have time for children. A chance for me to start again somehow. I hadn't ever discussed it with her, brushing away such thoughts as the romantic notions of an old man too much in love. But I had liked the idea.

The boy began at the feral school. I ended up being the one who dropped him there in the mornings. Lil was happy to know she could get off to work early. Charlie suggested we walk. It took us ten minutes along the pipeline track below the house if we didn't dillydally for the unicorns, crocodiles and giants. He was a funny little chap. Happy all the way down the hill and then in tears as I left, saying, 'Will you be here? I will miss you. What if I need you?'

His teacher said it was normal. That all the little ones went through it. But with Charlie it was hard. I hardly knew the boy. He was joyful one moment and full of fear the next.

'He'll make friends,' his teacher said.

The school was worse than I'd imagined. There was no rhyme or reason to how things were done. The children ran wild. The teacher was French, a woman called Verité with a stern face and an abhorrent dress sense.

'Isn't that dangerous?' I asked, seeing them climbing the large gum outside the one big classroom where all the children were taught.

'That's why they like it,' said Verité. 'Besides, it's not so high.'

'Do they have any sort of regular lessons?'

'They guide themselves,' she said. 'If they want to come in and work inside, they can. If they want to run in the wind all day, they can do that too.'

'But how do you ever teach them anything?'

'Mr Kennedy . . . Henry, isn't it? I know this school is unusual to many parents and grandparents, but give it some time. See if it works for Charlie.'

'He's a bright boy,' she said at the end of the first week. 'A most unusual child. A big heart. A beautiful heart. And he can already write his name.'

He wrote it over and over. Verité sent him home with crayons and coloured paper and he put his name up all over the house. He put elaborate drawings under our door when he woke up early in the morning. Lili pointed out that he always started with an horizon line and everything, though rudimentary, was in perspective. Gradually he put pictures side by side to tell a story on the same page. So the lizards began in the distance and then came closer until they were consumed by fire. The people went along in cars that tipped over cliffs. He titled his pictures. 'Cinderella's earthworms', 'One hundred blue tongues in the house', 'Where does the winter go?' And we had to write these on the bottom of the page for him.

After school Charlie and I would wander about the mountain or he made drawings at the table while I did paperwork or prepared the dinner. We worked in the garden together. We picked tomatoes from the little greenhouse, potatoes and carrots from the vegie patch. When Lil got home she'd run him a bath and get him in his pyjamas while I got the dinner on the table. One or the other of us would read him a story before bedtime. He often found it hard to get to sleep and liked us to stay with him. So Lil's and my evenings together got shorter and shorter.

Lili brought Suki home one afternoon. It was raining in great sheets, soaking the garden and overflowing the spouting.

'Sorry,' she said. 'Sorry to worry you both.' She was standing in the kitchen with a cup of tea in her hand, her bag by the door to her room. Charlie was on the couch watching afternoon cartoons, pretending not to notice her.

'Sorry. It was stupid. Someone gave me some stuff and I . . . couldn't say no. I know it's my weakness. It won't happen again, I promise.

'I know, Lili,' she said, 'what you must be thinking but I've been clean for years now. It was a stupid mistake. I guess you'll be wanting me and Charlie to leave? You don't need all this stuff in your lives. Kid and all.'

Lili said nothing.

'You can stay if you want,' I said. 'Take some time to sort yourself out before you go heading off anywhere.' It wasn't Suki I was thinking of. I was thinking of the way Charlie had taken to holding my hand on the way to school.

'What do you say, Lil?' I asked.

'It's your home, Henry,' she said.

'No, it's our home.'

'I'll go,' Suki said, looking at me. 'She doesn't want me. Never has.'

Still Lili said nothing.

'Lil, is it okay with you that Charlie and Suki stay a while longer?' I asked.

'Why not.'

And I think Suki and I both took something different from her tone.

'He seems to like school,' I said.

Suki nodded.

'Suki? Did Charlie's father get taken by a crocodile?'

She looked surprised. 'Of course not. Who told you that?'

'He did,' I said. 'A wee while back. And he's been telling the kids at school too.'

She shook her head. 'He couldn't possibly remember. He never knew him.'

Then she turned and went to her room and shut the door.

It wasn't ideal. None of it was ideal. Who knew what to believe? And Suki there sharing a room with the boy. A bed. We'd offered to get a single mattress for Charlie but she said no, it was nice having him to cuddle in the night.

'He likes it too,' she said.

They didn't talk much, her and him. He talked but Suki wasn't much of a talker. Least not when I was listening. Some days she'd sleep all day and Charlie would sing outside under the window getting louder and louder, and I'd take him walking to quiet him.

Silver Falls always got to him and he'd lie on the rocks and watch the river for half an hour or more. Once he fell asleep there beside me, flat out on the rocks, the afternoon sun on his back. When he woke up he said he'd dreamed the waterfall had run right into his shoes and washed a whole lot of black beetles out.

I watched Suki. I weighed up the risk of her. She was pale and had lost a lot of weight. She got a job at a pub in town doing afternoon and evening shifts. We put the boy to bed. Often she didn't get up till lunchtime. I continued taking Charlie to school. She'd bring home videos and watch them in the middle of the day. Sometimes on her days off she collected Charlie after school and took him into town with her. Sometimes he stayed with me. She hovered in our lives. Every Monday there was a $50 note on the kitchen bench. When I tried to say it was okay, we didn't mind feeding them, she said, 'We'll get our own place when we're . . . settled.'

She'd go off into the bush with Charlie beside her. Charlie told me they sat up on the rocks above the house and looked out to sea. He said his mum wanted to be a dolphin. Wanted to live in the cities under the sea.

'Are there really cities down there?' he asked.

'I've heard so.'

'Can we take *Venus* out when she's finished and find them?'

'Yes, but we'd best go at night so we can see the lights down below.'

'Can we go tonight?'

I looked up at *Venus*, unmasted, half a fit-out inside. 'It'll be a wee while.'

Suki and Charlie stayed on and we did not ask them to leave. The evenings were soft and quiet and it was light until 9pm. We no longer lit the fire every night.

After dinner Lil retired to her study to work. She came and went from the house and from us. She flew out, arrived home again, planned next year's guest list, did interviews, research, read endless books. I watched her on television and gazed at her soft lips, the curve of her cheek, her clipped measured voice, her smile bestowed at appropriate moments, and I missed her.

When we met at the awards dinner, she had been, at first, distant and detached. I thought perhaps she found us all beneath her. It never occurred to me she might be shy with people. That the camera gave her a sense of confidence she did not have on her own. Yet when one of the guests at the table that night delivered an opinion on the benefits of military service, she said, 'Would you still agree if it applied to all men over thirty-five?'

Once she said to me, 'There are two sorts of people. The

ones who want answers and the ones who love to ask questions. And I'm the latter. Maybe it's a control thing. But it's always the questions which fascinate me.'

'And me?' I asked.

'Ah, you are full of wonderful answers. It's one of the things I like so much about you. Of course I only believe half of what you tell me.'

'Which half?'

'You decide.'

TRACES OF CLOUD

FOR THE FIRST TIME SINCE I had come to live on the mountain, the arrival of summer weighed heavy on me. The days were long and changeable. The air had lost the bitter feeling. The frosts were gone. The deciduous trees had grown new leaves and the daffodils and snowdrops had wilted and dried. The paddock was bright green and the two sheep Jimmy and I shared were heavy with wool. The mountain had grown busier. It felt like every time I stepped out there was someone on the track or road.

This particular morning I had woken briefly at five and then drifted into violent dreams. I woke again as Lili was showering for work. The house was quiet. I dressed, kissed Lil goodbye and slipped silently outside. My legs felt steady under me and the air was delightfully fresh. It was good to be alone.

Lili rarely walked with me. She resided on the mountain but she didn't really live on it. Water was her medium. She swam at the pool and did yoga in South Hobart. Through summer she liked to swim at Seven Mile. I swam with her, and walked that long stretch of sand yet I wouldn't have wanted to live there on the beachfront. Like other people who dwelled up on the mountain, I was bound to the seasons and the fragile sense of transience that accompanied life on this old and beautiful beast.

White flowers had erupted along the path. They were sprouting off lean trunks and shimmering in the underbelly of the forest. Bright green moss gilded the track banks. I had always meant to find out the names of all the plants hereabouts. The birds too. Instead I knew just a handful of them.

Early summer flies lifted off the ground and buzzed urgently as I passed. I rounded the bend and looked up onto the higher hills directly below the summit. The bones of dead gums shone white in the morning sun, standing skeletons from the '67 bushfire amidst the lesser regrowth.

Nineteen sixty-seven. George had been born. My lineage. Lord Bingham. We were living in London, in the house in Belgrave Street. Having Charlie about the house made me wonder if I had ever known my own children. I had not been much use to them while I was in their lives and what a god-awful nuisance I must have been to them since. I had loved them. But I had never put myself out for them. They were never my first priority. My life was proof of that.

To a peer the world he lives inside is real and glorious. The rest of humanity, and indeed nature, is there to serve us. There is a proper etiquette for everything and we knew this from an early age. In the ruling classes there are racks of fine French wines in the chalk cellar and good brandy in the crystal decanters on the sideboards. There are generations of history accumulated in the family home. There is a safe for the jewellery. There are rooms for every purpose and all the fine things are in good supply. Some of the Persian rugs may be a little worn, and some of the rooms may have been closed to save on heating, but if things are not quite as the family had once enjoyed, it was still most adequate.

There was no need for a real job but, if asked, one undertook such a thing as a contribution to society. Or perhaps to stretch the mind. My friends were all of similar standing. There were the few nouveau riche who were included and tolerated, the ones who gave such fabulous parties and always had ready cash.

As a young man, it never occurred to me any of this would ever change.

I never bought off the rack, having my clothing made for me by my shirt-maker, tie-maker, suit-maker, shoemaker. My name and title meant I had been welcomed to sit upon several boards, for which they paid me a modest annual sum and put my name and title in their annual report. We had been peerage for seven generations. Everyone I knew (or cared to know) was in Debrett's. On the odd occasion I found myself outside my set I could immediately tell, if I had not already discerned it by the cut of his suit, what class of person a chap was by his accent.

There were times a fellow might run short on his allowance but that was easily remedied by a word with one's parents who would feel obliged to give a small lecture on the benefits of modesty and the dangerous attractions of the flashy life which was not something people of our sort aspired to. And then the matter would be solved by several hundred pounds, or thousand as the case may be, being made available. And should things ever become truly dire there was always a candlestick or two to sell, a couple of stones from the vault, the odd painting by some long-dead master that had become so ridiculously valuable it had been put away because the damn insurance companies wanted an arm and a leg to cover it. There were a hundred ways to sell a little here or there to remedy any major upset. And if the worst came to the worst, one could live with less staff.

When my father passed away, I inherited the title and took my place in the House of Lords. Wilson had ruined the economy. It was clear only the Tories could right the rise of the middle classes, stem the deluge of blacks swamping Britain like some dreadful backwash of colonisation and restore England to its rightful place of economic supremacy. My parents were great Labor supporters. My father, before his death, had been the party Whip. My mother was an ardent campaigner. We had some fierce fights about it. It did not change my mind. I ensconced myself firmly in a world that did not challenge me, with friends who had the same views as myself, and together we lamented the decline of the Empire and blamed the weak-minded politicians who had allowed immigration and unionism to get out of control. No one questioned the inanity of my life. Did it inspire me to have nothing better to do with my days than gamble, drink, suffer my wife and largely avoid my children? Of course not. But I was a fool, and the very worst sort of fool at that. A rich and privileged one.

If I had severe opinions, Veronica's were more severe. She loved England and the supremacy of all things Anglo-Saxon. She worshipped class and despised anything that wasn't. Her sister might have married money, but Veronica had married a title. In her struggle to become one of us, I sensed if not a deep wrong, at least an error of judgement on my part. I should never have married her. I had no idea what it would wrest from her to see her struggle to be something other than what she was. How she tried. I enjoyed the importance she placed on it. It made it so valuable. So far out of reach because of her birth.

She smiled when I won. Not then. Not in front of my friends. What a cold fish they made of her at the club. But at home, when we were alone, she would say, 'My lovely John. You shall make us poor with your gambling, but not tonight.'

She was sure somehow that she would manipulate greatness out of me, believing greatness to be my destiny. She wanted to be beside me when it happened. She would have died trying to ensure my place in history, and nearly did.

I have heard she lives alone, has never remarried, the dowager Lady Lucan as she calls herself. She does not live as one who was nearly murdered by my brutish obstinacy. But as someone who loved and admired me. When asked by a journalist why the lead pipe did not have the same effect upon her head as it did upon Sandra Rivett she said, 'Good breeding.'

—∎—

Traces of cloud lingered about the summit of the mountain. The track dropped into deeper forest and the rush of a river was loud. A sign said Fern Tree Bower and Silver Falls. Only the day before Charlie and I had walked this way. He had wanted to drink from a little tributary off the waterfall and had scrambled down, dipped in his hand and slurped the water off his palm, only to slip and fall backwards on the wet rocks as he attempted to climb up. I grabbed him but not before he banged his bottom. I found myself sitting on the riverbank with a tearful child on my lap.

I rubbed the boy's back and heard myself saying, 'Now, now. Be brave. It'll stop hurting in a moment.'

'No, it won't,' he wailed.

'Yes it will. You'll be fine.'

'How do you know?'

'I promise.'

How I wanted that promise for myself. I walked about with this thing in my head. Taking the same paths I always took, noticing water ferns and cushion plants, hearing magpies and seeing honeyeaters flit across the path, and all the time it was there and it wasn't going away. It was, in fact, growing, multiplying. I had no control over it.

The pain in my head had been quiet for several weeks. I took a chance and held on to my driver's licence. I hated the thought of being reliant. Especially on Lil. I didn't know how she'd take it. It worried me more than anything. I felt our age-gap and I did not want her to become my nursemaid.

At night when Lil and I lay together, I listened to her

breathing, the silence keen with unspoken words, but there were no words forthcoming. I hardly knew where to start, could hardly summon the energy for conversation, so busy was I with our visitors and my own grim thoughts. I kept hoping she would talk to me.

But Lil did not ask me how I was feeling. There were her silent lips against mine in the deep of the night. There was her body soft about me, her breasts in my hands. But away from the bedroom she was another women, not my Lil at all. She had withdrawn and I had no way to prise her out again. I was loath to press her for answers. I thought it might make her run, and that was the last thing I wanted. I had so little to hold her to me. I was a runner too. I knew how fickle was the solace of familiarity.

Michael Kennedy, who I knew in Africa, and gave me the use of his surname, would have said it was just the way the cookie crumbled. Some people smoked and drank and lived to one hundred and five, and there were vegetarians who died at thirty. You could never tell. Stan would say you couldn't live well if you didn't think well. If you got the right thinking happening, you could heal yourself. Jimmy would say you were lucky to get the life you did and make the most of it. And Lili? What would Lili say? I didn't know. There were so many things I felt I didn't know about Lil. I could ask her, but I suspected she would say, 'I don't think it helps to dwell on things.'

■

The house was still silent on my return, Charlie asleep unusually late. There was no doubt that I had adjusted to the boy and his mother. There was something about it that helped slow down the time and the months did not hang before me as something I must outlive but rather something I was living.

The curious thing about being Henry was how without pretence it all was. As Lucan, the quiet shelter of money had cocooned me. Here in the louder music of life, there was much to surprise me.

TRUSTING THE SHADOW

A SENSE OF URGENCY HAD overcome me regarding the boat.

I was fitting the bulkheads in the galley. It was precise work, designing the template, cutting the ply and fitting the pieces. The ply was the only manufactured timber on the boat. It was going to be finished with solid v-seam blackwood cladding to give a tongue and groove effect. All the doors and cupboards would be framed in huon. The whole interior was going to be finished bright to show off the beauty of the wood. The rainforest timbers had all come from various places on the island. Illicit timbers meant to be protected, or in short supply, but they'd come my way through the regular channels – government workers making a bob or two on the side. Some of them even wore their forestry uniforms when they dropped the timber off. Of course there wasn't any paperwork. Just cash. Everyone got a slice, all the way to the top I was told.

'Bloody idiots!' Jimmy had said when the trucks departed. 'In a hundred years they'll be saying what a tragedy it was, cutting down all the trees then replanting with some cheap crap only fit for cardboard. Wonder how their grandchildren'll thank them then. Jobs! Jobs my arse.'

The morning mist had lifted. It lay in the valleys below like a giant's breath. Away beyond the land the river looked as if it would leave a blue powder stain upon my fingertip. The line of horizon burned pale under a high stratum of soft grey clouds which seemed to have snagged on something further west.

Every sound penetrated and reverberated so that I heard the call of a rooster from the hill beyond as if it were right in the garden.

Suddenly I was aware of Suki climbing the ladder onto the deck. Charlie was at school.

'When are you planning on finishing her?' she asked, sitting down on the cockpit floor and looking in at me.

'Oh, ask me something simpler. Like, how long will it be before the mast's sanded? Or maybe, do you have any sails yet?'

'You're not well, are you?' she said.

'Oh, I'm well enough, Suki.'

I marked the ply with the pencil and scored it with a Stanley knife.

'So, is it terminal?' Suki asked.

'Suki . . . I think you're barking up the wrong . . .'

'Well, I'll be going. By the way, your doctor called. Yesterday while you were out. I forgot to mention it. Holloway,' she said. 'That's right, isn't it?'

She stood up.

'Said you'd missed your appointment. And Stan called a moment ago. Said he needed you to call him the moment you get in.'

I climbed up onto the deck and watched her disappear down the ladder.

Back on the grass, she called up, 'The oncologist Doctor Holloway. I looked her up in the phone book.' She paused then said, 'I don't know why you want to be so secretive.'

She had spied on me. She had sneaked around to uncover the truth. What would it be next? I climbed down, tossing the knife into the toolbox beneath the boat.

Inside the house Suki was putting on the kettle. I filled a glass with water then said, 'It's true.'

'You've got cancer?'

I nodded.

'Terminal?'

I nodded again.

'We'll go, Charlie and I,' she said. 'Bad timing.'

'I'm sure your mother'd like you to stay.'

'Yeah, right.'

'If you're going to stay, though, don't sneak around behind my back. If you want to know who Geraldine Holloway is, you can ask me.'

She looked away. 'Does she know?'

'Lil? Of course she knows.'

'She didn't tell me.'

'Look, I don't know what happened between you – '

'I don't think she gives a rat's about me.' She turned away and stared out the window into the trees. 'Did she ever talk about me?'

'No. But that doesn't mean . . .' I started.

'I might as well be dead.'

'No. Being dead's my business.'

She met my gaze and for a moment I got the kind of look I'd seen her only give to Charlie.

'Maybe I'll take Charlie off for a few days. See the island. There must be buses.'

'You're not that much trouble.'

'Give it time,' she said, but she smiled a bit. 'Would it be okay for Charlie to stay with you after school today? There's a course at TAFE I want to check out.'

'Sure,' I said.

I put her at ease. I made no waves in my life. I made no ripples. Did I want Suki here? If Lili wanted her daughter and grand-son to be here, that was up to her. I thought Lili would need all the family she could get soon enough.

I did not want to force my limited world upon Lili. She deserved to make her own choices. My simple life was reduced deliberately to three people. Lili and Jimmy and Stan. These were not people I trusted with the truth. They were people I trusted with my lies.

It occurred to me there was someone new I trusted. A boy by the name of Charlie. What did Charlie know of history? What did he know of Lucan? Nothing. But Charlie trusted a man called Henry Kennedy. It felt curious. As if I owed him something.

OBSERVATION OF SMALL THINGS

AND THEN, JUST AS DECEMBER started, Suki took Charlie down to the Saturday market on the waterfront. At four o'clock she arrived home without him.

'He's with some friends,' she said. 'I have to go to bed. I had a really late night and I've got to work later. He'll be fine. I'll get him in the morning.'

'We'll go and get him now,' Lili said. 'Tell us where he is and Henry and I will go and get him.'

'He's all right,' Suki said, her hand fidgeting with the strap of her bag, her eyes black and wide.

'Tell us where he is,' Lili said again.

'Look, he's my kid and I say he's okay.'

'I want him home,' said Lili.

'Like you never wanted me,' said Suki.

'This is not about you,' Lili said, deathly quiet. 'It's about your son.'

'Don't you trust my friends?'

'Do you?' Lil asked.

'He wouldn't come. I couldn't make him. He can be such a

brat. So Miro said to leave him, and I did.'

Lili said nothing. She gathered her bag, the keys, her sunglasses.

Suki pitched down on the couch, her head lolling against the backrest, feet bare on the carpet. 'It's cold in here.'

'It's warm outside,' I said.

'We'll bring him home while you have a sleep,' Lili said very evenly.

Suki closed her eyes and said, 'Fine, have it your own way. He probably won't even come.'

'I will not have him left on his own . . . with strangers!' Lil was angry now.

'He's all right,' Suki hissed at her.

'You don't know that,' Lil retorted. 'How can you possibly know that?' I had never seen her so furious.

As if defeated, Suki said, 'They were all there on the lawn. They're probably still there. Just ask.'

On the waterfront the cobblestones were jammed with shoppers moving from trestle table to trestle table. Children chased seagulls away. Couples were walking dogs up and down the grassy area. In the midst of a circle of people wearing Indian clothes, girls danced, spinning and shuffling on the grass while two men played large African drums with the palms of their hands. The smell of barbecuing sausages wafted over us.

We couldn't see Charlie. There were so many people. How were we supposed to spot a wee lad? The place was awhirl:

flapping flags, voices, music, buskers, peddlers, breeze blowing, cars passing, a pipe band playing away at the other end of the lawn.

Lil took my hand. 'Are you dizzy?'

'I'm okay.'

'He will be here,' she said. She had seemed calm again on the drive down the mountain but now we were here I could see she was angry again, or frightened.

I felt cold and a wave of nausea swept over me. I saw us driving home, no Charlie in the back seat. Miro, whoever Miro was, with Charlie, our Charlie.

We were standing in front of barrels of apples, bunches of spring flowers, small women in bright clothes, Tibetans, I don't know, calling out, waving ridiculously perfect carrots, radishes, lettuces.

'We are looking for a boy,' I said, 'a small boy.'

'What he wearing?' one woman asked. 'Lost boy!' she yelled across to the other women on the stalls.

'We're not sure. We don't know,' Lili said.

The woman called out again in her own language. Other women shrugged their shoulders. She turned back to us. 'No seen. We keep looking.'

Lil's hand pulled me on through the throng of people vying for second-hand clothes, porcelain bowls, spinning tops, carved maps . . .

Lil pulled out her mobile phone and dialled. 'No answer,' she said, 'she's not answering and I don't remember. I don't know what he had on when they left . . . did you see?'

Suddenly I had a picture of Charlie going out the door in his red T-shirt. It had a picture of a frog on it.

Lil pulled me away from the vendors and scanned the lawn again. The pipe band was moving down the grassy thoroughfare. Away beyond us the tin sounds of a voice on a megaphone carried from a rally outside Parliament House.

I became acutely aware of another little boy I had known long ago. How the same panic I felt now at the thought of never seeing a child again had driven me to snatch him and his sisters from their nanny in Green Park on a chill March afternoon and bundle them into a taxi. I had stolen my own children and taken them back to the Elizabeth Street apartment. Upon arrival I had announced that from now on they would live with me.

'But Father,' said George, 'what about my train set?'

'We'll buy you a new train set,' I said. 'We'll buy you anything you want.'

'It smells funny,' said Camilla, my four year old.

Frances, the eldest had said, 'What about Mother? She was expecting us home for tea.'

'I will let her know you're here with me.'

'But when do we go home?' Frances persisted.

'Once the judge says we can. All of us together.'

'With Mummy?' asked Frances.

'No, just us four.'

'Which bed am I going to sleep in?' said George.

'We haven't got any night things,' said Frances.

'Don't you want to live with Daddy?' I asked.

'I want to live with Daddy,' said my baby, Camilla.

'Where will the judge send Mummy to live?' asked Frances.

'How about I go up to the cake shop and find us some buns and maybe a jam roll.'

'Can we come too?' asked George.

'No, best stay here. I'll be right back. Frances will take care of you.'

'You were going to call Mummy,' said Frances.

'Food first,' I said.

I slid to the grass beside the nearest tree. A big, old, smooth-barked elm in a row of old elms the whole distance of the market. My head was pounding. My heart was pounding. God how Veronica must have panicked when the nanny returned distraught. She must have waited all afternoon for them to return. It would have got dark outside and still they were not home.

Lil squatted beside me.

'Are you okay?' she asked. 'We'll find him.'

My breathing slowed. I felt empty. I had kept them five weeks. Five weeks before the court hearing. I thought if I could prove I could take care of them, if they were well looked after, the magistrate could not possibly award Veronica custody. She was unstable. I had evidence: doctor's records, psychiatric evaluations. They would not be safe with her. But the magistrate didn't see it that way. He gave the children back to

Veronica and I was granted supervised access a few hours each month. Veronica was granted custody on the condition she employed a full-time nanny. That was in March 1973, the year before Sandra Rivett came to work for Veronica.

Lili was looking about and then very close I heard a little humming sound. I peered around the trunk of the tree and there, tucked between the tree roots, was Charlie, digging in the dirt with a stick.

'Lad!' I said.

He looked astonished to see me. A smile erupted on his face. 'Henry!'

'Charlie!' said Lili, and rushed at him, grasping him in her arms.

'Would you like to come home, lad?' I asked.

'How did you get here?' he asked. 'Can I bring my stick?'

'Sure. It looks a fine stick.'

'Hey, Charlie, where you goin' man?' came a voice and a tall, black man from the group of dancers ran up to us.

'We're taking him home,' said Lili stiffly. 'I am Charlie's grandmother.'

'You Suki's old lady? All right. He was going to stay with us. You want to go home, Charlie?' the man asked, bending down to speak to Charlie, reaching for his hand. 'You all right to go with these people?'

Charlie nodded. He touched the man's hand, said, 'Bye Miro, see you soon,' then turned and took mine.

Miro nodded to me and Lil. I hadn't seen an African in years. I wanted to shake his hand, ask him where he was from.

But instead I simply said, 'Thanks,' and walked away. Lil said nothing.

'Let's go,' said Charlie.

'Your mum's having a rest,' said Lili as we got in the car.

'She wouldn't let me bring my stick,' he said. 'It's from Jupiter. I can't get back without it.'

Charlie was quiet all the way up the mountain. When we arrived, Suki did not reappear from her room. Lili went in to check on her and came out saying she was sleeping.

'Didn't she have to work?' I asked.

'It's her responsibility,' said Lili.

After dinner we put Charlie to bed in our room. Lili said we'd move him downstairs later on. But we didn't. He lay like a sharp-angled pillow in the middle of us. At some point I left the two of them and moved onto Lili's couch in the window.

At dawn I awoke and went downstairs. On the fridge there was a scrawled note in red Texta. It said: *Don't fuck up my kid.* When I looked into the open doorway of the guest room, the bed was made and there was a small pile of Charlie's clothes and his toy box by the door. Apart from that the room was empty.

Suki had gone.

FACELESS

I WENT BACK UPSTAIRS. LIL opened her eyes. Charlie lay beside her, his head half buried under the blankets, fast asleep.

I showed her the note. She extricated herself from the bed and came downstairs with me.

A sparrow danced along the edge of the balcony, stooping to sip raindrops as it went. I heard Lil pull up a chair at the table.

'What did you say?' she asked, puzzled.

'Nothing.'

'Yes, you said something. Only it sounded strange.'

I gazed into her face and saw it was true. Something had uttered forth from me and I had been unaware of it.

'You sounded,' she said, 'like Sir Humphrey off *Yes, Minister.* Very proper. Very English.'

'You may suffer some loss of speech, or loss of comprehension,' Doctor Holloway had said. 'You may find people close to you tell you that you've used the wrong word. It's because it's in the motor cortex. In time it will affect your movement. In some ways it can be very similar to a stroke. But it will start very slowly. You may notice nothing for quite a while.'

But this was far worse than any lapse of awareness. I had spoken unknowingly. I had reverted to my true accent.

'Henry?' Lili said.

I walked into the bathroom and closed the door. In the mirror I looked into the face I had become accustomed to. The one which had emerged after vanity had been cut away. Nausea washed over me. I sat on the edge of the bath and waited for the black dots to disappear.

After the night of Sandra's death it was clear I had to flee. In South Africa I had many friends but I was too obvious. I had to duck my head round every corner, fear my height, my face, even my voice. So into Rhodesia I went, to an estate where private medical procedures were undertaken; clandestine royal births and operations which went unreported by the media. There a certain doctor also made it possible for people to leave their old identities behind.

He assessed me, reminded me, with the briefest of smiles, that there was no going back. Not successfully. And assured me that there were those still at large who were evidence of his craft. A certain recent President fallen spectacularly from grace. A music legend. People who had decided they wanted a life away from fame or infamy and who needed a new face to make it possible.

How I baulked at the idea of that operation! I had no desire for change. In fact I had spent much of my adult life attempting to ensure as little changed as possible.

I found it impossible to believe my life as a man of honour, a gentleman, might be over. I was cast out, yes, for my own safety, temporarily. My name would be cleared at the inquest and I could go home.

My friends and I would laugh about it over cigars. How Lucky nearly got done for murder! No use becoming some scar face no-one would recognise when I got back to London because I'd lost my nerve when the heat was on and had some nigger doctor carve me up.

No, I wouldn't do it. I would lie low. I would wait. So lie low I did.

In June 1975, an abominable seven months later, the inquest into the death of Sandra Rivett began. At the end of the inquest the foreman announced that Sandra Rivett's death was, 'Murder, by Lord Lucan.'

Three days after this news arrived a letter was handed to me. It was unsigned but I knew the handwriting of my brother well. He urged me to do whatever I must to hide myself. If I wanted any sort of life it could no longer be as Lucan, nor anyone resembling him.

So to the butcher I went. His knife pared cheek from bone, shifted the balance of nose and chin and the heaviness of eyelids. I dreaded the outcome. Why not simply immerse my face in boiling fat and save myself the trouble of the surgeon's fee? I had not anticipated that he would be such a craftsman. That my flesh was as sweet to him as clay to the potter. He took away the arrogant stare, the full lips, the straight nose. He took away my good looks and left me with a face I have learned to live with. It was not handsome. It was the face of a man who had not had the fortune I'd had, not the education nor the opportunities. It was a working man's face. He left only one hard scar, a line from cheek to ear. A convenient distraction from other more subtle scars, and a useful thing to make stories about.

'You will not unearth yourself,' I said to the man who still lived beneath my skin. 'You have no place here.'

I washed my face and patted it dry. I did not look in the mirror again.

Lil was still at the table when I returned.

'I want to help you,' she said, 'but I'm not sure what to do.'

'I can manage,' I said. 'You're going to be late for work.'

'I want to cancel work today. I'll call right now. Could we do that? Could we just go back to bed?'

'You're forgetting there's someone in our bed.'

'Then we'll use the guest room,' she said.

She walked ahead of me to the hall, opening the cupboard as she passed and taking from it clean sheets. She stripped the bed. She put Charlie's toys and books on the bookshelf. She put his clothes away in a drawer. Together we smoothed the fresh linen.

'You don't think she'll be back?'

'No.'

She opened the doors out onto the balcony and then, with a simple movement, undid the dressing gown she was wearing and let it fall to the floor, stepped over it and came towards me. She took my hand and sat down on the low bed with her legs folded beneath her.

'Take off your clothes, Mr Kennedy,' she said.

I sat down and undressed. She pulled me against her and held me in her arms, stroking my chest. We lay together and I felt the warm bumps of her spine, the tiny texture of hair invisible but tangible upon her back, the soft weight of her breasts against my chest, the hard line of her shoulderblade, the deep sweet scent of her skin, the hot moisture of her sex and later, when we were joined together, the rise and fall of her hips as she moved against me. Later still, I felt the warm flood of her around me and me in her.

Lili slept as she often did afterwards. Her little death. For ten minutes or more she slept, then stirred.

'I dreamed,' she said, almost before she realised she was speaking.

'What?' I asked.

'A crater, a hull of earth. Scarred. Raw and wide. There was . . . a deep crevice with bones, human bones, limbs and skulls. And yellow, seeping ooze under dark crusts that would break if I walked on them.'

'Where was this crater?'

'Inside me.'

Oh, Lil, I wanted to say, I know how hard it is to keep the

past buried. But if you don't, it will eat you from the inside out. I know that too.

'I am a bad mother,' she said.

'Lil, don't.'

'I am. Because I don't care if I never see her again.'

When I'd asked Lil, when we were new to each other, about her parents she'd said, 'I don't really remember my father at all. He disappeared during the War. And my mother died then too, when I was five or six. An aunt raised me. When she died I went to an orphanage.' I wondered what memories Lil had that made being a mother so hard.

'To know a man you must know his mother.' My mother Kait used to say it and it had worried me because I thought we were so dissimilar back then. I would have loved to tell her how I had changed my opinions on so many things.

For a man his mother is at the heart of him. She is in the smell of his skin and the taste of his food. She is the substance of his dreams and the beginning of his sex. She is in the books he fails to read and the letters he wishes he'd written. She is in the women he has sex with and the woman he marries. She is in the restaurant where he takes his first true love. She is in how he speaks to children. She is in the pictures on his walls, the colour of the paint he chooses for the hall. She is the sound of his need and the angle of his smile. She is the hope that lives within him and the limitations that he wears each day at his work. She is the song he has long stopped listening to which will never go away. She is his first bride, and she will be his angel when he dies.

But I began to understand, as I watched Lil and Suki, that for a daughter a mother was entirely different. I knew women could be unreliable creatures. They appeared benign with their soft bodies and quick smiles, their own particular promise of sensuality. They knew how to give and rarely how to take, which worked well for the men in their lives. But inside there was a hunger. I had seen it in Veronica too. Maybe they taught each other that, mother to daughter.

We waited all day but we did not hear from Suki. We waited two days and we did not hear from her.

I did not have any further slips in the following week. I spoke and the right words came out with the right accent. Lili seemed to have forgotten it. I passed it off as an aberration. Not as a warning but as an anomaly. It was as if, while I remained generally well, albeit a little tired, the headaches not too ferocious, the body pains not too noticeable, we could pretend nothing was going to take away our life together. Nothing would interrupt the home we had both found in the house on the mountain.

'Do you suppose she's all right?' I asked Lil one warm evening as I poured us wine.

'How would I know?' she said, eyeing Charlie on the rug building Lego before dinner.

'Surely she'll call?'

'In a year,' she sighed.

'But something might – '

'You can be sure it will. It may have already. Would we be the first to know? Hardly. It'll be the police. They'll come to the door one day and that will be it.'

I pulled her into my arms. Beyond the windows I could see all the way to Cape Bruny and across to Cape Raoul, those two far buttresses which marked the entry to the Derwent River. The sea breeze was up and the river was a broken mirror of amber light on a low chop.

Suki was gone. The risk of her had disappeared. I was relieved. My small world had returned, leaving with it just one unknown quantity. My dying brain.

THE FRIENDS OF GOD

'HENRY,' SAID CHARLIE, 'WHERE DO clouds come from?'

As we ambled through the garden and about the mountain he always had questions. Is that snow on the rocks? Can I drink from the puddles? Are there dinosaurs on the mountain? Are there worms as big as people? Are there caves where we could sleep one night?

'No, but there are huts,' I told him.

It was the first week of his school holidays.

'It's only overnight,' I said to Lili, 'and I'm feeling fine.'

'Are you sure?'

'It's half an hour.'

She did not try to talk me out of it.

'It will give me a chance to get some Christmas shopping done and hidden away,' she said.

We took two packs. Sleeping bags and food enough for dinner and breakfast, and a small axe for firewood. As we left, we passed by Jimmy's house. He was working at his outside table with his pen and a notebook.

'Morning, Shakespeare,' I called to him.

'Where you off to?' he said, looking up and grinning at Charlie and me.

'We're off to find a dinosaur,' I said.

'A brachiosaurus? A brontosaurus?'

'A celopheisus,' said Charlie. 'And Henry's secret hut.'

'It's a good day for it,' Jimmy said.

'We'll be back mid-morning tomorrow,' I said. 'If we're not back by twelve – '

' – I'll crack a beer. Watch out for snakes!'

'I've got my whistle,' Charlie laughed, holding it up.

At this time of the year snakes were all about. They slid out of the undergrowth into the pools of sunshine on the bush tracks. In the dappled light they could be hard to see and they did not like to be disturbed. I had told the boy to stamp his feet as he went about and sing! Sing as loud as he could. I had given him a whistle to blow if ever he was bitten by a snake. He thought it a silly thing and simply blew it all the time.

Jimmy had been very amused at my plan gone wrong. He said I was just going to have to trust the lad would be all right. It felt very risky.

Rain had come overnight and the track was damp underfoot. Leaves lined the bottom of the puddles. Charlie slipped his fingers into the clear water and picked one out, turned it over to see its brown underside and laid it back again. He bent his head and then looked up at me.

'It would be alright.'

'Not from the puddle, lad. There's a place just along . . .'

I indicated the way ahead and after another turn of the track we came to a run-off spot where the water splashed down into a gully. The bank fell steeply away, a massive tumble of rocks white with lichen before the deep forest of blue and green eucalypts, peppermint, stringy bark and myrtles, man ferns and wide-leafed grasses. The air was cold and bright though it was summer. Charlie's cheeks were pink and his breath came out in little blasts of steam. He drank from the falling water, his neck stretched, his hand holding firm to a rock.

He licked his lips and said, 'That is so cold I think it will freeze my teeth.'

We found the tiny side-track and walked between the trunks of gums and blackwoods, damp and pungent. There were outcrops of fungi on the bark, sepia-coloured with rims yellow as lemons. Along an embankment brown and cream toadstools grew, some the size of an eggcup, others big as a plate. Charlie was awestruck and insisted on looking at every one of them to see if there were tables and chairs, cups and saucers or any other signs of miniature life. I suspected his schooling had something to do with this newfound fascination with the fairy world.

The hut and another further on had been built by brothers who lost their wives in a boating accident. Carved on wooden lintels above each door were the names *Maria* and *Isabella*. Made from mountain rocks and timber, the huts were over a hundred years old. There were other huts on the mountain, secret places that were only discovered by word of mouth, or twist of fate. Jimmy knew them all. *The Mountain* as Jimmy called it, brushing aside its British name inherited from Lord Wellington who had never stepped foot on the island.

Charlie lay on his sleeping bag with his face toward the fire. The light darted in and out of the roof beams. He kept the silence at bay with his usual run of questions, moving on to the next thought only when he was satisfied I had answered him fully. 'Henry, how old are you? Will I ever be that old? How old will I be when I die? How old are the big trees? Will my mum come back? Will I ever have a sister? Did you have a sister?'

I answered him as best I could and we ate baked beans with bread we had toasted on a forked stick in front of the fire. Charlie's eyes grew wide at the rattle and clatter of possums on the roof.

'I lived in a hut even smaller than this a long time ago,' I said.

'Where was it?'

'In Africa,' I said. I made sweet tea with water from the billy and broke up a chocolate bar.

'Why did you live in a hut?' Charlie asked.

'I had nowhere else to go.'

'Didn't your mum want you?'

'No. No – I was a man by then.'

'Were there lions and tigers?'

'Lions and leopards. Snakes. Birds and butterflies. Millions of those.'

'What did you eat?'

'Not chocolate,' I said. 'Cassava. Polenta. And whatever we caught.'

'What did you catch?'

'Kudu, sable, antelope.'

'But why?'

'It was what there was.'

Charlie nodded.

'I will miss this place tomorrow,' said Charlie, 'but I am marvellously happy now.'

'Marvellously, hey. Do you know what marvellously means?'

'Big,' he said, 'and smiling?'

'That'll do, lad.'

I wanted him to grow up and be exactly the way he was right then. Buoyant. Hopeful. But life had a way of wearing down even the Charlies of the world.

'The voices like it here too,' he said.

'What voices?'

'My voices.'

'Ah,' I said. The lad had mentioned his voices before. Often at bedtime he told me about them. He seemed to think there were people all about him who were talking to him. I had put it down to imaginary friends but it wasn't quite like that. As time went on I'd become a little concerned the lad was slightly unbalanced. Heaven knows he was a strange mix. Could hardly identify a shirt but could do complicated Lego inventions and make up wonderful stories. Still the simplest things confused him, washing his hands, putting on socks, doing up a zip, remembering to shut the door when he came inside. Yet when he had been bullied at school and I had suggested he do a bit of bullying back, he had been mortified and said, 'But that might hurt their feelings!'

'What are they saying to you, your voices?' I asked.

'They say, "This is a beautiful place Henry has brought you to, Charlie." They say, "You are a beautiful friend to Henry."'

'Do you know them?'

'They are the family of Jesus and the friends of God.'

I looked at the lad. His wide open face. His bright, very dark eyes. His mass of dark blond curls. He looked so earnest. So innocent. I thought of his mother and the things she had done to herself and I didn't want Charlie to go that way.

'Do they ever say things that frighten you?'

'No!' He looked offended. 'They would never do that!'

'You never see scary things?'

'No.'

Then he asked, 'What do your voices say?'

'I don't have any voices.'

'That must be sad for you,' he said.

The boy slept and the fire warmed us against the cold breath of night that swirled about the hut. I lay awake and remembered Africa.

INTO THE UNKNOWN

ONCE I HAD RECOVERED FROM the surgery and my face was no longer bruised and swollen, I made my way to a hunting lodge near the Zambian border to allow myself time to adapt to my new circumstances.

It was the rainy season and there were few guests. A group of Americans stayed for a week or two, there was a waspish Belgian woman and her husband who showed only the barest civility, and there was a British doctor and his wife, both middle-aged, who arrived after a month or so. It was upon them I practised my new identity.

Max Marshall (my newly acquired name) was suffering from an illness (vaguely terminal I decided) but had always wanted to see the wilds of Africa. Marshall clearly had means and ample time. It worked too well. They were solicitous but not inquisitive. The doctor clearly had no interest in talking shop and my condition meant I was not expected to be out walking and shooting from dawn till dusk. What I did have was a camera and they thought me something of a nature enthusiast. It was all too easy.

One evening I could no longer resist the temptation and in some foolish attempt to prove my cleverness, to trade on the thrill of my notoriety or, perhaps, because inside I was morbidly lonely being someone I was not, I confessed my true identity. The doctor had heard little of the case, having been in India at the time, but his wife was deeply shocked. She took some time to fathom that beneath the new visage was indeed the old face she knew too well from endless press reports. The face of the man who had sought to deprive his children of their mother but killed the nanny instead. She made an early departure from the table and insisted her husband accompany her.

But it was that night which saved me.

After they had left, and the sitting room was all but empty of guests, a voice spoke from behind me.

'My, you are determined to ruin yourself, aren't you?'

'I do beg your pardon,' I said, 'are you addressing me, sir?'

'Young man,' he returned, 'following your most revealing conversation with the good doctor and his wife, you may have only days, perhaps hours, before your whole world collapses. Have you any idea of the discomfort you would experience in prison? I suspect the pistol on the table may be preferable to a life sentence. But you won't have that choice if you are caught. I'm surprised you have survived this far. Good God, John, come and sit by me. I haven't seen you in thirty years.'

He was an elderly man with a perfectly bald head and a very beautiful smoking jacket. Age may have dwindled his frame but not his character. Despite a slight stoop, he had about him the air of a man of impressive height and strength.

'I was unaware I was being overheard,' I said.

'Yes,' he said. 'Limited powers of perception are normal for your sort. Sit there so I can take a good look at you. Your mother sent me to find you. Got a cable. You're only two days from my home here. We knew each other well once, your mother and father and me. I had supper at your house several times when you were, oh, only so high.' He gestured to a mark near his knee. 'He would have been so interested in what's happened here, your father. Fascinating politics . . .'

'I don't believe . . .'

'No, quite right,' and he gave me his name, Edward Collins. I knew him even through the drowsy warmth of the brandy. He'd been in France through the Great War, Military Cross. Knighted. Retired to Africa of all places and had sprung up again helping the blacks in Zambia gain independence.

'How is my mother?' I asked.

'I expect she's fine, John. But no thanks to you. You must put all that behind you. Too late for regrets.'

'Look perhaps you're being kind but I can't say I like your tone. Nor your politics for that matter. But perhaps such things don't count for much here in Africa.'

'Ah, the great retort of the dull – social insult.' He finished the last of his drink. 'It is late. In the morning I am leaving for my estate. For your mother's sake, I invite you to join me. For your own sake, I suggest you meet me out front at 5.30am. Oh, not because I wish an illicit escape,' he smiled. 'I am a little old for such things. I sleep little and to save me the protracted inconvenience of insomnia, I always rise early.'

157

He stood without frailty and held out his hand. I had no idea of what to make of him so I shook it.

'There may be hope for you yet, John Bingham,' he said.

I was not in the least prepared for what I found on Collins' estate beside the lake. It was as if a manor house had been transported from the downs of Surrey and planted there. It was a rambling, two-storey mansion with arched windows, wide balconies and a large bell tower. A Union Jack flew from the flagpole and the brickwork was bright with orange and red flowers. Birds flew in and about the terraced garden and there was a rich scent of blossom. Drums rang out and the staff assembled in a long line to greet us as we stepped from Collins' immaculately maintained Bentley.

The vegetation was not English. The servants were not English. The scents, the sounds, the cry of birds, the parading staff, the ground beneath my feet was not English. Yet when I stepped inside the house all that was forgotten.

Here was a place which worked to British tradition. There were cocktails before dinner, coffee and port in the library after. There were early morning rambles about the estate to view the coffee and olive plantations. We had to check the bath for snakes and the lounge room for lions (one had found its way in only the month before), but it was a place of civilisation. My enjoyment of that, however, was short-lived. Edward Collins was determined to save me.

'I haven't asked you if you did it. No. I deliberately haven't asked you. These things are always so complicated and awful. If I harbour a murderer, then I think his anger has passed. If I house an innocent man, then it is time he learned to survive.

'Look at you,' he said. 'You are as blatantly from your class as any of that set. You can change your face, your hair colour all you like, but class sits upon you sure as a mantle and it is that which will catch you out. In order to truly survive you must give all this up.'

He indicated the trappings surrounding us. 'But can you? I very much doubt it. I suspect you don't really know how to live with true freedom.'

Collins' rules were simple. Meticulous punctuality. Absolute courtesy to all I met, black or white.

'It is simply a question of manners,' he said, when I objected to his request. 'You're out of your element,' he said, looking at me and patting my arm, 'but you must get used to that.'

After I had been there a month, he said, 'Now, you must stop dressing like the past.' He had allowed me the use of several of his dinner suits, shirts, pants and jackets.

'See what you can do,' Collins urged me, laughing. 'Treat it like a game.'

I tried a number of variations. Wearing a lounge suit with a rather unbecoming tie. Teaming a navy blazer with camel-coloured pants – a look I have never liked. It was all rather hopeless.

'I feel something like Rex Harrison but in reverse,' Collins chuckled. 'How do I turn you from Audrey Hepburn into Eliza Doolittle, that's what I'm wondering.

'What are we to do with him, Peter?' he smiled, turning to his manservant, a native black as night. 'All these years turning you into a gentleman and now we must reverse the process in this pathetic creature.'

I was furious to be spoken to in such a way. And to have Peter referred to as a gentleman was indescribable.

I went upstairs and packed my bag. I sat upon the bed and looked out at the lake lying like an opal under pearlised clouds. Collins had described it just so only the night before and it had struck me, this old man and his way with words. Until then I had given little thought to the look of the sky, the phase of the moon.

There was a knock at the door. It was the damn manservant carrying some garments.

'If you will excuse me, Mr. Marshall, the Bwana thought you might care to try some of these clothes.' He handed them to me, some faded khaki shirts and two pairs of pants.

'I am not sure about your foot size,' he said. 'But these may be correct.' He handed me a pair of work boots, well-polished.

In the morning I reluctantly dressed. I had never worn such poor garments. Collins hardly looked up as I entered the room. 'Morning Peter,' he said and kept on perusing the morning paper, cup of tea in hand.

I did not take my seat but stood frozen. Peter? What did he mean, Peter? And then it dawned on me.

Collins sighed and said, 'Whose did you think they were? My, they're a perfect bad fit.' After some time he said, 'Next we must work on your accent.'

It proved a more stubborn challenge than wearing the manservant's clothes.

'You need a whole new story, my boy. Think on that. A whole new past. When you find your past you will find your voice.'

Collins and I took walks in the forest to places he wished to show me.

'You know what keeps me young? Every morning I wake up to this view,' he said, spanning the vista of hills, lake, sky, 'and every day, though I have been here fifty years now, it is the most beautiful thing I have ever seen.

'And I sacrifice a chicken each full moon,' he added.

I dared not ask if he was joking.

'My family will be arriving here from England within the fortnight,' Collins said in late March. 'You are much too conspicuous and I will not lie to them when you have not yet learned to lie for yourself. So I am entrusting you to Peter. He will take you further up into the hills to a small village. You may return to the house in August, if you survive that long.'

The rains were coming to an end. I thought to flee. To take my chances in the wide world. See if I could find some quiet corner where I would be unrecognised.

Collins must have known this was on my mind. 'You see,' he said, 'away there in the north-west, the far ridge of hills? I have plans there for a lakeside retreat. Half-a-dozen houses. There are hot springs there. I suspect people might like that sort of thing. It's nearby to Peter's village. I have put a good man, Mkele, in charge of the project but I would very much like it if you could help him accomplish the quality of finish European tourists would expect.'

'I know nothing of building.'

'I have handbooks and there are excellent plans. Mkele himself is a builder. A fine craftsman.'

I looked at my hands. I had never attempted any form of manual labour. I had never picked up a hammer in all my life.

Collins noted my concern. He said, 'Dear boy, soon you'll have a story to carry you safe to the end of your days.'

CHRYSALIS

By the time Scotland Yard was combing Africa for me, tipped off by a sighting in Cape Town, and later another in Rhodesia, Lord Lucan had completely disappeared. It was a transformation none would have thought possible. But inside every misfit there is another man he might be, a better man, if only he were given the chance.

He was a hard man to kill, the seventh Earl. It took great persistence. Not on my part, but on the part of others. And none did more than Mkele. Collins entrusted me to his care, and Peter delivered me.

When we arrived at the village there were few people about. There were many pale mud-walled huts and a large wooden shed Peter said housed building materials. We put aside the bicycles we had ridden to reach the high village and Peter put his hands to his mouth and gave a long call. An answering cry came from the canopy of dark trees and tall grasses to the west. In a few minutes a party of men arrived carrying a small antelope slung on a pole. They milled in front of me and from their ranks came a most unexpected sound.

'G'day mate, I'm Michael Kennedy. They call me Mkele.'

A white man stepped forward. From his accent he was clearly Australian. He was dressed like one of the savages, his chest bare.

'You'll be Max. Collins said you needed looking after. You can't be living with them,' Mkele indicated the people behind him who stood motionless observing me, 'till you've been accepted into the tribe. Your hut's over there.' He pointed to a grass-roofed place on the edge of the trees. 'We brought you dinner. Enjoy it. Tomorrow we're off hunting for a few days, so you're going to have to get it for yourself.'

He thrust a small creature he'd been carrying into my hand. It was a porcupine with a dark fur and long black and white spines. I took the animal tentatively.

'They are a real pest in the gardens. And pretty good tucker,' said Mkele.

And then he spoke in their language and I could hear the men laugh together as they moved away into the village.

I had hunted many times in Scotland. Grouse. Pheasant. Pigeon. But I had never plucked a feather from a bird, let alone a spine from a porcupine. One never had to clean what one caught. Nor had I ever made a fire. I knew nothing and I suspected the rat Mkele knew it. It was a test. A joke perhaps. They wouldn't dare starve me. He'd be back any minute.

Tiny flies clung to the dead creature and buzzed about my face. Inside the hut there was a grass sleeping mat, a blanket, a pottery jug which held water. Someone had stacked some kindling by the door. There was no flint or matches. There was a knife in a leather case, a spear and a small axe. I was hungry and thirsty. I drank gratefully from the jug. Then I wondered where I must go to refill it. It was already growing dark. I stepped out of the hut and made my way toward the firelight and noise. Two bare-chested men stepped across the path and barred my way.

'I wish to speak to Michael. Mkele. Mkele. You will let me pass.'

One of them raised his spear at me. The other one gestured clearly to my hut, indicating I return there at once. Behind them the singing continued and I could smell meat cooking. I was famished. But no-one came with food or drink. Slowly the voices faded with the light. Eventually I drifted into an uncomfortable sleep on the hard earth.

When I woke at dawn the porcupine was crawling with ants. I kicked it from the hut. The village appeared deserted. I thought if I could only find some kind young woman she would give me food, or perhaps I could find leftovers. Coals were smouldering and fat marked the rocks at the central fireplace, but there was no food to be seen. Angry voices sounded behind me. It was my two friends from the night before. One of them rested the point of his spear against my foot, the other at my chest. Women and children began appearing in the doorways of their huts. They were talking and waving their arms, indicating I must leave. The young men jostled me back to my hut, picked up the discarded porcupine and waved it in my face, all the while talking very fast. Then they were gone, taking the dead beast with them.

What had Collins told me these past months? Which plants were edible? Which were poisonous? What animals lived here? I groaned at my lack of memory. I had hardly expected to be given a practical exam.

I took the knife and the spear. I was terrified of lions. I felt a fool with only a spear and a knife. I would have been lucky to bring down a mouse. I found nothing but a herd of zebra at the edge of the deeper bush. They looked at me with disinterest and though I attempted to get closer to them they moved away and I was left with ants climbing up my legs and biting me. I returned to the hut and lay down on the thin mat. In the afternoon thunder rumbled in. It began raining. This at least sent the flies away although the humidity was unbearable. My stomach groaned and by the time nightfall came I knew I would die. I knew nothing could save me. I would die from tsetse fly or malaria, I would die from some parasite or malnutrition. I would die of a bite from a black mamba or a cobra. Surely Mkele would return. He was hunting for my supper right now. I had only Mkele to help me, but as night descended again and again I went hungry, I saw he was clearly not to be relied upon.

On the second day searching for food I surprised a buffalo on the grassland. In my hurry to escape I fell and twisted my ankle. It swelled so severely I could hardly make my way back to the hut. The next day it was worse and I could bear no weight on it at all. My legs were covered in insect bites. It was so hot sweat ran down my cheeks and dripped into my eyes. I watched the door of the hut for any sign of life.

By the third day I was faint with hunger. How I would have welcomed a face, white, black, it didn't matter. I thought to retrieve the bicycle and get back to Collins, tell him I had been put in the hands of a madman who was starving me. I hobbled to the shed and found it locked. I screamed with frustration.

The water jug had been filled each day and left outside the hut, though I never saw who did it. I marvelled at how the water tasted of tea, soup, even gin at times. Had that been a knock at the door? Ah, no door. Who had spoken to me? No, that was a hiss. A snake? What sort of snake? Edible perhaps? I had moments of laughter, giggling at my own thoughts before silence returned. I could hear the village. All about me were people. I could hear their feet on the sandy tracks. Or was that a leopard prowling at night? I could hear voices whispering or was that the wind in the trees? I wanted to call out that I was dying. These people were killing me. But I couldn't. Let me die. Let's see how Mkele would explain that to Collins.

I lay and watched the sun move between the trees, its shadow passing from one side of the door to the other. I listened to the rub of my foot on the dirt floor as I moved, my fingers scratching at my scalp. I heard the rush of blood in my veins, my breath in my nostrils, my heart thumping fast and unsteady. I drifted in and out of dreams. The heat was abominable and flies settled upon any bit of skin they could find. Day became evening. On my back in the door of the hut I watched the night sky and never did the world feel so vast, and I so very small.

'You on a diet, mate?' Mkele said. 'Let's get you out of there. You stink.'

It was late afternoon. The day was cooling. The sun departing, scorching the sky with colour. They carried me to a river I had not even known existed. It was just a hundred yards away. They carried me like a log of wood and when we got to the river they threw me in. I came up gasping. I had never been a good swimmer. I tried to scramble up the bank but it was slippery and I kept sliding back. My ankle hurt dreadfully. Finally I fell down at the water's edge and, to my great shame, began to weep.

They sat me up against a tree trunk and placed a bowl on my lap. It had slices of deep purple figs in it. On the edge of the bowl was a flower. It had delicate white petals with a central crown of slender scarlet stamen reaching skywards. Looking up at the semi-circle of people gathered about me, I grasped a piece of fruit and popped it upon my tongue. The finest berries in England could not compare to the taste of that fruit.

The villagers began smiling at me. This seemed so wonderful that I started laughing. I don't know why I laughed. Perhaps I was a little mad. But then around me everyone else began to laugh too. Someone began singing.

Mkele put his hand on my shoulder.

'Well mate, I think we better teach you how to hunt.'

I should have hated him but all I could do was smile and nod.

LEOPARDS AND LIES

IN THE MORNING, AFTER BACON and two rounds of toast with jam, Charlie and I packed up. We stowed the billy and our rubbish in my pack, put the fire out. Charlie rolled our sleeping bags and we hunted for kindling to leave ready for the next person. As we left, Charlie swept away our footprints until no trace of us remained.

When we arrived back, Jimmy was working on *Venus*. He was sanding the cabin top ready for its first coat of paint.

'Ahoy there, young pirate,' he called to Charlie, 'where have you sprung from?'

'It's a secret,' said Charlie.

'You can't even tell me?'

'Nobody.'

We unloaded our packs. Lili was not home. There was no note but I suspected she was swimming at the pool. She often went on Saturdays. Two kilometres up and back, up and back. Charlie climbed the ladder onto the deck and leapt off the stern several hundred times, or so it seemed, as Jimmy and I worked.

'By the way,' Jimmy said, 'we're staging a protest this Tuesday. The Premier's launching a new book on Aboriginal history and we're going to picket him on the steps about the centre.'

The push for the Aboriginal centre was on again. After deliberations and round-tables, the bodies of the woman and her baby were to be entombed at the site. No other bodies had been found.

'Will that do any good?'

'We're sick of waiting. Being Aboriginal in this place boils down to a few tourist boards along the roadsides. A sign at a lookout. But if it's got anything to do with now, let alone a future, they don't want to know about it.'

We talked on for a while, fiddling around with a few things on the boat. At last Lili appeared. I felt like I hadn't seen her for a week.

'Jimmy's staging a protest about the land transfer on Tuesday. You going to get your mates to cover it for him?'

'Are you, Jimmy?'

Jimmy grinned.

'Jimmy, would you like a bit of training?'

'What sort of training?' asked Jimmy.

'Handling the media.'

'So I sound like a politician?'

'Better than that.'

'Sure.'

Lil smiled. 'Okay. Well, let's make a cup of tea.'

Jimmy winked at me. 'Got the inside lane now.'

'I can't promise it will help,' said Lili.

'Got nothing to lose . . . can't lose when you're down the ladder about as far as it's possible to go.'

'Hush,' she said. 'You are not an apologist. You're a leader.'

'Ah,' said Jimmy, looking a bit stunned.

'It's the first rule,' said Lil. 'Always take the high ground.'

'And the second rule?'

'Say one thing but make it clear and strong. So when they cut you into a three second grab on the news, they take what you wanted to say, not what they wanted to catch you saying.'

Jimmy rubbed his head. 'Okay, I'm listening.'

After Jimmy left I held Lil beside the sink and buried my face into the nape of her neck. There was a vague scent of chlorine on her skin. Charlie bounced about telling her his recollections of the walk and the hut and our night together.

'Henry lived in a hut in Africa!' he said.

'Did he now?' Lili said, pulling away and looking at me.

'Didn't you, Henry?' he said.

'Aye, laddie. With the lions and leopards.'

I winked at Lili. She smiled curiously.

He ran off saying, 'And the snakes.'

Lil said, 'He believed you.'

I shrugged. 'Bed-time stories.'

'Have you ever been to Africa?' Lil asked.

'Nowhere near it.' I picked up the newspaper and wandered to the couch. I breathed very slowly. How had I thought for a minute the boy would not say anything? I had slipped up. It wouldn't do. Africa. I had run to Africa and years later when I left Africa, I didn't look like Lucan, I didn't talk like Lucan. I was a new man with a new name and Lucan and all his mistakes were left behind. Henry Kennedy had never been to Africa. He had come from England to Australia looking for ghosts. Lil knew that.

When I had concentrated on the news for a good few pages and my pulse had slowed, I said, 'So how was your day? Did you have a good swim?'

'Oh, yes, hardly anyone in the pool.'

'It was nice what you just did for Jimmy.'

'It was easy,' she said.

I got a sudden flash of her life when I was gone. Her here in the house. Jimmy and Pearl next door. Jimmy coming over to cut wood for the fire. Yes. She'd need him then. Who else would she have when I was gone? Who did she have before I arrived?

I hadn't even talked about it with her.

'Lil, I want you to have the house.'

'Do you?'

'Of course. It's our house. Your house.'

She sat next to me and laid her head against my chest. 'I'm a bit sad.'

I put my arms around her and kissed the top of her head. The weight of lying to her was heavy on me.

'Are you feeling okay?' she said.

'Aye, Lil, I'm bearing up.'

A SCOTTISH WINTER

CHRISTMAS EVE WAS UPON US. The third Christmas since Lil had come into my life. Charlie was in bed and I had checked twice to make sure he was really asleep. The lad had not been himself these past few days. We'd had tears over little things – not being able to go outside because it had been raining. Not wanting Rice Bubbles for breakfast. His Lego not going together the way he wanted. I thought he must be missing Suki. I had wanted to take him up to Silver Falls again but since our trip I'd had several dizzy spells. I did not want him to suddenly find himself with an invalid half an hour from the house.

He had spent the morning working a lump of yellow play-dough on the table, building volcanoes and roads and driving cars along it. Every now and then he'd let out the sound of an explosion. Other than that he had been unnaturally quiet. Lil suggested he help her with some shortbread biscuits and he'd seemed enthusiastic but then he'd said he was tired and took himself off to his bedroom for a while.

He'd insisted on carrots along the back path for the reindeer.

I read him *The Night Before Christmas*. Lil had picked it up in town for me just yesterday. He had never heard it and made me read it three times over.

My head was aching. The vomiting that now often followed breakfast and kept me nauseous through the morning had passed, but the day had been disrupted with bright flashes of pictures and sounds I could not quite grab hold of. As if my brain was searching for something it had forgotten but was desperate to retrieve.

With Charlie settled for the night, I sat in my chair by the fireplace and watched Lil wrap an orange kite and place it under the fresh cut pine tree. The scent of the tree filled the room and confused me. Her hair was pulled up in a clip and she looked as if she was thirty, not forty-something. In the background Bing Crosby was singing *Have yourself a very merry Christmas*. Every now and then Lil joined in for a bar or two, humming, not singing.

Lil disappeared and came back with a large heavy box wrapped in gold paper and bound with a red ribbon. She refused my offer of help and lowered it unsteadily to the floor then pushed it under the tree.

'Don't ask,' she said. She went into the kitchen and returned with a bag of carrots. 'Do you think you're up to gnawing them a bit to make them look like . . . well, like they've been chewed by a reindeer?'

She sat down on the rug beside my chair. She liked the floor, did Lil. Despite her love of furniture, she liked the floor to sit upon best of all.

174

She took a carrot from the bag, broke it in half and proceeded to gnaw at it. 'There!' she said laughing at her handiwork.

Lil, whose sole gesture to Christmas until now had been holly earrings.

'Tell me what happened for you when it was Christmas,' she said. 'When you were a boy.'

Do all of us become something in order to be with people? What had Lil become to be with me? I had no idea, but I knew there must be a price. This was my price. I must continue to lie to her.

'Argyle,' I said, 'was one of those stone homes with four dormer windows in the slate roof, both front and back. It was surrounded by pathways and garden beds, an orchard and greenhouses. It snowed there every Christmas.'

Lil placed four carrots with chewed ends on the floor and said, 'Reindeer evidence.' She looked up at me and said, 'When I first learned about England I used to think it would be just like that.'

'Dinna mention the damn English. We were Scottish. Any resemblance is mere coincidence!'

'Sorry,' said Lil, smiling.

'Sometimes we'd run about and play football in the snow on Christmas day. My father had been quite a champion in his time.'

'We should have done that for Charlie,' said Lili.

'What?'

'Got him a soccer ball. How old were you then? When you

were still in Scotland? Hang on,' she said, getting up. 'I have something.'

She returned with two small glasses and a bottle of madeira. She kissed me and said, 'Merry Christmas.'

I took the bottle and looked at it. 1934. It was dusty and bore the classic Spanish words printed straight onto the dark glass and an importer's label.

'Where did you get it?' I laughed.

'Well, it's a birthday present a day early.' Her face had such wide brown eyes. Her smile was perfect. She was wearing a white linen shirt and jeans and her feet, as always inside the house, were in small leather slip-ons.

'You are spoiling me,' I said.

'Well, if you won't let me throw a party . . . '

'I hate parties,' I said.

I removed the cork stopper and poured a glass for each of us. I held my glass to hers.

'You are a mystery to me,' I said to her.

'Mr Kennedy,' she said.

'Ms Birch.'

My heart ached as I looked at her. Lil was not one for declarations of love but she showed her heart in her face when she looked at me. 'Go on,' she said. 'Christmas.'

Did she believe me? There was something so innocent about Lil at such moments. 'I like your voice,' she had once said to me. 'I think you could persuade me to do almost anything.'

'Well,' I said, savouring the madeira warm in my mouth and smooth on my throat, 'The Christmas I remember most was when I was nearly ten. I remember my da came home and it was a wild night. He'd been away and we were all excited at his return. My mother sat by the fire. And whether it really was like a Christmas scene from an old colour template in a *Boy's Own*, or whether it's true, I'm no longer sure.

'My da was smoking his pipe. Hugh was needling him for information about what he'd brought back with him, what Christmas treats he might expect and da was laughing and saying, "Patience is everything, Hugh." And then he said, "But I do have a surprise for you all. I have accepted an offer to sell Argyle Biscuits."

'The room was silent as snow. "Douglas," I heard my mother whisper. "Aye, they've made a fine offer and we will be set for life with it, Beth," he said.'

Lil smiled at me as I mimicked my parent's brogue.

' "But this is our life," my mother said. "Well, we are about to have a new one, Beth," Da replied. "I have a Directorship at United Foods. We must be settled in London by March." "Leave here?" she said. "Leave Scotland?" I remember jumping to my feet and shouting "No!". Father laughed and said, "Sit down, ye wee bairn, there's no call for a drama. We are, simple as that." He leaned forward and took my hand and pulled me onto his lap. "Hush there, laddie," he said. "Twill be good for us all."'

I stared into the fire and Lil was quiet.

'I was too young to understand, but I knew there was much more to it than he shared with us. I knew it because my mother's face was empty as she tucked me in.'

'Maybe she sensed that something terrible was going to happen. She died the next year, didn't she?'

'Aye.'

'It must have been very lonely for you after she was gone.'

'When we went back to Argyle for holidays I used to see her coming up the white driveway from a walk on the moors. I think my da used to see her too which is why he sold the house.'

Perhaps it was what had made me a gambler. I loved to risk. As I spun my stories, I shivered with a strange mix of fear and elation, but to those who observed me I was a picture of calm. And until yesterday I had always thought I would go on being in control.

Yesterday I had called Charlie 'George'.

'Who's George?' he asked.

'My son, of course.'

'Where is he?'

'Right in front of me,' I said, thinking it all a game.

'But I'm Charlie.'

And then it all shifted and I was standing on the driveway. Lil was unpacking groceries from the car and a little boy with sandy curls was looking up at me.

Lil did not look at me as she passed.

'I'm not George,' Charlie said emphatically.

'Let me help,' I called to Lil. 'Let me carry something.'

'It's fine. I can manage,' she said.

'Don't you ever call me George again,' said Charlie, taking my hand as we walked to the back door together.

'Henry?' Lil asked. I had left off my story. Bing Crosby had finished. The night sounds seemed far from the house. Our glasses were empty.

'I was thinking of Charlie,' I said.

'And George?'

She looked at me and I wondered if I had spoken his name again.

'Who is George?' I asked innocently.

'I don't know,' Lili said, staring at her efforts under the Christmas tree, 'but I think you should.'

'I don't,' I said, shaking my head.

'Yesterday, you said he was your son. You thought Charlie was him.'

'I don't have any children.'

'Yes,' she said slowly, 'but it is possible to almost forget.'

My heart sank. She suspected. She sensed the lie.

'You know,' I said suddenly, 'I did have a friend when I was a boy about Charlie's age. His name was George.'

'Ah,' said Lil.

This was not good. I hated having to make something up on the spot. I liked to practise. But this had been too big a slip to simply ignore. It needed smoothing over.

'It's not uncommon,' said Lil. 'People often start thinking about their childhood when they are . . . when they're sick.' She looked at me. 'I've been reading about it.'

I slid my hand over hers on the arm of the chair. We looked into the fire together.

'Where do you think Suki is tonight?' I asked.

'I don't think about it.'

'Don't you think it strange we've heard nothing?'

'I heard nothing for years.'

'You don't think we should call the police? Report her missing?'

'She's not fifteen any more.'

'So you don't think she may need you?'

'She knows my number.'

'Lili, you have never said whether she has . . . well, a mental problem.'

'What do you think? Is it normal the way she is?'

'Why would she do that to herself?'

'I don't know.'

'I think we should take Charlie to see someone.'

'What do you mean?'

'I didn'a want to worry you. But he tells me he hears voices.'

'Voices?'

'Yes, I can't be sure if he's making them up. Like imaginary friends. But he seems very certain about them. He doesn't seem to think it's a game.'

'How do you mean?'

'They say, "We love you Charlie." And, "You're a beautiful boy, Charlie." They tell him what kind people we are. It must be noisy for him hearing all that,' I said. 'I wonder how he concentrates at school.'

'God knows what her pregnancy was like. Maybe it did something to him. Maybe she took something.'

'What was her father like? Is there a history?'

'No. No – nothing.'

Lil did not talk about Keith Birch nor his suicide. She did not appear emotional about it. On the contrary, it was as if it bored her to discuss it.

'It wasn't . . . ?'

'Clinical? No.'

'I think we'd better take him to see someone.'

Lili sighed. 'As if we don't have enough – '

'Charlie is not a problem.'

'No.'

'We're both tired,' I said. 'Let's finish these carrots and get to bed.'

'After all, you are almost sixty, old man,' she said.

Yes, on Boxing Day I would be that as well. George was twenty-seven now. Frances thirty and Camilla, my baby girl, would be twenty-four. Somewhere in London it was Christmas Eve and there was no present from me under their trees. No card with a foreign stamp. No place at their table for their father. Did they dine together? I wondered if they ever sensed I was still alive. Did they ever mention me? Would they have liked me to come home? Or did they think me a murderer, and never want to see me again?

I had tried to write to them over the years. I had sat down at various desks and begun. And then I'd torn the letters up. Watched them burn in the fireplace. I was already dead to them. I had to let it rest there. I had to let it be.

THE OBVIOUS PERSON

LIL LAY ASLEEP ON THE couch with her head on my lap. I had covered her with a blanket and she was making a little whistling noise as she breathed.

It was Christmas night. The large gold box with the red ribbon had turned out to be a TV and video all in one. 'For our bedroom,' said Lil. 'So even if you're in bed, you can't miss my programme.'

'Och, Lil,' I said. Another thing to clutter up the bedroom. But it was a strange thing too. As a rule Lil didn't talk about her show. She'd talk about the research, or a particular person she'd interviewed, but not the end result. Not the hour of air-time she commanded each week. Sometimes I watched it and told her so. But this was the first time I had ever sensed she wanted me to watch her. That it mattered.

I had given Lil a painting. It was a woman emerging from water. It was a Barbie Kjar – a black line drawing with only the bathing cap red. It made me think of Lil and her laps at the pool.

'It's one of the only sports I can do that doesn't require

communication with anyone else,' she'd said when first I asked her about it.

Charlie was long asleep in his bed. We had eaten, played, gone for a walk in the rain. We had flown his new kite in the paddock when the weather cleared. Pearl and Jimmy had come for lunch and had stayed until after tea.

Now the dishwasher was stacked, the benchtops cleared and the fridge full of leftovers. We had drunk too much champagne and several reds, and the madeira bottle beside me was half empty. Lights were still flashing round and round on the Christmas tree. Lil was snoozing and I was watching *It's a Wonderful Life* on TV.

I glanced at Lili's hands holding the edge of the blanket. The small gold bracelet on her right wrist, the simple gold band on her left ring finger. It was not a ring from her marriage, she had said. She had found it in a second-hand shop and liked it.

The movie was nearly over. Jimmy Stewart was with his friends and family. Everything had worked out. Life was good and life was wonderful. He'd got to choose, Jimmy Stewart. What luxury. What luck.

Next year, I thought, I'll buy Lil a ring.

But in my bones I knew there would not be another Christmas.

Careful not to disturb Lil, I stood up and did a very dangerous thing. I went into her office. Turning on the light, I searched the shelves for it. I knew it was there somewhere. I had seen it. I had been unsettled to discover it, but had made nothing of it. She had countless works of investigative journalism. It was not unusual that she had this particular one.

It was a modest volume with an aqua dust jacket discoloured from being in the sun. Richard Deacon – *Escape!* The front cover read: *'The Mogadishu Hijack, Donald Woods, Kim Philby, Lord Lucan, Alfie Hinds, Jeremy Cartland.'*

When I'd first seen it I'd been a little disappointed it was not me in the front cover photograph. That honour went to the serial escapist Alfie Hinds.

I flicked through to my chapter. Chapter Three, 'Into Thin Air'.

At ten o'clock on Thursday, 7 November 1974, the chatter in the saloon bar of the Plumber's Arms pub in Lower Belgrave Street, London, was disturbed by the dramatic entrance of an hysterical woman, bleeding from the head and in a state of near collapse.

'Help me! Help me! she cried. 'I have just escaped from a murderer!' For a few seconds nobody seemed to know what to do or say. Then, bursting into loud sobs, the woman cried: 'My children! He's in the house. He's . . . murdered the nanny. Help me!'

The landlord dashed forward to catch her as she seemed about to fall, then gestured to his wife to help her while he went to the telephone and dialled 999. Somebody called across to him: 'That's the Countess of Lucan. She lives just across the road.'

Veronica Lucan's home was at 46 Lower Belgrave Street, only thirty yards away. One man left the Plumber's Arms to look at the house; he came back to say it was in almost complete darkness. Within a few minutes an ambulance arrived to take the Countess to St George's Hospital. She told the police who came to her bedside that 'It was my husband who attacked me.'

Two night patrol police officers, Sergeant Donald Baker and Constable Christopher Beddick, went to No. 46 and forced open the front door. At the far end of the hall their torch light revealed fresh blood stains on the wallpaper. At the bottom of the stairs leading to the basement breakfast room was a large pool of blood . . . Naturally the police officers' first thought was for the children. They went up two flights of stairs and entered a room in which they found a bedside light on and a bloodstained towel lying across a pillow. Then, in the nursery on the top floor, they saw the two younger Lucan children, George (Lord Bingham), aged seven, and Camilla, aged four, asleep in their beds. Beside them, silent, frightened and seemingly quite bewildered by all that was happening, stood ten-year-old Frances. Sergeant Baker quietly said 'Hello' and tried to sound as reassuring as possible. 'Where is my mother?' asked Frances.

'She's fine. She'll be back quite soon . . . Now what about getting into bed and going to sleep?'

He tucked her up and shut the nursery door. Then he and Beddick recalled the ominous pool of blood below.

Together they went down the basement stairs to the dining area which was in darkness except for light which filtered through the slats of the Venetian blinds. There was some broken crockery on the floor. In the kitchen the light of their torches picked up a bulb lying on a chair. Sergeant Baker directed his torch toward the ceiling, there was a light fitment but no bulb. Picking up the bulb, he placed it in the fitment and the light came on.

Then turning into the breakfast room, the officers saw what appeared to be a United States mail bag from which blood had seeped through. The top of the bag was folded over, but the cord was not pulled. When Sergeant Baker opened the bag he saw inside the body of a young woman with black tights on her legs. He felt for her pulse and decided she was dead.

It did not take long to establish that the body in the sack was that of the Lucan family nanny, Sandra Eleanor Rivett, an attractive twenty-nine-year-old, who had been married to a Merchant Navy seaman, but had separated from her husband in April that same year. She had not been with the Lucan family very long, but all who knew her testified to the fact that she was very fond of children and liked her post at No. 46.

The police surgeon was called and he certified that Sandra Rivett had died as a result of multiple head wounds . . . A piece of lead piping, carefully and somewhat curiously wrapped in Elastoplast, some eight to ten inches long and weighing two and a quarter pounds, had been found in the nearby cloakroom. It was bloodstained and therefore assumed to be the murder weapon.

I put down the book, overwhelmed, remembering suddenly that night in the depth of winter and how cold the kitchen had been. How the light from the street cast a blade across the floor. Had the pipe been heavy in my hand? Had it taken much to wield it? It is never good to expect the best of people. Especially oneself. One is likely to be disappointed.

'What are you doing?' asked Lili.

I jumped perceptibly and spun around. She was standing in the doorway with the rug from the couch about her shoulders.

'Sorry,' she said, stretching and coming toward me. 'Didn't mean to frighten you. Is it still Christmas?'

My heart was racing. Lil squeezed onto my lap and picked up the book off the desk. She flicked through the pages of photographs – *'The wedding of Lord and Lady Lucan in November 1963'*, *'Lord Lucan at a backgammon tournament in Germany'* and further on *'Lord Lucan with Dominick Elwes'*.

'I think he drowned. Don't tell me you're about to discover the pleasures of non-fiction?'

It was an ongoing joke between us.

'I do read non-fiction.'

'Oh, newspapers! Hardly non-fiction,' Lil laughed.

'Are you being elitist?'

'No. Not like he was. Revolting man.'

'Oh?'

'Can you imagine? You only have to look at the inquest to see what awful types they were. They lied for him, all his friends. I would have loved to have seen them catch him and bring him to trial.'

'Do you think he did it?'

'Killed her? Of course he did.'

'What makes you say that?'

'Oh, he mucked it up. Meant to kill his wife. All those gambling debts.'

'Och, you're very learned,' I teased.

'I could never understand how he managed to kill the wrong person. I remember I wanted more than anything to be a journalist in London. I mean, you think you'd know your own wife.'

'Maybe he didn't do it. Maybe it was someone else.'

Lil shook her head and flicked through the other chapters.

'Unlikely,' she said. 'I think usually crime is simple. Usually it's the most obvious person.'

She turned again to the picture of Lucan and Dominick Elwes. We were laughing. Really laughing. I had a cigarette in my hand. Dominick was one of my dearest friends. He committed suicide not long after I disappeared. I blamed myself. Somehow it had unhinged him entirely, the whole fiasco.

Lil looked at me. 'You could almost pass for Lucan. Of course, you're more handsome,' she said, kissing my cheek.

'Really?'

'You and Jimmy and a bottle of something and you start giggling just like that.'

I could see she was more than a little drunk from the Christmas festivities.

'Och, you're a cruel woman.'

'It's perfect! Here you are after all this time. The very naughty Lord Lucan. Oh, tell me you're him!'

I closed the book. 'Come to bed with me, ye wee beastie.'

'You be Lord Lucan. And I'll be Lady Lucan,' she said. Then she leaned against me and said, 'But you can be sure there'd be no sex tonight if that was the case.'

'You are wicked,' I said. 'Although I'm sure you're right.'

Later, after I was certain she was asleep, I slipped from the bed and returned to her office. I took the book and thought to burn it in the fire. My heart would not stop racing. What a fool

I'd been! What an utter fool. She would remember it in the morning. She would go and hunt it out. She'd flick to the page with Dominick. She'd read about the children. The boy called George. She would walk out of her office and look at me with her interviewer's eye. If the book wasn't there in the morning she'd be puzzled. She'd ask me where I'd put it. Her books were her pets. She'd be distressed until she found it.

Could she really believe I might be Lucan? Was I so absolutely Henry Kennedy that she would never doubt me? I felt the sweat upon my body. I felt the tremor in my hand as I put the book back upon the shelf. There was a chance she would not remember in the morning. Perhaps she would make nothing of it. But if she suspected, would she tell? I was certain she would.

I looked at the clock: 1:23. It was my birthday. Henry Kennedy was sixty years old. Not my real birthday, on that score I had been sixty for eight days, but Boxing Day had been an easy lie to remember. I thought, not for the first time, that I should have deducted a few years when I became Henry. Made myself five years younger, ten even. But it was just another thing to remember. And it was too late now. It was too late for many things. It was certainly too late to be caught.

Not now, not now. I am too old, and too ill, and too desperate.

I was a desperate man in those early months after I left England, but it was a desperation borne of anger and shock. Now I was desperate because of the contentment that lived in me and made me want to cling like a drowning man to my home, the view out over the river, the mountain, the feel of

Lil's skin, to these fragile threads I had sewn together to protect me and warm me.

I had managed my risks. What would I have to do to manage Lili? I felt the race of discovery running alongside the race of decay and I wondered which would win. Perhaps the race was not over after all. If I had still been Lucan perhaps I would have made sure her brakes failed on the mountain road.

But I could no more have harmed Lili, nor allowed harm to come to her, than I could the small boy who slept across the hall from her study. Lucan may yet rise up and shatter our small world, but I would die fighting him.

TWENTY-SEVEN LIVES

CHARLIE AND I SAT ON the wooden sleeper which served as a garden edge. It was his favourite place. His fingertips, the front of his T-shirt and the corners of his mouth were stained red.

'Do you think there really is a Santa?' he asked. 'Here, have some more,' he added, offering raspberries in his hand.

'I'm done for now, laddie. Put them in the bowl. We'll have them for dessert.'

'It's more fun eating them in the garden.' He paused. 'But is there?'

'What?'

'A Santa? You are not listening to me.'

'I'm just a wee bit . . . distracted.'

'Tired,' he said.

I tried not to use the word. It sounded like such an excuse but I felt as though I could sleep all day. I had not told the boy I was dying. I could not bring myself to do it. Even Lili was reluctant. So instead I got slower about him. I took more naps as the weariness in me grew. I felt myself becoming dislocated from the city below and the news in the papers. But the boy was a thread, a good firm thread to keep me tied to the days and moments.

The sun beat down upon my back. Charlie's face was shaded by a soft orange hat.

'Do you think there's a Santa?' I asked back.

'Well, I think there must be. How else do all the children get presents all over the world?'

'Indeed.'

'Someone at school said it was just your mum or dad dressed, up but it can't be.'

'Why's that?'

'Because my mum wasn't here but I still got presents.'

'I guess it could have been Lili or me?'

'That's ridiculous,' he said, 'you can't get up on the roof.'

'What about Lili?'

'She's too small. She couldn't drive the sleigh.'

I nodded.

'I like it here,' he said eating more raspberries. 'Did you always live here? Oh, no. You used to live in Africa.'

'I've lived lots of places.'

'Me too,' he said, 'but this is a really nice place.'

'What other places have you liked?'

He shrugged. 'I don't remember. That's funny. I don't remember. I just remember being here.'

'Me too,' I said.

His shirt was inside out and his shorts back to front. Although Lil and I helped him most every day, the mysteries of getting dressed were still beyond him. He'd go off to his room after breakfast and within two minutes he'd call out, 'Henry!' When I got there he'd be sitting on the floor in near despair. 'There aren't any shirts!'

I would pick one out from the pile in the cupboard where all his shirts lived and he would look astonished as it unfolded and took on the familiar shape. 'You're a genius!' he'd say, hugging me.

A cricket struck up somewhere among the lettuces.

'How are your voices, Charlie?' I asked.

'They're good. Thank you for asking.'

'You know, Charlie,' I said, 'Lil and I were wondering if you'd like your voices to be a bit quieter. So it's easier to go to sleep. Or to hear the teacher when you go back to school. Would that be good?'

'I don't know. Maybe.'

'Well, there's a fellow called Mr Jarvis. He's good at that sort of thing. We thought you might go and see him with us.'

'Do the voices speak to him too?'

'I don't know. Perhaps you could ask him.'

'You don't have to worry about me, Henry,' he said, putting his arms on my legs and leaning into me.

'I know, laddie.'

'Are you going to ask him about being tired? Maybe he could give you some beans.'

Beans were Charlie's description for energy. If he ran out of beans, he ran out of puff.

'Aye, I could do that.'

'Do you think it will snow tonight?'

'No, it's summer. It won't snow until winter, I hope.'

'Is that a long time away?'

'Not really.'

'I will love to see the snow. Will we be able to eat it?'

'It's not the same as raspberries. It'll give you a tummy ache.'

'So do raspberries if I eat too many. And then I have to go to the toilet.'

'Yes.'

'Henry?' There was a long silence while he stared away into the forest watching the treetops. 'Do you think my mum is okay?'

I took his hands and turned them over and inspected their grubby palms.

'I'm sure she is,' I said.

'Will she be here when the snow comes?'

'I don't know.'

'I think she will be,' he said. 'I think she'll come home then.'

Some days the relentless enthusiasm of a five-year-old was too much for me. His noisy games, his chatter. I longed for the quiet hours after he was asleep, or the times Lil took him off in the car and I could have the house still and silent. There were times I'd rather have had Lili to myself. There were days I wanted to lie in the hammock I had slung between a couple of wattles and not be disturbed. I'd send him away then. Tell the boy it was high time he started playing on his own. And he'd go, running off unperturbed, as if it was me missing out, not him. I noticed occasionally my tone had got sharper with him. Only a day or two back I had growled at him for pouring water on an ant nest.

'Don't you know you're killing them? You're drowning them. They're going crazy because they're in a panic. How would you like it? Some great giant drowning you and your family? I'm disappointed in you, Charlie. I don't want to see you for the rest of the afternoon.'

How quiet the verandah became. The sandpit suddenly just a pile of sand. The paddock empty. I refused to call him. Later, I dozed off and woke to find him sitting on a chair beside me.

I reached out a hand to him and he put his in mine.

'I was giving them a drink,' he said. 'I thought they must be thirsty on such a hot day.'

He made friends with a boy along the road – Mitch. Lili encouraged it. Organised for the boys to get together when Mitch came home from his school in town. They traversed the paddocks, beating the bushes with sticks, playing swordfights, raiding the cherry tomatoes, and making cubbies under *Venus* with the tarpaulins. Since Christmas he'd fallen asleep more quickly at night but he still called out in his sleep. Sleep for Charlie was like a wrestle with unseen forces. He shouted and yelped. Yet he remembered none of it.

I worried about the boy without his mother. But I liked our little trio. For however long it lasted, it seemed to keep at bay the shadow of darker things.

■

In mid-January, Charlie, Lil and I took a trip to Bruny Island and stayed in Stan's holiday house down there. It was a patchy week with grey days and sudden showers though it was meant to be midsummer. We fished off the rocks and spent hours looking for crabs. One night we lit a fire on the beach and watched the sunset across the d'Entrecasteaux Channel.

Charlie lay on the dark sand and watched the flames awhile, then blurted out, 'What's past space? How do we get to be alive?'

'There's nothing past space,' Lili said. 'That's all there is, space.'

'That can't be right,' said Charlie.

'How do you think we get to be alive?' Lili asked him.

'I think we are stars that fly right down to earth and we already have our clothes on.'

'Do you now?' Lili said.

'You know,' said Charlie, 'we only have twenty-seven lives.'

'Oh,' said Lili, 'only twenty-seven. How many have you had already?' she asked.

'This is my first one.'

Had Lili ever mentioned the events of Christmas night? Did she talk again of Lord Lucan as she went about putting candles on my birthday cake on Boxing Day; as she cleaned away the pine needles that dropped to the floor when the Christmas tree wilted; as she pondered the newspapers through the holiday period? She did not. She had become more and more preoccupied with my health. She tended me. She bought me new slippers and a dark blue robe. She organised a massage for me with a shiatsu therapist.

On Bruny as we walked along the beach at Cloudy Bay, I asked her, 'What would you do if you knew you were dying, Lil?'

'Oh, I think it would depend. If I could still travel I should like to go to Venice. I never went there. And Antarctica to watch the whales and maybe ride on a dog sled. I should like to take you with me to New Orleans for the jazz festival. But if I wasn't able to go far, I think I would get out every movie I ever wanted to see and re-read every favourite book.'

'And you?' she said after a pause.

'I just want to sit. Sometimes it's like all the world is right here.'

'Will you tell me . . . if there's anything?'

'Last wishes, Lil?'

'Yes.'

We discussed radiotherapy; politics; Charlie; the water levels in the dam; the colour of *Venus'* hull; the bird life that crossed the sky and darted about the garden; the scheduling of time for meals, for Charlie, for appointments. We needed a schedule now. I no longer drove so I relied on Lil in a whole new way.

'I don't care, Henry,' she had said, 'I don't want you driving any more. You have to think of the other people on the road.'

'She's right,' Jimmy had added when I had complained to him. 'I don't want you coming down the road if I'm coming up. Maniac.'

Lil quietly put the Land Rover in the shed and my keys disappeared off the hook in the kitchen. I hated it. Having to be transported everywhere like an invalid.

'Could you at least drive my car?'

It was a damn effort having to get into that little green Ghia. With my limbs turning to lead, it was more than I could manage. But I didn't want to admit it.

'I could learn to drive it,' said Lil.

Did she ever look at me in any way that seemed suspicious? Curious? She did not. If she remembered discovering me with the book on Christmas night, or even the words that had passed between us, she made no mention of it. It was like so many other domestic moments. Forgotten. But I did not forget it.

On the blue and white sign at the beginning of the long driveway it said *Mental Health Services*. A vast 1920's red-brick house had been converted to a public building complete with concrete stairs and disabled access. Inside I expected to see people who were unbalanced or retarded, but in fact everyone appeared to be so disappointingly ordinary. Benjamin Jarvis was very short, with round pink cheeks and a thick shock of dark hair. As he welcomed us each with a gentle handshake, I noticed that Charlie took his hand with great delight, saying, 'Hello, pleased to meet you.'

We sat in a sunny room at the rear of the building. The walls were decorated with pictures of planets, birdlife, plants and wildlife. Charlie told Jarvis the names of all the planets and their moons.

Jarvis chuckled and perched himself on a red vinyl chair around a laminated coffee table. When Charlie had finished, he fixed his bright blue eyes on Lil and me. 'So, tell me what brings you here.'

I recounted some of the conversations I'd had with Charlie. When I had finished, I said, 'Would that be about correct, Charlie?'

'Yes,' he said, spotting a box on Jarvis' desk. 'Is that the new Space Lego?'

'Ah, yes,' said Jarvis, leaning forward and grabbing it. 'Would you like to build it? Someone gave it to me just today.' He looked quite delighted by such a gift.

'Can I?' said Charlie. 'That would be great!'

Jarvis watched Charlie rip open the box. He passed him scissors for the small cellophane packs of blocks inside. Then in a subdued tone he said, 'Charlie, I'm just going to talk with Henry and Lili for a little while. Are you all right to play there while we do that? You can listen to what we are saying. If you want to add anything please do.'

'That's fine,' said Charlie.

Jarvis turned to us. 'Is there any history? Any family record?'

'I gave some detailed information regarding his mother . . . when I spoke with . . . when I first made enquiries,' said Lili.

Jarvis looked around at the orange folder on his desk. He flicked it open and regarded the notes there. I thought how there, for him to see, was the story Lili had never told me. I looked at her and wondered at my own reluctance to push her into some grand confession of the awful years when Suki stopped being someone she knew.

'Yes. Yes. I recall this when I first read the file. But it's always nice to hear it first-hand,' he smiled at Lili and at me.

I shook my head. 'I'm not the boy's grandfather, of course.'

'But Lili, you are his grandmother?'

'Yes, that's right. It sounds terribly old, grandmother.'

Jarvis scanned his notes further. 'And Charlie's mother is still away?'

Charlie continued building, humming to himself at the little table.

'Yes.'

'This has been a longstanding problem – the substance abuse?'

'Yes,' said Lili.

'Charlie,' he asked, gazing at him, 'how are you going at school?'

'Good.'

'Who do you play with?'

'I don't know their names.'

'He goes to Zoey,' I said, by way of explanation.

'Ah, yes,' said Jarvis making a note in the folder, 'the Zoey school at Fern Tree.'

'But he doesn't,' Lili said quietly. 'He doesn't play with the other kids. He plays on his own.'

'No, I don't!' said Charlie.

'Do you miss your mum, Charlie?'

'Sometimes,' he said.

'What do you do when you miss your mum?' asked Jarvis.

'I don't know. Just feel sad.'

'Do you like living with Henry and Lili?'

'Yes,' said the lad.

'Is anything worrying you about your mum being gone?'

'I'm scared I'll never see her again.'

'Yes. Of course. Lili and Henry say sometimes you have friends who aren't real. Is that true?'

'No.'

Jarvis had a very soft voice, not quiet but gentle and soothing. He said, 'Do your friends at school play with the other children too?'

'They just play with me.'

'Can the other children see them?'

'I don't think so.'

'But you see them.'

'Yes.'

'Sometimes, Charlie, when we're lonely we invent things to make us less lonely.'

Charlie nodded and continued to put the Lego pieces together.

'Do you think your friends at school, the ones that no-one else sees, do you think they might be like that?'

'No.'

'Do you have other friends, Charlie? People who everyone can see?'

'Mitch is my friend.'

'He lives along the road from us. They just moved in over

summer,' Lili explained.

'Good,' said Jarvis to us. 'It's a positive sign if he can make friends. What I would like, with your permission, is to see Charlie on his own and to also have a session with the two of you.'

'Of course,' Lili said.

'Charlie, would you come and see me again?'

'Why?' asked Charlie.

'Because we're all a little bit concerned about how you're going at school. And with your mum being away.'

'Oh,' said Charlie. 'Can I play with the Lego again?'

'Yes, you can,' said Jarvis.

'Okay.'

Jarvis spoke with Charlie a few minutes longer as the Lego model was completed and Charlie briefly flew the small spaceship about the room before placing it upon the table saying, 'There, it's all done. Enjoy your new toy.'

'Thank you, Charlie. Well, I'll see you very soon. We'll go and find the appointment book and see when we can find a time.'

When we returned to Jarvis, he had already had his session with Charlie and he reported on how very active and bright Charlie was. He said he would undertake two intelligence tests to see exactly where the boy was at.

And then he said, 'But it's the two of you I wanted to talk to. It's very rare, extremely rare for a child to present in such a way. Imaginary friends are quite common but there seems a much deeper issue. Hallucinations, an altered sense of reality, are very unusual in a child of this age. There is no link, medically, with this and other things which might surface later. But I think we must be careful.'

He put his fingers together and stared down at them in his lap.

'Clearly, these people Charlie talks about are very real for him. But they are also benign. In fact they seem to give him great reassurance. What's important is that he gets to tell fact from fiction. He learns to understand what is real and what is not.'

Lil nodded.

'So apart from doing some work with Charlie, I would like to hear a little about each of you. Tell me, Henry, how do you find Charlie? He's new to you. You have no children of your own?'

I shook my head.

'How has it been having a child in the house?'

'He's a nice lad,' I said. 'He was very upset when his mother overdosed back in October and then around Christmas he was a bit fragile, but lately he's been fine.'

'And you're both at work? Who looks after him?'

'Well, I'm not working much at present, so he's been home with me. Lil's on holidays since New Year and soon school will be back.'

'Henry's not very well,' said Lili.

'Ah,' said Jarvis.

'Brain tumour,' I said.

'I see,' said Jarvis. 'So there's a lot going on for the boy besides his mother.'

'He doesn't know about Henry,' said Lili.

'We've not told him,' I said.

'Is it operable?'

'No,' I said.

'I see. So what is the prognosis?'

'Och, I'll be here this year, I hope.'

'Ah. I'm very sorry to hear that.' He sighed and stared out the window for a moment.

'And you, Lili?' he continued. 'You have been through a great deal with your daughter. Now Henry has this tumour. How are you feeling about everything?'

I watched Lili for a sign then. A sign that she felt more than she let on. She sat up a little straighter, flicked back her hair, used her steadiest voice. If she was upset she held it back with the consummate skill of a professional.

'He has no-one else. It's only right we take care of him.'

'Charlie?' said Jarvis, a twinkle in his eye.

'Of course,' said Lili, not flinching.

'Do you believe his mother will come back?'

'No, I don't think so,' said Lili.

'You see, children can be so much more perceptive than we give them credit for. He observes a great deal, Charlie.'

'Do you think he really hears voices?'

'I think he thinks he hears voices. What those voices are I'm not sure yet.'

'But it wouldn't be right to tell him. Not yet, about Henry?' Lil asked.

'Perhaps just begin gently. Tell him Henry is sick.'

'He knows that bit, the lad,' I said.

'Yes, but it helps to hear it from you. Tell him the truth. Assure him that even though his mum is gone for the moment, you and Henry are here to look after him. That he'll keep living with you. I think it's very important he knows he belongs somewhere.'

'But what if she never comes back?'

'Then she never comes back.'

Lili sat back and looked at the floral curtains and the mobiles hanging from the ceiling.

'Henry,' said Jarvis, 'do you feel comfortable to let Charlie know you are dying?'

'No. Not at all.'

'Why is that?'

'Because he doesn't want to believe it himself,' said Lili.

'Aye,' I sighed.

'Well then, I will continue to work with Charlie and we will see how he goes. But take some time for each other too.'

He smiled at us.

'Time is such a wonderful thing if you use it well.'

HERE'S TO YOU, SANDRA RIVETT

I THOUGHT OF JARVIS' ADVICE and imagined on the drive home the conversation Lil and I would have.

'Lil, there's something I've been meaning to tell you. There's another woman in my life. Her name is Sandra Rivett and in 1975 I was found guilty of her murder. Of course you'll remember Sandra Rivett yourself after all your interest in the case. So you see, despite your best intentions, you have liked Lord Lucan. In fact you've built a home together these past three years. You know I never had a trial. It was only an inquest but it condemned me. And most of Britain thinks I killed her too. That's why I live here, so far away and why I make sure I have so few friends. There's not many people you can trust when you're not who you say you are . . . '

'Such different people, you and I,' said Lil, breaking the silence as we took Macquarie Street up onto Huon Road. 'Such different lives before we came here.'

'You know,' she continued, 'I think we should move into the guestroom. Before it becomes difficult. I should hate for you to wake one morning and not be able to get down the stairs.

And I think Charlie would like to have us close by.'

'Where will he sleep?'

'I thought I could make my study his room. And I could move my desk upstairs?'

Lil was right. I'd got dizzy and lost my balance on the stairs a couple of times. But leaving our room?

We were onto the stretch where the sun filtered through the trees and the mountain lay to the right of us, hazy and purple in the afternoon warmth. I grew up with the long green lawns of England, the structured gardens and polite hedges, the landscape manicured within an inch of its life. In Tasmania, the land runs on and on in khaki-coloured wildness; long blue shadows of hills stretch into an infinite silence of sky. There's nothing English about any of it, and that could have made me homesick. But it didn't. I found myself grateful for being permitted to live somewhere so effortlessly magnificent.

'Only if you promise when it's time, at the end, I can go back up again. So I can have the view,' I said.

'All right.'

'I want to die in my bed, Lil. Not in a hospital.'

'All right,' she said quietly.

'Can you organise a nice day too? Sunny, bit of a breeze?'

'Please don't joke about it.'

'Ah, Lil, it's better than crying.'

I wondered if by the time we got there I'd even know which bed was mine.

We passed the few houses clustered along the road edge and then we were around the first hairpin bend and the mountain had us. I wound down my window and smelled the pungent air. It was my favourite moment on the road, rounding that bend and then the next corner. The green light of the trees, the fresh, clean smell of rain and cold and growing forest. Almost home, I always thought.

'I was born up in the hills,' said Lil.

'Near Saigon?'

'No. Saigon was later. After my brother died. Bai Gian it was called. North-west from Saigon. It was very remote. Peaceful.'

'I didn't know you had a brother.'

'He was just a baby.'

'How did he die?'

'I want you to start the radiotherapy,' said Lil.

'Lil, we've been through all that.'

'I know but Geraldine and I have been talking and it's ridiculous you won't.'

'Geraldine Holloway?'

'Yes.'

'It's not – '

'What? Not my business?'

'That's not what I meant.'

'Yes it is. Since when has this been anything but my business? Who's going to have to see you deteriorate, Henry? Who's going to have to wheel you into the hospital? Who's going to order flowers for your goddamn funeral?'

'Lil.'

'What?'

'It's too late.'

'Too late for what?'

'To start fighting.'

'Geraldine says it's not. It would help – '

'I don't mean the tumour. I mean you and me. Don't let's fight, not like this, Lil.'

For a few moments we drove in silence. We passed the turn-off to the pinnacle road and then we swung round the corner past the tavern. Shredded grey clouds were coming across from the west. She sighed. 'Would you like to go back to Scotland?'

'No. Do you want to go back to Vietnam?'

'No,' she said.

'Why not?'

'Do you believe in war?' she asked.

'I think sometimes it's necessary. But I don't like it.'

'In the village where I lived the Republicans – the army of South Vietnam – killed many people. It was the early sixties. Bai Gian was a little bit like Ayers Rock or Mount Warning. The Viet Cong used it as a base because it was holy. In 1963, the Americans came into Bai Gian. What the Republicans had left standing, the Americans destroyed. Mostly they came in helicopters but sometimes they were on foot.'

I looked across at Lil. Her skin was almost luminous it was so pale and fine. She stretched her fingers and then her hands resettled on the steering wheel. I resisted the urge to lay my hand on her leg.

'During one American attack, a girl had hidden with her mother and a baby boy in their home. It was one room, the sort all of the village people lived in. The baby had just been born. The mother was bleeding badly so she had not been able to flee. The father had gone to get help the night before but he had not returned. The little girl had gone out in the early light to look for him but she could not find him. She thought he had probably been taken prisoner. It happened often, and then eventually people were released, or their bodies turned up in the ditches beside the rice fields. Her father would never have left them alone unless he'd been captured.

'The little girl waited. She kept checking to make sure her mother and the baby were both alive, they were so very still. Then the little girl heard voices. Foreign voices.'

We rounded the last bend before our turn-off. I had a moment's irrational thought that Lil would keep driving and miss the turn, but she indicated and the car accelerated up the steep section of the road, Lil changing down through the gears, taking the blind corner slow.

'American soldiers burning the last of the homes,' said Lil, glancing across at me for a moment, her eyes dark and her face now slightly flushed. I had been half-thinking this was some story from her days as a foreign correspondent. Someone else's story. But I saw suddenly that it was not.

Lil's voice was growing quieter as we neared the gravel driveway. 'The girl began trying to rouse her mother but the mother could not lift her head. The girl ran from the house to alert the soldiers. She saw one of the men coming toward her with a metal ball in his hand. He was tossing it up and down. She knew these balls. Like all children she had been told never to pick them up if she found one. Never to pull out the pin.

The soldier tossed the ball high into the air as he watched her. She screamed at him to throw the thing away, her mother was in there with a new baby. She pointed wildly and tried to run back in the house but another soldier grabbed her and held her in his arms while the soldier with the grenade pulled out the pin and lobbed it into the open doorway.'

We had arrived outside the house. The fading sun was sending orange fragments of light through the windscreen.

'Lil,' I whispered.

'I was taken to Saigon. I have no village to return to. No altar for my ancestors. As a journalist I worked in Bosnia, Iran, Afghanistan, Palestine, El Salvador. But it didn't matter how horrific the things I saw were, I couldn't forget. People like to think that war is necessary. That the end justifies the means.'

She turned off the car engine and her voice quivered.

'It is a cheap and terrible lie.'

THE BEAST BENEATH MY SKIN

AS WE MOVED THROUGH THE evening, Lil said very little. But then Lil was often quiet. She had a way of completely withdrawing into herself. Though it burned in me that night to confess myself to her, I bit back the words and let the silence between us grow cold.

I had read in the paper of a young lad over in America who sold his soul for $275. I wondered what he had done, or what he feared he'd do, that he wanted to be rid of it so badly. A poor price for a soul, I thought. Especially a relatively unused one. He was only seventeen.

I didn't so much sell my soul, as invite another to come and take its place. Someone who would take over Lucan's wasted life.

I understand now that Lucan's addiction to chance was as real as Suki's addiction to heroin. Her poison, at least, was illegal. But gambling attracted no such wrath. It was perceived, at worst, as an embarrassing habit. For a man of my class it was the accepted thing. One had to find something to do, after all. That it was slowly ruining my children's hope for a decent education, my marriage, my health, was never raised by my friends.

I found it a relief to be noticeably good at something. I breathed the cigar smoke. I enjoyed the rippled laughter, the snap of cards, the tumble of dice, the clatter of pieces on the backgammon board. The numbers came and went, bringing with them exhilaration or complication. I liked the eternal evening where daylight never came. My meals were on the house, my credit always good.

Addiction is a beast that befriends us. It offers comfort, reassurance, excitement. We think it distracts us from the emptiness but in truth it feeds it, until the emptiness is so big that everything, and everyone, is gone.

Veronica was the only one who dared raise it with me. I thought her vulgar and inappropriate. Whose money was it, after all? If I wished to play with it, then play I would. I loved the rush of cold stillness which descended upon me when the stakes were high. The higher the stakes and the longer the run of losses, the colder the calm. And then I won. Always, eventually, I won. Or so I told myself. Unfortunately, when my friend James sold the Clermont, the new owners began closing down the old relationships and calling in the debts. My credit was not extended.

I think on the eighth of November, when the day dawned bright and grim, and Sandra Rivett lay in a London morgue, it was the first time I had seen the sun rise in years.

In the years preceding 1974 there were no wars to fight, no battles to try my hand at. John Bingham, the seventh Earl of Lucan, paddled in the pool of privilege with his friends, waiting for something to mark his days with greatness.

The third Lord Lucan, my great-great-grandfather, had wanted to create a modern estate. The farming methods he proposed did not require tenants. Four years in a row the potato crop failed in Ireland. By 1848 three million of Ireland's poorest were dead. And the poorest of the Irish lived in county Mayo on the Lucan estate. He began evicting and continued to evict his tenants throughout the famine. People died of hunger and cold literally on the sandstone steps of his vast home. The House of Lords rebuked him. He refused to back down. It was his land. He would do with it as he pleased.

Later he instigated the fateful Charge of the Light Brigade. Half the troops died, yet he wore the blame with dignity, refusing to accept guilt. He sued for libel when the media accused him. He lost.

In my early twenties I began to think of him as a hero. Mistakes may be made, but leadership, endeavour, honour; all these things showed what a man was made of.

Luck demanded greatness of me. Where Veronica tried and failed for she had few rewards to offer me, Lady Luck bestowed stellar moments upon me at haphazard and irregular intervals. She had me win big, very big, at my first attempt. More than £20,000 playing chemin de fer. I threw in my job at a merchant bank, the only paid employment I had ever taken after my stint in the Guards. My father's death had afforded me an inheritance that gave me our home in Belgravia and a suitable income from investments. I was not hugely rich, but undeniably comfortable. My win ensured I had ready cash. I would live the gentleman's life.

I arranged the most precise schedule for myself. I kept note of all factors and when I found a winning combination, I seized upon it and would not vary from it. I knew if I lived my life to a perfect timetable the system would work.

I did not change the route from home to club, from club to gambling house, from gambling house to home. It was deeply perturbing when Veronica and I reached a point of total disrepair and I was forced to take an apartment. But even this I chose for its proximity to my routine deep in London's West End.

It is easy to see, now with hindsight, that my world was unravelling. I tried to assure myself I was drinking no more than usual, losing no more than usual. I became fixated with the belief that if my children could live with me I would remain the Lucky Lucan my friends knew.

But I lost custody of my children. With that I lost my Luck.

It was the bleakest time of my life and it went from bad to worse. I was cut off from the only people in the world I truly cared for. I became more and more desperate.

As I held Lil in bed that night, I wanted more than anything to hold back her memories. So they could never hurt her.

'Are you okay?' she said. 'You have been so quiet tonight. Did it shock you? This afternoon in the car?'

'Aye, Lil, it did.'

'I thought after what Jarvis said it was important to tell you. To not be afraid to tell you.'

'Why would you be afraid?'

'I don't like to remember.'

'You can tell me anything, Lil.'

'Can I, Henry?'

'Of course.'

There was a long silence. The moon appeared in the bedroom window between two long skeins of cloud.

'I shall miss being up here,' I said, 'when we move downstairs tomorrow.'

WIFE AND MISTRESS

'WHAT'S UP WITH YOU?' JIMMY asked on Tuesday night.

'Nothing. I'm fine.'

'That's not what I see,' he said.

'Was I just an easy catch, Jimmy? A bit lonely, no ties. Nice house. An older chap. Nice bank account. Someone who could put her up and keep her comfortable?'

'Lil? Pretty harsh thinking.'

'Aye. It is.'

'I think Lil was pretty comfortable herself before she met you.'

'Maybe she just wanted to start again. Away from her daughter.'

'Maybe she fell in love. And you with her. And I seem to recall you looked fit enough to live out a century.'

I drank the beer in front of me slowly. The wood heater was smoking as usual, filling the room with a mild London fog. The tavern was almost empty. The tourists had gone home and only a few locals hovered around the edge of the pool table in a curtain of yellow light.

'It's natural you'll try to pull back. You know, so it doesn't hurt so much, losing one another,' said Jimmy.

I have not been good with women. I had not meant to cause them harm.

It was Veronica who kept me, that dark November night, from killing myself. When the vision of a speedboat with the cocks open bubbling down into the Channel came to me, it was the image of Veronica which stopped me making it real. In the wee hours between midnight and dawn, it was my Veronica of old I held out my hand to. It was she who grasped me firm and hauled me back to life.

Because of her, or in spite of her, I vowed to live on.

Little did I know that Veronica had grown from someone who idolised me to someone who despised me. She would have done anything to be rid of me.

Why did it take Veronica until the next day to name me as her attacker? How did she know Sandra was dead if she had not been into the kitchen? Why was there blood on her shoes? Sandra's blood? After all, she claimed she was herself attacked upstairs and never entered the kitchen. What could she possibly have to gain by having her husband sent to prison?

With me out of the picture, Veronica gained a certain peace. I could no longer trouble her. She gained the assurance that the house would not be sold, the estate no longer plundered for the debts of a gambler. Would she have been willing to use the nanny to free herself and her children from the blight of her estranged husband?

Nannies had come and gone so often from the house

perhaps they seemed expendable. The perfect decoy so that it would look as if the wife, not the nanny, had been the intended target. I mean, after all, who would trouble themselves to kill a servant? And of course, she herself would be wounded in the attack. She would fight bravely, so very bravely, that the man would desist and she would run for help, this heroine who had defended herself and her children from the attacker. What name would she give her attacker? 'Why,' she would whisper to police from her hospital bed, 'it was none other than my husband, Lord Lucan.' And then she would win, Veronica. She would win the three most important things in my life. George, Frances and Camilla. Not because they mattered desperately to her. No. She would win at all costs because they mattered desperately to me.

It was a scenario all the investigators never imagined. She never divorced me through all these years, so legally, as my wife, she would never have been allowed to testify.

'You're not alone in this,' said Jimmy as we got into his car for the short drive from tavern to home.

'No, Jimmy?'

'I'm not just saying it.'

'I am the desire to disappear. I am an experiment in aloneness.'

'You're a failed experiment and you're drunk.'

Lili and Jimmy were slipping away from me. I supposed Lil would live on in the house although maybe she'd sell it. Move nearer town. Maybe she'd get a place on the beach. Someone else would live up here and see the river away beyond the gum trees. Hear the magpies calling, the wind blowing, watch the clouds moving east.

Damned is how I felt. Damned to be a traveller when I would have been so happy staying home.

THE PROMISE OF REDEMPTION

I WONDERED MANY TIMES WHAT happened to Michael Kennedy after I left Africa. Perhaps he too was a fugitive, this man who had been entrusted with my care, who had left me alone to starve in my hut. I resented him. I resented everything about my life.

For two years Mkele and I worked on Collins' tourist dream. We harvested timber and milled it with double-ended cross-saws. We baked bricks in a kiln constructed to Collins' specifications. I adapted to a diet of beans, peanuts, maize. The food and the water did not agree with me. Many a night I spent running from the hut and my difficulties did not end with my stomach. My head was awash with a hundred thoughts and all of them were inexpressible to these people.

My feet grew mould which cracked open the skin between my toes. I was forced to give up my boots and walk about barefoot, a factor that did nothing to improve my humour. My mouth erupted in abscesses and there was no dentist to fix it. I was given leaves to hold in my mouth but they did nothing to improve matters and I went about for several weeks in the most awful discomfort. I caught my hand between two logs of wood and nearly tore my thumb off. I thought I would lose it to gangrene. I fell into a dreadful fever. In the end Mkele brought me a powder. He said it was a mixture of dried snake and bat's blood. I was too delirious to resist. In the morning I was quite better. In a few days it was as if the whole thing had never happened.

The bungalows beside the hot springs began to take shape. The long months of intense dry heat were broken at last by the rains. And with the rain came Peter. 'Mr Cartwright, the Bwana's family are here again from England. They are inspecting the new works tomorrow. The Bwana says you must stay well away. He suggests you remain in your hut.'

Strangely I no longer feared discovery. Who could possibly recognise me? Though I washed in the river, I was sure my stench was powerful. My clothing was thin and bleached by the sun, my beard had grown long. The village children laughed at it and wanted to feel it. Mkele had offered me a razor and a mirror but I had no desire to look at my face. My fingers were torn and mended so many times they were unrecognisable to me. Nevertheless I had begun to sleep better than I had ever done in my four-poster bed.

Collins' family had arrived again from England? Had I been here longer than I had thought? Had a whole year passed? Was it Christmas and I had not known it?

I waited all day for Peter to speak with me again. Two children brought me food. How strange it seemed that I had taught my children so few skills. Save for playing piano with Frances, I had mostly been responsible for teaching them how not to do things. I reprimanded them on how they held a fork or spoon, how they spoke to their relatives or carried themselves in public. I had rarely taken time to teach them a song or a story, certainly not how to cook or sew. There were servants for such things.

When I finally emerged from the hut at sunset, Peter had already departed.

'How long have I been here, Mkele?' I asked.

'Not long enough. Gotta finish the job, mate.'

But with the return of the wet our work on the bungalows slowed. And Mkele began in earnest to teach me to hunt. He was a master hunter. British hunting with its baying hounds and fleeing fowl is like a pantomime compared to the real thing. In the cool of evening warthogs came, grunting and rustling through the long grasses to the river's edge. They were a vicious foe. One wrong move and they would disembowel you, or tear the skin from your bones. Mkele taught me to wait for their smell, to watch for the tiny flash of their eyes catching the moonlight.

Finally one night I shot one, a great boar, heaving and squealing. I laid down the rifle and took the heavy cudgel from my side. It is good to kill with a single blow but it does not always work. The creature reared at me, slicing the air with its tusks. I beat the creature, bringing down blow after blow.

I remember Mkele looked at it then he said quietly, 'The head is good tucker if you can keep it intact.

'Frightened you, eh?' Mkele said as we carried the pig back to the village.

'Not really.'

'Maybe you're just one of those sadistic types.'

'I hardly think the creature suffered.'

Over time I learned to hunt with only a spear or a knife. The hunt became not a giddy terror but a slow, deliberate dance.

Mkele disappeared for a few days and when he returned he said, 'The Bwana is pretty crook. His family is staying on.'

'What's the matter with him?' I asked.

'He's ninety-three, you know. Won't live forever.'

'What would you do if he died?' I asked.

'Not much use most places, hunting. But building's a good trade. Get work pretty much anywhere. You're going to need a job when you leave here too, yeah?'

'I hadn't given it any thought.'

'Look, Max, I figure your safari tour didn't just leave you behind. You're going to need some help if you ever get away from here.'

'Did you have anything in particular in mind?'

'Well, it's like this, you may know a thing or two about building now, but the thing you don't have a clue about is how to get on with people.'

'I see.'

'So, I reckon, if you want to survive in the real jungle, then it's time you dropped the holier than thou shit.'

■

Collins remained in an unstable condition. One of his daughters stayed on. I had no calendar. I had not notched the poles of my hut like some Robinson Crusoe. I had no idea if it was May or July or even September. There were nights so cool the pools by the river's edge were covered in a thin layer of ice. The days were long and never still. All about us the vast land changed colour and temperature. From the largest beast to the smallest blade of grass everything was moving.

'What will happen to all this?' I asked Mkele.

'I expect there will be some other mad Englishman happy to buy it.'

'Collins' family won't keep it?'

'There are unhappy memories here too,' he said, but did not elaborate.

I briefly imagined myself lord of this estate, the great Bwana. But I knew that though these people were accepting of me, they had no fear of me as they had of Collins. In any case, I reminded myself, I had no funds to finance such a vast project. Besides, I would require a far more insignificant life if I were to remain at large.

I could no longer exactly recall my children's faces. I would catch glimpses of them, a profile, a smile, a moment of remembered domestic life. I lost hope I would ever see them again. It was as if they lived on another planet, one I had visited for a brief moment and would never have the proper spacecraft to return to again.

By the time we completed the six bungalows, the dry season had been and gone again. Mkele and I stood back and surveyed the thatched roofs, the individual jetties jutting into the calm water, the pathways we had made, and bordered gardens we had planted.

'Next week,' Mkele said, 'Collins wants us up at the big house.'

I folded up my blanket and swept the floor of my hut. We set off at dawn and made good progress, crossing the last hill as the sun was sliding behind the mountains. I raced Mkele the last few hundred yards. Peter came down to meet us. He was dressed in an impeccable safari suit, his face and teeth so clean he looked as if he'd been polished. I looked across at Mkele and he grinned at Peter. 'Guess you'd like us to take a bath before we come inside?'

'You both have baths awaiting you in your rooms,' Peter said. 'Dinner is at eight.'

Turning to shake my hand, Peter said to me, 'You have learned how to smile, Mr Marshall. Welcome back, sir.'

In the mirror in my room a wild man looked back at me. A man who appeared to be on the verge of madness or impulse. Gone was the assured look, the satisfied gaze. The surgical scars about the eyes, mouth and nose had all but disappeared. But it was my eyes that were most unfamiliar to me. Something had stripped me of the anaesthetic of civility and I do not think I have ever quite managed to replace it.

Collins was visibly stooped and frail but he welcomed us with great ceremony. I was surprised to see a wilting Christmas tree in the library.

Confused, I said to him that surely it was not that time of the year.

'Dear boy, it's 1977! Ah, I see Mkele's done a splendid job with you. Splendid.'

When I made my way up to my room at the end of the evening, I stood for a long time out on the balcony and reflected. Dinner conversation seemed to have abandoned me. I no longer knew anything of current affairs or politics or society. Nor did I feel any desire to. I lay on the bed with its white linen and it felt too soft to give a decent night's sleep. At some point in the night I moved out onto the balcony and slept there without pillow or cover until I awoke to the sound of the dogs barking on their morning walk.

I stayed and worked on the estate another two years. Mkele stayed on too. We spent nearly a year hacking a road from the eastern end of the estate through to the high lake. I confided to Mkele that my name was not Max Marshall. I told him other things too, about dead bodies in the kitchen and inquests gone horribly wrong.

'You're going to need to be a whole new person, if you're going back out there,' Mkele said. 'And blimey, mate, the one thing you're really going to have to lose is that accent.

'What name shall we give you, then?'

We were in the rowboat fishing on Collins' lake at dawn. The place was alive with birds – pelicans, spoonbills, cranes and geese wandered the shoreline and flamingos made spectacular landings on the pink surface of the lake.

'James? No, sounds like a butler. Bill? No, too ordinary. Frederick? Marcus? Timothy? Henry?'

Henry.

'Henry who?'

'Kennedy's a good name. Lucky and unlucky, depending on who you are. It's free for the taking.'

'Henry Kennedy. I suppose I could get used to it.'

'Scottish!' said Mkele. 'Let's say he was Scottish.'

'Kennedy is Irish.'

'Well, your grandfather married a Scottish lass. You can do a Scottish accent, I'll bet.'

'Och, now wot on airth gave ye that idea?' I asked.

'Bugger me,' said Mkele.

'I spent a lot of seasons in Scotland. Grouse and what not,' I said.

'Grouse, eh, old chap,' he said, imitating me. 'It's perfect! But you'll need to have it down pat. Can't slip. Never. Have to be good enough for any Scotsman to think he's found his kinfolk.'

'I will be a star pupil.'

Henry grew strong. He bathed naked in rivers. He crafted furniture. Henry delighted in a bird call, in rain falling, in the smell of the earth after the rain. Henry quietly took a black woman to his bed and liked it. Then he took another. He woke early and climbed the hill to watch the African dawn. At night he read late by candlelight. He liked silence.

Edward Collins declined slowly. It exhausted him to hold a book or paper so often I read to him. Collins must have owned five thousand books or more. I had used his library to study architecture, engineering, building, horticulture. Though he had all the classics in literature and poetry, at this time of his life Collins only wanted to hear, of all things, children's stories. I made my way through *Tom Sawyer*, *Treasure Island* and *David Copperfield* through those long warm afternoons on the verandah. But it was *Gulliver's Travels* that set me upon my course. For there, early on in the book, Swift had written:

'We were driven by a violent storm to the north-west of Van Diemen's land. By an observation, we found ourselves in the latitude of 30 degrees 2 minutes south.'

'Van Diemen's Land,' said Collins. 'Nice out of the way sort of place. My mother came from there, would you believe? Most wonderful woman in the world. Spent her early years there running wild by all accounts. Father was a governor. Used to be a penal settlement for the British. It's called Tasmania these days. I still have family there – from Mother's side. I could help get you settled if you thought it might be suitable. And I'm sure dear Michael would have a few ideas too. I seem to recall he's spent a bit of time there, our resident Australian.'

Edward Collins was as good as his word. There were papers

waiting for me when I arrived in Tasmania making me the owner of a tract of land up on the mountain above the capital city. (*In case you ever want to put those building skills to use*, Collins had written.)

Several months later a letter arrived from Mkele, in a beautiful copperplate I could never have expected. *It is with sadness I write to inform you of the passing of our dear friend and benefactor. He wanted you to have this small token of his affection.*

Enclosed in a wooden box was a plaque, beautifully carved. It bore the words *Spero Meliora*. I remembered the inscription well – it was emblazoned on the family crest that had hung above the library door. It meant in Latin *I hope for better things*.

Though I wrote back, I received no response from Mkele. I never heard from him again.

FUCK AND OTHER CHILDREN'S NAMES

CHARLIE'S SCHOOL HOLIDAYS DREW TO a close and pain became my companion. Pain lay in wait for me. It caught me as I woke. It woke me as I slept. It stalked me in my dreams. All my life I had rarely dreamed. Oh, a glimpse here, a fragment there, a nightmare half remembered in the light of morning. Suddenly I was getting villains, heroes, blood and beauty, music, conversation and every type of story imaginable.

Within a few short weeks I found myself with a body made of rusted iron that creaked and squealed at every movement. My head ricocheted with pain when the medication wore off and I could keep no food down. Much of the time I slept and when I woke, the pain soon found me. Some days I found myself weeping for no other reason than it was all I could do.

Illness did funny things to me. Made me love food I never liked and weather I never liked. Bloody rain, I used to think. Can't get a thing done on the boat. But through late February I listened to it falling and it was like music. Two fluid things, me water, it water, hearing one another; like two instruments lying side by side, a flute and cello maybe, finding the sound we shared and playing it.

Jimmy came and went most days. He worked on *Venus*. The smell of paint drifted into the house.

'I reckon we'll have her in the water by May. The hull's come up a treat,' he said, sitting awkwardly on the edge of the bed.

'What about the sails?'

'The guy from North came up last week. They're underway. Main, genoa and a storm jib.'

'Get them to invoice me,' I said.

'The winches arrived.' He unpacked them out of the bubble wrap and handed them to me. They were heavier than I remembered. Shiny, beautiful things.

'May,' said Jimmy, 'so you'd better be getting back on your feet.'

Lili sponged my face and wiped my hands with a cool damp cloth and her face was that of an angel.

The suddenness of it had thrown me. The illusion it would not really get me was gone. Somehow getting through Christmas and the warm, soft fruit days of that short summer, I had made myself believe it was not going to come true. Yes, there were daily irritations and reminders, but the spiralling debilitation took me from functional to very limited function in a matter of weeks. It left me with little to do, and a mind too active suddenly for the body in which it found itself.

232

I lay on the couch watching the sky turn from blue to sapphire as the days passed; watching wind scud through the trees, sending the silver birches into paroxysms of light. There was a sense of emptiness those days when Lili was at work and Charlie in class. My world was confined to the house and the deck. Pearl picked Charlie up from school and Jimmy said it was perfect for her. They kept the lad till Lili got home. Lil employed a housekeeper, a rather dour woman, Mrs Flannery, who came each morning and cleaned and tidied the house and cooked me a warm meal at lunchtime. She was an excellent cook and I found myself served the food of my childhood – mashed potatoes, good stew, vegetable soups and apple crumble with custard. But my appetite was a disappointment to her.

The boy had his visits with Jarvis and Lil went too. Of course I was not well enough to go. I was relieved to have escaped the psychologist. I had no idea how I was going to lie to someone who spent his life discerning the undercurrents in people's lives.

Sometimes I heard my children playing in the paddock, George and Frances and Camilla. Sometimes Veronica wiped my brow, running her finger across my hairline like she used to.

'Still got your lovely hair, my handsome man,' she said.

I asked her if the house was still the way I remembered it.

'I had to sell it. I had to sell your robes too, your beautiful ermine collar,' she whispered. 'But I have all our photos still. I tried so hard to hang onto everything we were.'

I thought at times I really was dear Fergus whispering in his bed at night. The twelve-year-old lad, Fergus, who Mkele and I invented. Fergus Kennedy, who so wanted to lead a big life he renamed himself Henry.

'Ah, Mother,' I would whisper. 'Mother.'

And other times I thought of my true mother, and all she had gone through to save me in the years before Sandra Rivett, when she watched me all but bankrupt the family. And the years after, when she had sent Collins to find me, and in saving me that last time, lost me completely.

Not long after I had arrived in Tasmania, I was in the city library flicking through a file of the *Times*, an indulgence I allowed myself in the anonymity of my new surroundings. Hobart felt so far from England, so entirely remote. A small article caught my eye. *The Dowager Lady Lucan passed away on Sunday . . . mother of Lord Lucan who disappeared in 1974 after the murder of the family nanny.* I walked out to my car. I sat for a while in silence staring at the traffic passing, the people walking up and down the street. I went down the hill to the cathedral. Inside it was quite empty. It was the first time in many years I had entered a church. I knelt in the silence. I don't remember what I said, but it was my own version of goodbye. God gave me no comfort.

'Sometimes, he seems to be lost back in time,' I heard Lil say to Geraldine Holloway at an appointment in Holloway's office.

'You mustn't worry if you find yourself talking a great deal, or remembering things very vividly, Henry,' Geraldine

Holloway said. 'It's all part of the metastases altering brain function. It may pass or it may worsen.'

What cool grey eyes, she had, Doctor Holloway. What painful effort to get to her rooms from the car, even though Lil had parked in the gravel courtyard at the back of the building.

'She will do a home visit if you want,' Lil had said.

'While I can, I will keep moving this wreck,' I had replied, patting my legs.

'Stan. Stan. Did I tell you how I hated England?'

Stan had arrived in the mid-afternoon. He had brought up some contracts we both needed to sign for new projects he was taking on.

'Yes, Henry. You told me last week.'

'Lil, can you get Stan another beer?'

'It's fine, Henry. Oh, okay, just make it a light. You don't have to do this any more. We can remove you as a director.'

'I'm not unfit yet,' I said.

'How can you be sure?'

'Because you will tell me.'

I signed, initialling every page but it was hard to hold the pen, as if even that took an inordinate amount of strength.

'Okay,' he said, 'I'm telling you this is the last time.'

'Och, am I that bad?'

'You have more important things to do than sign paperwork. Now go on, tell me about England.'

'I was ten, eleven. I remember gazing across those neat,

green fields and hedgerows and I longed for Scotland and the sea. In Surrey, the sea might as well have been a thousand miles away. 'Do you know Surrey at all, Stan?'

'No, Henry, never left Australia.'

'How can you be an architect and not have travelled?'

'Dunno,' he said, patting the arms of his wheelchair.

'There is nothing Scottish about England. Save perhaps for frost. In the mornings I'd walk an entire circle from the kitchen door out around the garden to the Great Park and back leaving a dark trail of footprints – proof that I had been there.

'By then, I was Henry. My father was irate when he got my school report. *Henry does not always apply himself sufficiently to his work. He has a mischievous streak that has had to be curbed on a number of occasions.* "Who's Henry?" he bellowed at me. "Who the fuck is Henry?"

'"Father," I said, "you said it was our big chance here in England. I couldn'a with conscience remain as Fergus when I do not think it will serve me well for the long road upon which I am travelling." I remember him laughing at this and he would recite it to his friends.

'So Henry I became,' I continued. 'My father was never one to hold anyone back. He found it hard to remember though, and would start off saying "F . . . Henry," for years after. It always made me think he was about to say "Fucking Henry".'

'I thought about calling you fucking Henry on a number of occasions,' said Stan.

'Aye, with good reason, I'm sure.'

Young Fergus who became Henry and grew into a man and left England to make another life for himself after the death of his father in the car Henry was driving. This is the man Lili and Jimmy and Stan thought they knew.

Stan and I sat in silence and then Lil emerged from inside.

'I'll walk over and get Charlie,' she said. 'He's off at his friend Mitch's house. Back soon.'

The day was drawing to a close. Birds flitted along the edge of the trees. My gaze lingered on the bright shining river, the straggly trees, the sheep in the paddock sitting staring out to sea. The sun had disappeared behind the house and the shadows were growing long on the deck. A crow made its way up onto the eaves.

I must have nodded off because the next thing I knew Charlie came bounding out the door onto the balcony.

'Stan!' he said. 'I didn't know you were here!'

'Hello, Charlie,' said Stan, reaching out and hugging the lad. I blinked at Charlie. Lil came out from the house and stood behind me, her hands on my shoulders. She kissed the top of my head.

Stan turned back to me. 'I have to go,' he said. 'Be gentle on yourself.'

'Did I drift off?' I asked.

'Not a bit,' said Stan. 'I'll be up next Saturday.'

He shook my hand, kissed Lil, then wheeled himself down the long curving path he'd made especially when the house was built, so he could come and go as he pleased.

I had created the stories to serve me. I had hidden myself

deep inside them. But I knew it was not good the way things were going. I saw how Lili watched me. I could not be sure if her gaze was curiosity or sadness. Certainly there was something Lil was unhappy about.

STAINED GLASS

I BEGAN TO EXPERIENCE PAIN in my hips and pelvis, my right leg. Holloway suspected more growths in my hip joint. The tumours in my head began enhancing something called my reticular activating system so at night I was troubled not only by the dreams but also by long periods of wakefulness.

I had frightened Lil several times. She would not say what I had said or done. Only in the morning she'd say, 'You must be tired.'

She wrapped her arms around me and laid against my body and it seemed as though we almost melted together. All the worry went out of me then with her head against mine, the length of her legs and stomach gentle against me, her hands soft, relaxed in the curve of mine. And for a few minutes the pain would forget me.

How long the hours when I lay alone, hoping the pain would lie quiet if only I managed not to attract its attention. How agonising the simplest act of rolling over to take a piss in the jar Lili brought for me.

——■——

Try as I did to keep the past shackled, ever more urgently the events of the seventh of November, 1974, rose up and snapped at me. Voices that whispered to me in the night, 'Lucky? Oh Lucky, you did marry beneath you, didn't you? Never any good come of that. You should've known better. You always wanted to be important, eh Guv'nor? People know you now! Bloody infamous! That's real recognition for you! And anyways, paying off the coppers is common practice to people like you, isn't it?

'Paying off the debt collector is much harder. Oh, yes, Lucky. Them nice Kray brothers who loaned you such a lot of dosh. And the Family, after the boys was locked away, who showed you every kindness. Years of it, Lucky, for you to have your fun with. Ooh, you was a naughty boy, eh Lucky. Did you think you could get away with it? You was dead wrong about that, weren't you, Lucky? Dead wrong. The Family, they never forget, and they never forgive.'

'Why do I have to be the one to love you?' said Lil. 'Why this place?'

She was sitting on the chair beside the bed, helping spoon soup into my mouth.

'It's a nice place.' I looked around at the timber ceiling, the cream walls, the theatre of clouds beyond the glass.

'I mean this place,' she said, poking her chest.

I was silent.

'Why Henry? Why will you not fight it? Why will you not

even try?'

'Because I don't want to.'

'I don't understand that.'

'Not everything has a happy ending.'

Sometimes when two people love each other there is no way to say what pain it can cause. Someone is loving more. Or less. Someone is hurting. Because it's not just this love you feel. It's all the other loves. Love is not a season or a drug. It is not a tonic or a fragrance. Love is a memory. It is a memory we lock away inside ourselves when first we feel it. Love is a fragment from a stained-glass window. We want to see its entirety. Yet we hold only a single, coloured piece.

I could not grasp at life to keep Lil from feeling pain. In going this way, there was no deceit. No pretence. Let the burden of my care go quickly from her. Better quick than slow and tiresome. Did I want to die? Somewhere beyond my initial fear of it, I did. I was weary. Weary of my game.

As she sat beside me, as I watched her in the house, I wished I could bottle the soft sweet scent of her and take it with me. Would we meet again, Lili and I? Would life turn and twist and reincarnation perform its magic so one day I would smell her skin again, as Stan would have me believe? Or were there only worms to know my heart, and darkness to welcome the part of me Jimmy called my soul?

Some nights I lay awake and saw Lili's face and it brought with it a thousand pictures. Some days as I watched her it felt as if my heart would surely drop right through the bed it grew so heavy.

'I don't want you to die,' she said. 'I want you to stay with me until I am old, too old even to kiss.'

'That was never going to happen,' I said.

'I'm not going to cry.'

'No.'

'Why does 'I love you' always sound like an excuse or an apology?'

'Does it, Lil?'

'You made me feel like a woman who had no memories of being a girl.'

'Lil.'

'Time is running out for us – '

'Not just us, Lil. Everyone.'

'But I can hear it now.'

It was both beautiful and heartbreaking letting go of the paddle, floating away down the river. There was in my life now a kind of strange quiescence I had never known. Would I have loved Lili this way if I had not been leaving?

If I were to stay, would we go on, she and I, loving like this?

And Charlie? This little boy who knew what it was to sit on the verandah and do nothing but watch a sleepy black spider crawl from an upturned bit of bark and make its way under a pot plant, bottom left facing the world but head and legs, safe at least, from sight.

Charlie who brought me, cupped in his hot child-smelling hands, a ladybird, ever so gently holding it up for me to spy through a tiny hole between his two thumbs, saying, 'See see.'

'It's too dark in there for a good look,' I said.

'Quiet,' he whispered, 'ladybirds have very gentle ears.'

'How do you know?'

'Because she could hear her children even though they were in London.'

'In London?'

'When the fire was burning.'

I looked down at Charlie as he uncupped his hands and the beetle crawled about, then, in a wink, took flight and was gone from us.

In the end I gave in. Not because I had hope. But because I saw that Lili and, to my surprise, Jimmy needed to feel they were doing whatever they could to allay the inevitable.

'You're a stubborn bastard,' Jimmy had said. 'You're not going quietly, are you?'

'I'm doing my best.'

'Why would you miss a chance for a few more months with Lil?'

'Don't you think she'd be better without a patient?'

'Oh, that's rubbish and you know it.'

Jimmy had opened the doors from the bedroom onto the deck. It was a cold autumn day and the air was beautifully fresh. A row of poplars on the southern side of the hill beyond had turned yellow.

'May was looking good for *Venus*, but it'll be June I suspect,' he said.

'Ah.'

'You'll never get on deck the state you're in. Lil said you might get some movement back with the radiotherapy.'

'Aye.'

'Why would you pass it up? The pain eased a bit? I never took you for a masochist.'

I wanted to tell him the pain was my sentence. The one I never served, and here it was, twenty years of purgatory fitted into one.

'You'll like the galley. The nav table works just the way you wanted it,' Jimmy continued.

'I'll be needing an interesting set of charts, eh.'

'I could look into that.'

'Where do you buy those, do you suppose?'

'Oh, I expect the Buddhists have some. The Muslims have quite nice ones. The Catholics have a set but I don't much like theirs.'

'Ah, Jimmy, you're the only one with enough guts to make fun of it.'

'Better than drowning our sorrows.'

'Aye, especially when there's only herbal tea in the flask.'

'So will you get some radiotherapy?'

'If it will make you feel better, Jimmy.'

'I'm glad you've finally realised that I'm the one suffering here.'

■

I went four times over two weeks to lie under the machine. My skin was burned as if I'd been too long in the sun. Red pen stained my skull where they shaved back my hair and noted the growths beneath with small crosses. On my chest too they marked the tumours. Those had remained perversely stable in size, unlike the ones in my head. They also irradiated the new tumour in my hip.

We waited two weeks and had another CT scan. Geraldine Holloway ordered another round of radiotherapy. My skin had barely recovered from the first treatment and I went through the whole process again. My gums bled.

Lil took leave from work. The weather was calm and warm and there were days when we sat out on the balcony and watched the light in the gum trees. She read or dozed on the bamboo lounge she'd found at a second-hand store that summer.

I had grown thinner, my belt needing extra notches, my shoulders gaunt in my shirts. My face in particular had grown leaner, my eyes brighter and yet hollow. The scars on my face which over the years had grown indiscernible were coloured again from the radiotherapy. Perhaps because my face was thinner, or because the illness had pared away some level of pretence, I felt like my old face was re-emerging. A last hurrah.

The therapy worked. The pain in my limbs eased up. The headaches diminished and only occasionally my eyes gave me sharp and stabbing pain. My medication was reduced which made me less tired. I was more alert and interested. Lil said I was more settled at night. I was not talking as much as I had been.

The shining autumn days went on and on.

Jimmy said the legislation for the land transfer looked set to go to the Lower House in June and the Upper House in July. They'd be breaking ground by Christmas if all went well.

Stan came up with nonalcoholic champagne because the Howroyd place had been nominated for a national award.

We had a wake for Molly Watkins, who at the age of sixteen had had to be put down. Jimmy said he'd spent more time talking to that dog than any person he'd ever known. He built her a coffin and he and Pearl decorated it with pictures of Molly running, sitting, smiling. I'd never seen Jimmy cry before but he cried that day. We sat up there, Jimmy, Pearl, Lil, Charlie and me, above their house with a few beers between us (ginger beers for the lad and me). We told each other stories of Molly. I sat on the tree stump and looked at the fresh earth where the hole had been dug. I didn't want to go in the earth in a box. I didn't like the thought of it at all. It wasn't a bad place to be buried. The view was good. But I didn't want to rot down there.

Jimmy banged a picket in the ground. It had a plaque he'd carved. It said, Best Friend.

'It's a mighty title,' I said.

'I might make you one of those,' he said.

■

Charlie finished his sessions with Benjamin Jarvis. Lili said Jarvis thought that for now there was a notable improvement. Charlie was making friends at school. He'd stopped talking about the voices, although when I asked him he said he still heard them.

'Can you hear them too, now?' he asked, surprised.

'Well, I have a few of my own these days,' I said.

'That must be nice for you.'

Lili made toffee apples for Charlie's class to celebrate his sixth birthday. The blackberries were finished along with the apricots, nectarines, cherries and peaches. A whole season of sweetness, of blue mornings and afternoon sea breezes, had come and gone.

Life took on the illusion of repair.

'Reintegration,' Lil said. 'You're reintegrating.'

'It's like I've been outside life.'

She massaged my neck, her hands working the muscles. She worked on me every day. Places I couldn't bear her to touch two months ago loved the steady strength in her fingers.

I found myself looking out at life with newness, with shyness, as if I was not quite sure I was welcome.

Don't think it's over yet, I said to myself. Never forget this is the pattern. You win a bit. You win a lot. But in the end . . .

LABILITY

I MADE MY WAY TO the bathroom and it struck me that the sun had moved along the horizon. It now fell onto a different corner of the bathroom floor. I saw the way Lili had folded a towel by the shower door so I didn't have to reach for it on the rail.

I knew I would never understand exactly how a woman loves, nor even why she loves, but when she loves it is a gift.

Back in the bedroom after my shower I called out to her that I could not find my shirt. I had left it on the dresser but it was gone. She walked in and picked it up from beneath the dressing gown I had thrown over it. She bent and without a word slipped on my socks and shoes for me. I stood with the help of the frame and she reached forward for my fly.

'My favourite part,' she smiled, as she carefully pulled up the zip I had unwittingly left open.

'Not much use now.'

'We'll manage again yet. Just you wait.'

Lili could sense a shirt. The shape and vibration of it, or any lost item – be it toothpaste, butter, a pen. As if she had, long before she had searched the room, a hint, a feeling of where that item was.

It's like the fridge. I thought. Butter must be on the top shelf because that's where it was meant to be. I had no clue what butter even looked like if it was not on the top shelf. When I looked, it was as if all the other shelves were invisible.

Such thoughts arrested me. Simple things became so loud in the silence of my day.

Lil deferred her trips to Sydney and Melbourne to interview guests. She recorded at the local ABC studios in Hobart and did as much as she could via satellite. They were keen to keep her happy. She'd been offered a job at Channel Nine doing current affairs again.

And then one afternoon she arrived home and said, 'Henry, I spoke to Suki today. I asked her to come back. She'll be here at the end of May.'

I could not find what I wanted to say. I wanted to know how it had happened. How had Lili known where she was? Lately it had been harder to find the words. As if vocabulary was slowly leaving me.

'She's much better. She's been in a very good clinic. I didn't want to trouble you. I know it's not ideal. I can tell her not to come. I didn't mean to upset you,' Lili said.

Tears were running down my cheeks. I hadn't realised. I shook my head.

'Charlie,' I wanted to say. 'Happy for Charlie.'

She smiled. 'You're not sad then,' she said, running her fingers under my eyes to wipe away the wetness.

I shook my head again and then I was laughing. Laughing.

I felt happy.

'Lability,' said Geraldine Holloway. 'It's an effect of the metastases. You might find yourself crying or laughing for no apparent reason, Henry. You might find yourself feeling things much more deeply. You mustn't worry about it. It may come and go. Some days you will feel quite normal and other days, you may be disoriented. It can be unsettling to those around you.' She looked at Lil as she said this.

'You may not even notice what is happening. Some patients become distressed because they cannot control their feelings, their language. Others seem to be quite unaware that anything unusual has happened.'

Despite the radiotherapy, the tumours continued to grow in my head. Geraldine and Lil talked of palliative care when the time came. Nurses who would share the twenty-four-hour administration of my medication for pain relief, organising adjustments to the house. Devices to make taps turn on and off easily, ramps up and down stairs for the wheelchair when I lost my mobility completely.

I said, 'There'll be no need for the ramps.'

'Henry,' said Geraldine.

'The house is already well-equipped,' I said. 'My business partner is a paraplegic. He designed the place for easy access.

250

Never thought it'd come in useful for anyone but him, mind.'

'Well, then,' said Geraldine Holloway. She paused, as if considering her words carefully. 'You may begin experiencing light and sound intolerance. After a certain point the nerves running out from the brain will be squeezed against the hard edges of the skull. This will cause a stroke, Henry. You might experience some level of paralysis but it will not be painful. It's likely by then you may not know those close to you. You may slip into a coma. You must plan for all this. You and Lili.'

Stan had long since hired freelance project managers to do the stuff I'd done at work. We'd begun resolving the financials. He brought up an independent valuation of the business and said he'd buy me out.

'Can you afford to?'

'I can. Didn't do too badly in ten years, did we?'

'I think you're being too generous,' I said, looking at the figure at the bottom of the page.

'Well for once maybe it's working in your favour.'

'It always worked in my favour. It was you who did that to people. Made them feel they could trust you.'

'It was a team effort.'

I looked at his wheelchair and my walking frame and considered the team we'd become.

'I used to think positive thinking could really heal people,'

Stan said. 'But somehow it makes all that feel shallow, seeing you like this.'

'Why is that?'

'You don't deserve this, Henry.'

'How can you be sure?'

'I'm sure.'

'The morphine may affect your lucidity,' Geraldine Holloway explained. 'It can cause nausea. We need to adjust it to give you maximum relief but minimum side-effects.'

I nodded.

'You must have been on morphine after the car accident?' she asked.

'What car accident?' And then I remembered. 'Oh, aye.'

How busy I had been playing out my fiction. My carefully constructed stories to explain the scar on my face caused by the horrific accident where my father had died; how after the accident I had become estranged from my brother Hugh, drifting across Europe from one job to another, learning skills on building sites. Eventually flying to Sydney and then, later, making my way to Hobart.

'Would you like me to try to track down Hugh?' Lil asked.

'He's dead, Lil. A couple of years ago. I had a telegram. I didn't tell you. No point. It's all over, Lil. I'm the last.'

'Dead? How?'

'It was a heart attack. His lawyers wrote to me.'

'But you never spoke with him again?'

'Oh, we found our peace in our own ways.'

'Do you think he still blamed you for your father's death?'

'I don't think so.'

'Then perhaps you can stop calling out to him in your sleep,' Lil said.

'I'm sorry.'

'It's okay.'

'Don't leave me, Lil,' I said, feeling her arms about me as I drifted into sleep.

'I'm right here,' she said.

THE PRODIGAL DAUGHTER

SUKI RETURNED. CHARLIE TREATED HER like a visitor he was pleased to have come and stay. He had grown two inches since Christmas. Because we had moved downstairs, Suki went upstairs to our old bedroom. Slowly the house was becoming less mine and more Lil's and Charlie's and Suki's.

Suki made me foul herbal tonics and squirted homoeopathic drops into my water. She could be kind in a way I had never imagined or expected. She had put on weight and it suited her.

Snow had been falling for two days. The purity of light, the hush of noise, the load of snow on ferns and branches, the banks at the edges of roads turned from mud and foliage to pristine white hedges. And the air. The sweetness of it. Charlie had never known snow before. School was closed. He and Lili followed the snowplough down the mountain to go and buy supplies. Suki settled herself by the fire. She had begun a university degree by correspondence. Social work. She was reading from a book she had open before her. Chopin was playing on the CD player, piano concertos.

' "*At death, one must give back everything that one has been given and more besides, in the form of thanks, and still have more than one started with. Only then may we pass the Eagle. It is not possible to cheat.*" '

'I hadn't been counting on eagles,' I said.

'I saw one once, when I was out of it. It flew right between my eyes.'

I watched the snow steadily piling up outside on the balcony.

'Do you mind?' she said.

'Not really. And some days, yes, very much.'

'I should say thank you.'

'To whom?'

'For what!' she said. '"For what" is the question.'

'Okay, for what?'

'Oh, for Mum, you, Charlie.'

'And Charlie's dad?'

'Why thank him?'

'For Charlie.'

'Yeah. Yeah sure.'

'Do you know where he is?'

'No.'

She sat and stared out the window. 'I only knew him for a few weeks one summer. He was some guy from Melbourne who was camping up at Byron. He came up again the following year but I just couldn't tell him.'

'So he still doesn't know?'

'I ran into him a few months back in Sydney. It was the

weirdest thing. He's in advertising. He's got a wife and another kid now.'

'Maybe you should tell him.'

She nodded slowly and went to the kitchen to make tea. She brought back two mugs and two protein bars. She sat the drink and food beside me, ripped open the wrappers.

'Charlie would like it, to have a dad somewhere.'

'I never knew my dad,' she said. 'I mean, I didn't have one, so why should Charlie? The normal selfish thinking.'

'But wasn't your father . . . Birch? . . . Lil was married to?'

'Keith Birch? Is that what she told you? I was born a whole three years before he and Mum got married.'

I looked at her and blinked.

'See, it's what people, parents, like to think. That kids get screwed up on their own.'

'But he suicided . . .'

'Yes, why was that? I barely remember him. Just that he used to sit me on his knee and brush my hair.'

She leaned forward over her bent knees, nearer to the fire. She stretched her hands out as if she could run the warmth right through her body that way. She let her head flop forward.

'You don't know about Vietnam, do you? She's never told you.'

'Of course she's told me.'

'What did she tell you?'

'About her family being killed by the Americans. Going to the orphanage.'

'But not about having me.'

'Maybe Lili would prefer to tell it herself.'

'I think she would have done it by now, don't you?'

'You're not making sense.'

Suki sighed.

'She won't say. But she didn't go straight to the orphanage. She spent years with an aunt in Saigon. Whatever happened to her there, that's what's wrong with her. She won't say. She can't. I tried and in the end I left. She can't really love anybody, Lili. It's like it's not there. Maybe it's different for you, but it's how she is with me. More than three million American soldiers came and went from Vietnam between 1963 and 1974. And in 1971 I was born. Put it together yourself. Why do you think she is like she is? Miss squeaky clean television personality.'

'I don't want to know, Suki,' I said.

'Do you think it will make it go away?' she said. 'I tried that.'

'She's your mother. She gave you a better life.'

'She should have had an abortion.'

'No, Suki, no . . .'

She smacked her mug onto the hearth. It cracked against the stones and sprayed hot tea onto the carpet. The wood went black and smoke and steam billowed up.

'You don't get it, do you? She doesn't get it either. I wasn't trying all these years to blame her. I was trying to belong to her.'

Suki lunged away, across the room, through the back door and out into the snow.

■

When Lil got home, the fire had sputtered back into life. She came in carrying bags I knew were heavy with celery and carrots and powders from the herbalist. Charlie was carrying two small logs of wood and he gave them to the hearth as if they were presents.

'There you are, Grandad,' he said.

'That's my boy,' I said. He'd never called me Grandad before.

He came over and leaned on my leg and said, 'How are you feeling today?'

'Better for seeing you.'

'Would you like to build a snowman?'

'Maybe tomorrow, Charlie. Maybe tomorrow.'

'Where's Mum?'

'She went out for a walk, Charlie.'

Lili kissed me. Seeing the broken pieces of cup in the fireplace, she picked up the dustpan and broom by the hearth, and using the poker to dislodge the coloured shards.

'What happened?' she asked, glancing at my mug still beside me on the table.

'Lili, can I go out in the snow, too?' asked Charlie. 'I want to build another snowman.'

Lili nodded and smiled.

'Just out there, where we can see him,' I said.

'This one's going to be huge,' Charlie said as he disappeared into the laundry with Lili.

When he was gone, complete with gumboots, coat and hat, Lili came and sat on the arm of my chair.

She said again, 'What happened?'

I took her hand. 'Ah Lil.' I brought it to my lips and said, 'You must be the only woman in the world who pretends she is older than she is.'

'What?'

'It doesn't add up. Suki three when you married Birch. I never guessed. I didn't know.'

'Where is she?'

'Gone. Gone out.'

She was silent a long time. The she said very quietly, 'It's not her's to tell. She doesn't know.'

'Lil . . . '

'I could have crushed her head with a rock,' she said. 'I could have thrown her under the wheels of a passing truck. Instead I fed her opium oil on my finger to keep her quiet while I worked. And when she got too big, I took her to the orphanage on Rue Catalan and left her there. They were over-run with the war, but there was nothing I could do. I begged them to take care of her. I promised them I'd bring money. And I did. It was a better life than most children.'

'Lili . . .'

'Do you hate me? Do you want us to go?'

'No.'

'She must go. We can't live like this.'

'This is what living is, I think.'

We sat there and watched the fire, my hand holding her hand, my mind making pictures of her I did not want to see. If Lili had known how to cry, she would have cried then. Her face looked like it had watched a thousand deaths and every one of them sadder than the last.

After a while Charlie called us and Lil helped me from the chair.

Charlie was pretending to dance with the snowman, saying, 'Hello snow lady, would you like to waltz?'

Suki appeared around the edge of the house.

'Mum,' yelled Charlie and ran toward her. She bent down and pulled him into her arms and kept him there hard and close for a long time. When they walked toward us and came inside, Suki did not look at us.

I took my meal in bed. The house clattered quietly with dinner preparations, Charlie's chatter and the sound of the evening news on the television.

When at last Lil came to bed I waited until she was quite still beside me before I said, 'Tell me about Saigon.'

'I can't,' she whispered.

'Is it true?'

'What did she say?'

'That Keith was not her father.'

'Yes.'

'Who is her father?'

'I don't know.'

'Why Lil? Why don't you know?'

'There were so many of them. It has been hard to think of her as my daughter sometimes. More like a bill for services rendered.'

Part of me wanted to shed her then, wanted to peel her off and discard her like an unwanted hair caught against my clothing. And part of me wanted to tell her no harm would ever come to her while I could hold her in my arms.

'Did you not go to the orphanage?'

'I did, but much later. After Suki was born. Before that I worked in my aunt's brothel.'

'No, Lil.'

'After they blew up my mother and brother they loaded me into a truck. They took me to a camp and then another and finally they took me to her place. They said she was my aunt. My father's sister. I had never met her before.'

'But they must have seen it was . . . how old were you?'

'Nine. I expect they got a good price for me.'

And she lay there and held my head and stroked my cheek and kissed the skin of my eyelids and said, 'It's okay. It's okay. It's like it was another person. Some other person. Not me at all.'

'Tell me,' I said.

'I cannot,' she whispered.

'Please, Lil.'

The curtains were open. Moonlight spilled onto the bedspread.

In the mother-of-pearl darkness she said, 'Promise me you will forget it as soon as I've finished telling it. It's a story you heard about someone you don't know.

'It's not really mine, this story. It belongs to every woman who has nothing else to sell. Or who has lived through a war and tried to save herself from death. It's not about sex. It's about our infinite ability for cruelty.

'I thought about it,' she said, 'when Suki turned nine. I thought about dressing her up and sending her into the arms of a man. I could never have done it. But it is what Aunt Lhien did. She dressed me up and sent me into the next room and the men came. Other girls lived in that house. I remember thinking how many nieces my aunt had. They lit the men's pipes when they came to smoke opium. I was the youngest. My aunt's little treat for the ones who liked that sort of thing.

'I didn't know what it was. Their faces sweating in the heat. The ceiling fan that blew the smell of them down on me. The pain they caused me. The stickiness they left on my legs, my stomach, my face. Afterwards Aunt Lhien would feed me honey on a teaspoon. It came from a silver tin on top of the wardrobe in our kitchen and only I was allowed it. A single teaspoon. I would sit out on the back steps with the spoon melting its warm contents into my mouth and watch the laneway with its cabbage leaves and sunning cats and slit of smoggy sky, the pigeons over the way walking the gutters of the warehouse.'

Lil sat up suddenly and shed the bedclothes. She stayed there on the side of the bed with her back to me. I reached out to her but let my arm fall before it touched her.

'One of the men was a regular visitor. He would always cry afterwards and read aloud from a Bible before he left. I was very interested in that book. What was it telling him? He tried to teach me to read. Aunt Lhien was not to know, he said.

Sometimes I saw him in the street when I was running errands for my aunt. He would pretend not to know me.'

She stood and walked to the window, the fall of her nightshirt silver in the half-light.

'I began to see words everywhere. On buildings, newspapers, the whole world had words and it was like a land I was not allowed to visit. Then one day I followed him when I saw him in the street. I followed him to where he worked at the orphanage school. He was a priest, a teacher. I could hear the children chanting, singing. Some days I would go there very early and climb the tree and stay there all morning listening and watching, glimpsing him through the open windows, his back to me as he wrote on the blackboard.

'One day he stood beneath the tree and called up to me, "If I see you here again I will tell your aunt."

'I fled. But the next day he came to visit me. He did not want me to take off my clothes. He said he was very sad. He said if I never mentioned what had happened between us, never ever, then I could come to his school and learn with the other children. His name was Keith Birch.

'The first morning he taught me to write my name. Li-Le.

'By then I was twelve years old. He asked my aunt to have me come to him. He paid her well for it. And instead of sex, I became a student. It was hard to stay awake sometimes. My work took most of the night. When I was fifteen my aunt became very sick. We were forced to work in the bars and clubs, even on the streets, because my aunt no longer brought them to our house. I stopped taking the herbs she had always given me and I fell pregnant.'

Lil's eyes caught the light and for a moment she looked like a strange shy animal I had captured. She moved a fraction and the image disappeared.

'The war was getting old. Everywhere there were beggars, amputees, refugees. I was the oldest student at the school by then. I helped to teach the little children to learn their numbers and letters. I was scared. There were terrible stories of women dying trying to have abortions. Keith was worried. Anxious that I look after myself. Not keep working. But I had to work to feed myself and the other girls and to get medicine for Aunt Lhien.'

'You were so young.'

'Much worse things happened. Many women were kept by men for months with no pay and forced to do terrible things. Others died of infections that went so long untreated they could not walk. Some were raped and beaten; it was not unusual. And so many died. In the mornings they'd be face down in the canals. They were murdered in the camps. There is nothing honourable in war. Only what you hold in your heart. So many people held nothing. Nothing at all. Or worse than nothing. I held on to the idea that my child would have a better life. That she would not live as I had lived.

'I did not realise how much it would remind me, every time I looked at her, as she grew up. Sui Khi. But Keith always called her Suki and it stuck. She was happy at the orphanage with the nuns. And then when she was two years old there was the fire which destroyed my aunt's apartment block. And we were alone.'

She slid open the door onto the deck. From the bed I watched her breath make clouds in the icy air.

'Keith was going home to Australia. He said the war was nearly over and the Communists would not want Catholic teachers. He asked me to come with him. He said he was going to give up the priesthood. He was going to live as a normal man. He said he would take us both with him. Suki and me. "Come as my wife," he said.

'So we were married and after a lot of bribery and paperwork, I was allowed to leave Vietnam. I arrived in Sydney as Mrs Keith Birch. He arranged my enrolment at university. I was eighteen, the same age as the other students. We pretended I was twenty-one, so it wasn't so unusual that my daughter was three. I graduated and got my first job at the ABC as a cadet and then one day he drove into the Blue Mountains and hooked a hose up to the exhaust pipe.'

'Did you love him?' I asked.

She slowly closed the door and stood there looking back at me but her face was in darkness. Her voice was very quiet.

'After he died I missed him. It took me by surprise. The house was so silent. The phone did not ring. It was as if he had brought my life to life and without him there was no life of my own. I did not love him. I could not love him. I think it killed him in the end. I did not trust him with her. Inside, I could never forgive him. I think it was all he wanted.'

SPIRAL

Jimmy had been wanting to smoke me. He said he'd just light a few leaves and the smoke would wash over me. It was a cleansing. I agreed to do it. But I reckoned it would take a furnace to cleanse me now.

We did it on his land, up above the house. In the centre of the clearing there were a few logs drawn about a fire pit. There had been fires there before. The ground was black with a big circle of charcoal. Jimmy was setting a fire over the dead coals. Laying kindling, small sticks layered with larger sticks and wedges of wood he'd brought up from the woodpile in a barrow.

It was Sunday afternoon. No-one else about. When he had the fire crackling away, he asked me to come stand by him.

'It's just a chance to let things go. Worries. Thoughts. Anything you don't need any more.'

He pulled a branch over to the fire and tore off a couple of fans of leaves. He stuck them in the fire and when they'd caught he blew them out so they were smoking and smouldering, the eucalyptus giving off its own particular scent of bush and earth and peppermint.

He let the smoke drift over me. He walked around me and fanned the smoke with the leaves. I closed my eyes because it made them sting. I tried to breathe nice and slow so I didn't choke.

'You want me to die of lung cancer first?' I said, attempting some levity, but he just said, 'Relax, Henry. Just breathe and let it go.'

I breathed and my eyes saw red light. I rubbed at them. They were dry with the irritation of the smoke. Red spirals turned in front of me. Jimmy was saying something in his language. It sounded like the rise and dip of oars, the morning call of magpies. The smoke was strong in my nostrils. I coughed and choked and opened my eyes and spat out onto the ground.

I looked up at him. My eyes were watering. I shook my head.

'That it?'

'How do you feel?'

'Like a tandoori chicken.'

The leaves continued smoking, the breeze blowing the smoke away in little puffs across the clearing. My back was sweaty. My head felt light. My hands began shaking.

I found a log by the fire and sat down, waiting for the world to stop spinning. I thought about the little red crosses on my head, about Lil and the men on her body. I thought about Molly Watkins rotting under the earth. I leaned forward and vomited into the fire.

'Sorry,' I said.

'Oldest medicine there is, the fire. Doesn't mind you throwing up on it at all.'

Which was lucky because I vomited a few more times and Jimmy kept waving those smoking branches around me and singing and clapping. The spirals turned in front of my eyes, little stars ran in lines before me, I thought I heard Charlie laughing, Lil singing. I laid my head in my hands and cried. I couldn't blame it on the smoke.

I felt pretty good after it. I didn't tell Jimmy but I figured he knew. When I got home I went to bed and slept like a baby until dawn.

THE ASSASSIN

I NOTICED AT BREAKFAST A few days later that something had changed. Lil was saying to Charlie, 'It's gymnastics on Friday, isn't it? We'll have to remember your runners. You go put them in your bag when you've finished your toast.'

At dinner that night she said, 'I'm doing some research on colonial music. I thought it might be fun to do a concert – a sort of period ball – as a fundraiser for the Community Centre. I hear Parliament's set to see it go through unscathed. Maybe Jimmy could organise some of their music too. Some traditional dances.'

It went on. From a trickle to a flood. A flood of words from my Lil, as if a radio I had never known was on was suddenly audible.

Instead of simply putting Charlie's fresh pyjamas by the fire she'd tell him they were there.

She got out a quilt I'd never seen before and told Suki how she started it years ago to give to her when she got married. She said, 'Maybe I can finish it over winter. You'll just have to take care of the husband bit.'

Suki half-smiled. Lili laid her hand on Suki's head.

She said, 'I think I'll go into town a bit later. Before it gets too late. I'll buy a hot chicken and we can have it with those tomatoes we preserved; some kind of potato bake and a winter salad.'

Perhaps if I had said to her then, in those weeks after, as she and Suki found ways to laugh together, 'Look, I have not been telling you the truth either,' it would have been easy. But I did not. There was no warrant for Lili's arrest. There were no bodies that needed explaining. Yes, it troubled me, what she had been. Yes, I was appalled at night lying beside her when I thought of it. But here she was a woman now, and who she had been as a girl, as a young woman, seemed long ago.

Would Lili have kept my secret? Sex is one thing. Murder is quite another.

I was drinking too much those weeks before Sandra's murder. I was stretched with every moneylender I knew. And I knew quite a few. There was pressure, unbelievable pressure to find some cash.

'It's my wife,' I said. 'She has the house, the bank accounts tied up in her name.'

Some businessmen are more patient than others. And £45 000 is a deal of money even today, but in 1974 it was a staggering amount to owe.

My debts worsened every week. I told them it was my wife who held the key. She would not divorce me so I could not gain access to the accounts, the family trust. That is what I told the men in their double-breasted coats and bowler hats who pretended to be gentleman bankers but were, in truth, thugs in tailored clothes.

They scared her out of her wits, the moneylenders. Telephoned her in the dead of night. Whispered to her when she was out shopping. But she did nothing. Refused their demands. Thought it was me setting her up.

So one night they sent a bloke to free those funds up once and for all. I had a tip-off. A last-minute warning. 'Lucky, if you ever want to see your old lady alive again you had best get to that house of yours before 9pm. We thought we'd have a little word with her in person.'

I had made dinner reservations at my club. I had been planning to flee to France with the children in the coming weeks. I had even borrowed a friend's car so as to be able to leave incognito.

It was too late. It was all over for Sandra. Oh, unhappy day when she changed her night off.

My children were in that house. I was just in time to wrestle the hired man off Veronica after he came at her on the stairs.

She was badly beaten about the head. She knew it was not me who attacked her. It was me who had saved her. But what choice did she have? She thought I had arranged it all and had very nearly succeeded in achieving my aim.

It was beautifully done. The true criminal mind is an educated thing. They had set me up. You do not mess with people of that ilk and think you can get the better of them.

Who would ever believe me?

I may as well have killed Sandra Rivett. It was my life, my luckless life that had brought about the girl's demise.

Through my actions I almost succeeded in killing the mother of my children. For all that might have been acrimonious between us, she was still my wife. We had not been happy but a man does not harm his wife.

I was not guilty, nor was I innocent. People thought that I fled the law. But there are things far worse than the law.

I laid low in Ireland after my escape. In Africa I waited for the police to find someone who would talk. Some low-life to confess to the crime. No one came forth. The ranks had closed. The Lucan silver went to auction and paid off various debts. Some of the debts were never paid. The ones which had attracted no paperwork. No doubt there are still people waiting for me to surface. People who do not like the ledger left unbalanced.

In all these years it has never been solved. I am painted as a murderer. But why would a man of my standing trouble himself to do such a thing? Would I bother with a lead pipe when a handgun with a silencer is so much more civilised? Would I bind a lead pipe with Elastoplast when I struggled even to know how to bandage a cut upon my child's thumb? Would I mistake my wife of almost a decade for a young woman one month in my service? Would I stuff a body in a mail sack when I had never so much as taken the garbage out, let alone disposed of a corpse?

Imagine me the assassin. A blundering British Earl with

barely an education in classics. In a strange way it has become easier and easier to believe I was such a villain. For surely only a fellow callous enough to commit the vile act would have been clever enough to disappear without a trace.

SINEAD O'CONNOR

VENUS WAS READY. HER PAINT and brass were sparkling new. Her mast varnished, the cleats and fittings in place, everything was ready for the mast to be stepped. Her new sails lay in bags in the forward hatch. On deck the winches gleamed, the navigation equipment was fitted. Down below Pearl and Lil had organised the upholstery. The purpose-built galley items were stowed – pots and pans and heavy-duty crockery. Lil and Jimmy had even stocked the ship's library.

What were we waiting for? We were waiting for me to say I was ready to go out for a sail. They would never take her without me. So they must wait. Either for the day I could, or for the day when they could go without me.

There is more to such things than opening a bottle of champagne. We needed a crane to lift her from the paddock onto a specially fitted semitrailer. We had to get her off the semitrailer into the water. I had seen boats in other people's back yards. A dream started and, for whatever reason, never completed. I'd seen boats looking like they were all but ready to sail if only the long grass that grew beneath them was actually the sea. Sometimes I wondered if the sheer logistics held such boats back from union with their proper element. Or perhaps the transition from dream to reality is harder than we imagine. It's hard to work so long on something and then stop. It's hard to imagine what would take her place.

Jimmy and Lili would organise it all. It wasn't the difficulty of moving her that stopped me. It was the empty space I knew would be there behind the house. We'd have a day sailing and we'd put her on a mooring. I'd come home and she would be gone. I had no way of driving myself to be with her. She would be afloat, far from sight. This was my world. This house, this stretch of land, these people. I wanted none of it to change. Not even for the chance of a sail on a boat I'd spent ten years completing.

It was July. Lil's birthday had passed. Technically she was turning forty, but she insisted on being forty-three. She said it was too late to change it now. Pearl made her a cake covered in white icing with flowers all over it. I wondered if Lil had confided in Pearl about Vietnam. I did not ask. I did my best not to think about it. She was my Lil, here and now.

We were deep into the footy season. It was round sixteen: the Eagles versus Carlton. The Eagles dominated all afternoon, then lost by a point. There was a Lord Carlton. He had been a friend of my father. But I kept quiet about that. Afterwards, because the weather was clear and crisp, and the wind had died, Jimmy and

I sat out the back and had a beer or two. He had cleared some ground away from the house and made a fire.

'It's too lovely to sit inside but too bloody cold to sit outside. So this is my compromise,' he said.

He sat sipping his beer and staring at formations of early birds heading north and the black chinks of land where the river found her boundaries. I looked into the fire and enjoyed the heat on my face and hands and knees. Jimmy and I both knew I might not last until the Grand Final. My body had wasted away until I felt like a praying mantis. Some days speech was difficult. Strange anomalies had begun happening when I spoke. I did not always notice them, but other people did.

Jimmy was pointing out two hawks wheeling above us.

'We're looking good. Legislative Council's all set. Premier's been very supportive.'

'Good.'

'There was something about giving those two people, that mother and baby, some sort of purpose beyond their death. They could've stayed there forever – faceless, nameless. Now they'll be the start of something new.'

I nodded.

'Stan reckons we might be breaking ground by December.'

'It's grand news.'

Jimmy put his arm about me.

'I would have loved to have seen it, the centre,' I said.

'You may yet.'

'You don't have to do it.'

'What?'

'Pretend.'

'I'm just beating about the bush really. What I wanted to talk to you about was your funeral. So, cremated or buried?'

'Cremated. I'm sure about that.'

'Any ideas about the service?'

'That Pia Jesu piece I heard on the radio last week.'

'I'll find it. Where do you want the service, then?'

'Here? Right out here.'

'And who would you want to do the service?'

'Maybe Mick Malthouse dressed up in a cassock. Or what about Sinead O'Connor? I always thought she looked like the Virgin Mary.'

Malthouse was the coach of the Eagles and Jimmy loved him.

He grinned. 'I reckon it's better than a wedding, a funeral, 'cause you've only got yourself to please. And if it all mucks up, you're not even around to feel disappointed.'

'Write my epitaph, will you, Jimmy?'

'You better give me some starting points.'

'Well, let's see . . .' The pain moved down my back and settled in my hips like a burning coil of wire. It made the breathing come out a bit up and down. 'Here lies Henry Kennedy, may the angels seduce him.'

'The sum of a man's life is not in the love he won but the love he gave away,' said Jimmy.

'You've been reading too many desk calendars, Jimmy Owens.'

'Thought that one was okay. Made it up myself.'

'Ah, you're a Hallmark poet.'

'I'll take it as a compliment that I have mass appeal.'

We watched the evening star and the moon coming up right on the horizon, red and huge.

'Would you do the service, Jimmy?'

'I'm no priest!'

'The way your people did. Would that do for me?'

'Why?' he asked. 'Why our way?'

'I want to get bedded down here. In this earth. I don't mean buried. I mean, who I was. I want it bedded down here for all time. I have a feeling you could do that for me.'

He leaned across and took my hand, then, in both of his.

'You're a crazy bastard.'

'Where do our spirits go, Jimmy?'

'They go to be with our ancestors.'

'They'll not be wanting me.'

'Oh, they will. A spirit finds its way home with or without a guide.'

'I don't want to go back there. I want to stay here.'

'I don't know if such a thing is possible.'

'Isn't there a ceremony? Your people must have had ceremonies for strangers.'

'There were no strangers. And the ceremonies are forgotten now.'

'So what do you do for each other?'

'We paint ourselves with the ashes of the dead. We burn leaves, we clap, sing.'

'Would you do that for me, Jimmy?'

He hesitated. 'Leave it with me a day or two . . .'

278

'You can have longer than that,' I said, 'I'll be around at least a week.'

We both grinned. Then he said, 'It doesn't matter where you come from, Henry. It just matters that you were here.'

MARRYING LILI

Lɪʟ ʜᴀᴅ ᴅʀɪᴠᴇɴ ᴜs ᴅᴏᴡɴ to the beach. I always liked it here at Seven Mile. The shoreline changed so with the tide. Some days, when the surf rolled in, the sand was soft and deep. Other days, when the tide was out, it was wide and flat with mirror puddles and long rippling shallows.

If Lil had been beside me then, I might have told her the story of Henry having sex for the very first time on the grey stones under Dalrymple Pier with Morgaine MacTavish. Maybe I had told it to her already. I couldn't be sure.

How tired I was now of the stories. The denial of some inner man buried so deep I was afraid to see his face, for surely he was as decayed as Sandra Rivett in her grave.

Charlie and Suki were flying his kite. It was an orange dragon with a rainbow ribbon tail that rattled and snapped in the breeze. I sat near the washed-up seagrasses at the top of the beach where they'd settled me on the rug. Lil was far away from us all, along the beach in her red coat. I wanted to walk after her and have her turn and see me, this raven-haired woman with her pale gold skin. Being close to the sound of waves with the breeze about me and the sand beneath my shoes, there was a longing in me I knew now was not for love. It was for something like love. Something close to love, or bigger than love. Some sound, some feeling, some music I struggled to hear.

Suki said that the best thing there could be in life was a rewind button like on the video player. So you could rewind back past the silly comment, the thoughtless deed, the irreparable mistake, and have the moment over. She'd said it when she had apologised to Lili for telling me about Vietnam.

'I don't want to spend my life destroying things,' Suki said.

'We know,' Lil said. 'Life's too short, isn't it?'

There's a whole chain of events that leads to a moment and you can't see the moment coming until all the dominoes are falling.

Whether I was Henry Kennedy or John Bingham, I had made a mess of understanding women. Until Lili.

I thought often of how we might be, she and I, old together. Now sex was beyond me, I was surprised how gentle I felt about everything. Locked in our half-moon curve together, I didn't feel any less or more a man for not making love with Lili before we went off to sleep. I felt good to be there with her, loving her the way I did.

There were so many things I'd never know now. So many moments I'd never live. It had slipped by me. I'd been so busy planning and thinking and precious little of it had ever resulted in anything good. Anything which had made me truly happy. Perhaps happiness wasn't what I'd aimed for.

I'd like to have bought a piano. I'd like to have read more books. I should have owned a dog – not a doberman like my other dogs, but a kelpie who smiled when I came home at night. I should have sailed *Venus* all the way down the river on a bright summer morning and come home on the sea breeze. I should have turned away from the tables after the first win and never picked up the dice again. I should never have abandoned my children. I wish I'd planted a whole hill of raspberries. Ridden a motorbike again. Married Lili.

A BREEZE AND A HELMSMAN

LIL TOLD ME SUKI WAS not Sandra. She shrugged when I said Sandra again.

'Suki,' she said again to me. 'This is Suki, not Sandra.'

I knew it was Suki. I didn't mean to say Sandra. Of course I didn't mean to say Sandra. I had best say nothing at all. I had best say nothing. Nothing at all to Sandra.

Lil said to Suki, 'Don't mind him. He just does that. He can't help it. It's the brain malfunctioning because of the tumour. It's called perseveration when they get the word wrong. Doctor Holloway told me about one patient who said, "Oh Jesus Christ"' over and over. She was a devout Baptist and was very upset by it but it didn't matter whether she wanted a piece of toast or to close the curtains, all she could say was, "Oh Jesus Christ."'

Suki smiled when I said Sandra but Lili did not smile. I worried that I would begin calling her Veronica.

Strange dark tissue distorted my life and would not let me keep my worlds apart. How could I tell my brain to behave itself?

Sandra left the room but Lil stayed and brought me a glass of water. I could see *Venus* across the paddock. Snowdrops had come up and made an ocean of white underneath her, like sea foam floating her there, waiting for a breeze, and a helmsman.

'Have you taken anything?' Lil asked.

'No.'

'It would help.'

'Would it?'

'You mustn't be cross with yourself. It's not your fault.'

Yes it is, Lil, I wanted to say. It is all my fault.

Who would they be burying, these people? They had taken me into their lives, they would mourn me when I went, but who would they be burying?

Some days I hated their kindness. My deterioration was repulsive. I was nothing more than a creature they had to feed and change. A creature slowly being stripped of the veneer of acceptance I had given him. Lil would never have loved Lucan. None of them, if they had known me, would ever have befriended me.

They tiptoed around the house and whispered in the passage, telling Charlie to be quiet. At night Lil would hold me and I felt like a thief. The unshed tears dripped back down inside me, eroding my cells like slow acid.

'I hate myself like this,' I whispered.

Lil turned me towards her and kissed me. Our mouths moved and swam together and I filled myself with this ragged love.

■

Stan had come by a week or two back with a solicitor to witness the papers. I had left everything to Lili, save for *Venus*. I had left her to Jimmy along with my toolbox – the solid mahogany toolbox I'd made myself. The box was marked with a hundred dings and knocks and scrapes, many of which had happened on our long afternoons together on the house or on *Venus*. I'd set up a trust fund for Charlie to put him through a good school when the time came, and university. Lil would be surprised at the bank account; she'd never have to work again if she didn't want to.

I could plan for the future but I could not lay the past to rest in the same way.

THE APOLOGY

My dear Michael,
I HAVE had a traumatic night of unbelievable coincidence. However I
won't bore you with anything or involve you except to say that when
you come across my children, which I hope you will, please tell them
that you knew me and that all I cared about was them . . . I gave
Bill Shand-Kydd an account of what actually happened, but judging
by my last effort in court no-one, let alone a 67-year-old judge,
would believe – and I no longer care, except that my children should
be protected.
  Yours ever,
  John

Michael Stoop had lent me his Ford Corsair two weeks prior
to November 1974. When Michael's car was found abandoned
at Newhaven the day after Sandra Rivett died, the police
found in it a length of lead piping remarkably similar to the
murder weapon.

No evidence was found which indicated I had been near
Sandra's body. Not a single fingerprint nor footprint. The

coroner and his jury overlooked this. I had no chance to defend myself. It never went to trial. The inquest jury determined the cause of death. 'Death by Lord Lucan,' they had pronounced. Death *of* Lord Lucan would have been a truer verdict.

Veronica sat on the window ledge. I saw her there. She was wearing a pale blue suit, her hair quite grey and her face turned to the view beyond the glass.

'Hello, John,' she said without turning to look at me.

'I never went near Sandra's body,' I said.

'Now, John, are you still on about that?'

'There was not a thread of mine on her body, nor on the sack.'

'Don't come to me for pity, John. Do you know how the press have plagued me? The women's magazines. The gutter journalists. They are less than human.'

'You could have saved me.'

'Believe me, I tried, John. I had grown weary of it.'

'I had no trial.'

'Ah, John. Guilty or innocent? Hmm?'

I did not answer her.

She turned to stare at me and her eyes were black and she smiled at me with her old woman's mouth. Everything about me disappeared. I was in greyness. There was no room, no window, no walls. There was no pain. It was gone as if it was never there. I swung my arms and waved my head. There was no tiredness. There was no heartbeat. The grey was unchanging. It was as if the air was a fog but there was no fog.

I waited for her to change it back. I fell heavily to the floor.

'Guilty or innocent?'

'Please, Veronica. I was wrong.'

She did not answer. The fog was dense and I did not like it so close to me. I did not like the way it came all around me. I did not like the silence.

'For God's sake, I'm sorry. Please, Veronica, it was all my fault. I'm sorry!'

The pain came at me in a ricochet of molten fire up my spine. The room rushed back to me. The window was empty of her form. I was drenched with new sweat. I realised I was on the floor screaming, watching Lili's legs come hurrying towards me.

BUTTERFLY

Jimmy came and worked on the fireplace. He cleared a big circle of grass. He raked the bare grey earth so the fire was surrounded by a spiral going slowly outwards.

'Are you planning on roasting me then?' I asked.

I was in the wheelchair on the verandah, the late sun warm on my face and legs. Lili had tried to make me wear a hat but I wanted to feel the heat harsh and strong on my skin.

'If you like,' he replied, 'though you'd be tough as jerky.'

'You don't think it could wait a bit longer?'

'It's not meant to make you nervous, Henry. It's meant to reassure you things are being taken care of.'

Charlie sat beside me on the deck. He had brought me a long piece of dried grass to chew and one for himself. He was leaning his head back into his hand, his elbow crooked, like he was all grown-up.

'Mum said if you're falling you have to imagine you've grown wings. She said if you do that, you'll never get hurt.'

'It's a risk,' I said.

'What's a risk?' he asked.

'Jumping off high places.'

'Not if you're a bird,' he said, 'or an angel.'

'Have you ever seen an angel, George?'

'Oh yes, in a book. And I think one night in a dream.'

'Did it speak to you?'

'No. It was just standing on a bridge.'

We watched the clouds.

'There's a dragon,' he said, pointing to a cumulus mass with a head and body and a fiery dragon breath.

'George,' I said, 'there is something I need to tell you.'

'What?'

'I'm not going to be around here much longer.'

'Are you leaving?'

'Aye.'

'But where will you go?'

'I'm dying, lad.'

'I know. My mum told me. Why are you dying?'

'Well, my old body doesn't want to go on any more.'

'Have your beans run out?'

'I guess so, lad.'

We sat for a while in silence. There he was, one foot in the country of adults, and the other firmly upon the island of childhood.

'Butterflies only live for a few days,' he said. 'They make their cocoons and turn into butterflies and then they die.

'Will I die soon?' he asked.

'Not for a long time yet I hope. Not until you're an old old man with lots of grandchildren.'

'Like you.'

'Aye, like me.'

Grandchildren? The idea was almost too painful to contemplate.

Time drifted on and still he did not move from me, picking up bits of stick which had blown down onto the balcony, breaking them, holding them back together, asking broken or not broken? He made a tunnel under the table and sneaked up on me saying, 'I am a big green snake coming to eat you.

'Is it nearly dark?' he asked, looking up at the mountain behind us. 'It's been such a fast day. I only just had breakfast.'

'Some days are like that,' I said.

'When you die,' he said, 'do you go up through the clouds?'

'I don't know, lad.'

'Will we be able to see you?'

'Maybe.'

'Will you wave to me?' he asked. 'Will you wave and say . . . '

'Say what, George?'

'My voices say you are a kind man. They say that even though you call me George you can't help it. You know I am Charlie really.'

'Do they, lad?'

'They say you don't have to worry any more. They say that dying is okay. I'm not sure about that but they say it is. It's just like a little rest.'

'Do you often hear your voices?'

'Yes. Mostly I see them these days too.'

'What do they look like?'

'They wear long blue clothes.'

'How many are there?'

'I think there are forty of them.'

'Is forty very many?'

'Just enough.'

'You know what, George,' I said. 'Don't ever forget your voices. They are your friends. If anything ever happens to you, you listen to your voices. They'll help you.'

I looked at the boy's face. Would he remember me in years to come? How I wanted him to.

It was coming, the end. But I could not quite believe it.

PRESENTIMENT

SANDRA RIVETT BROUGHT ME PEPPERMINT tea and offered me yoghurt she had brought home in her raffia bag. I sipped the tea very slowly. I wasn't sure what Lili made of Sandra. But nobody asked me. And it felt good to know she was here with us. I liked George having a good nanny to take care of him. He seemed to like her very much. And Sandra seemed very fond of him too. I liked seeing her happy. Happy and safe after all.

'Thank you, Sandra,' I said.

'You're welcome, Henry.'

'I'm so glad you're all right, Sandra.'

'Yes, I'm much better.'

'It was a terrible time. I never wanted any harm to come to you, you know that, don't you, dear Sandra?'

'You were kind to let me stay.'

'You're safe now.'

'I know.'

'You will stay on, won't you? The boy needs you. Dear George needs you and he seems to like you so.'

'Yes, I'll stay. I like him too.'

'Good.'

She smoothed the sheets across in front of me. 'You're not to trouble yourself,' she said. 'Everything will be fine. Lili will be home soon and we'll bring you some dinner. I've made pumpkin soup.'

'Ah.'

'I know, Henry, but you have to try.' My appetite had slipped from me suddenly. I found it hard now to keep anything down.

'Is George about?'

'Charlie's in the lounge room building Lego. Would you like to see him?'

'Ah, let him play. They're young for such a short time. What about the girls?'

'There aren't any girls, Henry.'

'Are you sure? Maybe they're with their mother.'

'Yes, maybe you're right.'

'You will look out for them, won't you? It's getting late.'

'Yes, Henry.'

I looked out over the valley. Forest. Combined species living in collaboration, in silent agreement, surviving, dying and birthing. Forest. Provider of oxygen. I was no longer a tree, I decided. Thinner, weaker. More fragile. I had gone from tree to fern.

I could hear Sandra in the kitchen. I wondered if Sandra Rivett was a tree, what sort of tree she would be. Was she a pine or a gum, a myrtle or a maple? Or perhaps a cedar. Some chap was singing 'Blue Hotel' in a mournful voice. I felt like a man left hanging by his fingertips on the cliff's edge so long, he had given up any option but falling. Falling had gone from frightening to miraculous. To go from this hanging on to perfect, graceful, momentary flight into the abyss.

I wanted to walk again on the mountain. I wanted to see the boy grow. I wanted to stay here with the sunshine coming in the window and the wind blowing and Lili coming home up the driveway. But I realised this was my allotted time for life. No matter how it happened, this was my sum total of life as Henry Kennedy.

Lili would be disappointed with me. She would say, 'I cannot understand how you don't want to hang onto it with every fibre of your being.'

But was it a matter of struggling? Or was it about forests, and going when your time was up? Did a giant eucalyptus lament its passing? Did an oak, split in two by lightning, long for something other than its destiny?

The days were already warmer. The snowdrops in the paddock had been joined by a mass of daffodils. The strange light-headed feeling lingered upon me. Like two gins on a warm February evening.

I was surprised how fast the days went. Sandra Rivett sat and fed me and changed the water by my bed. The district nurse came, Wendy Darling. Such a lovely name. I asked her to read me stories and take me to Neverland. She laughed and patted my hand. She said she was much too old to do such things, and anyway, I was not a lost boy. Even Nick Powell, our GP, had started making house calls. He looked at me with his brown eyes and said, 'You're doing very well, Henry. I'll see you in a few days.'

Afterwards I could hear him and Lili talking. Sometimes Sandra Rivett joined them and Wendy the nurse. All these people making plans. I made no plans. I liked the view out the window. I liked to feel water in my mouth as Sandra or Lil held the glass. I liked the warm washer Wendy used when she washed me down, and the way she plumped the pillows.

But it was Sandra Rivett who put on the Chopin I loved and seemed to know better than anyone how much sunlight hurt my eyes and how to adjust the curtains and the sheet so that I was, for a while, completely comfortable. It was Sandra who understood when I needed to see my son and, when the weight of the boy had become too much upon the covers, would usher him from the room.

'But Mum,' he would say.

'Now Charlie, Henry's had enough for a little while. You can come and say goodnight later.'

Dear Sandra, after all these years she and I had finally solved our conundrum. She was safe. My family was well and happy. It was like a riddle I finally understood. Time went on and on yet time could not be made or reclaimed or given – only taken away.

It meant I could finally forget. I could finally forget that terrible night. Had it been twenty years? Twenty years gone so fast, like a marathon I had been running. Finally I had crossed the finish line only to discover there was no-one else running my race.

∎

On the seventh of November, 1974, they called me on the telephone. 'Lucky, we're going to pay your old lady a visit tonight. You come and see her with us, Lucky. Eight forty-five sharp. We'll have someone meet you.

'See the wife has the money, hasn't she, Lucky?

'So if we want the money, we have to get rid of the wife, right?

'That's what you said, wasn't it, Lucky? The wife has it all tied up. But it goes to you if anything should happen to her.'

I rushed to the house early. I parked the car in the laneway at the back. I rang the doorbell to try to raise Veronica. But there was no answer. I used my key. I waited in the hall. The house was quiet but for the faint noise of the television set upstairs.

'Evening, Guv'nor,' said a voice. 'You're in good time. Nice night for a bit of funny business. Now, not a sound.'

He slipped from the cloak room into the hallway. He was a tall fellow. Similar build to me and dressed in a dark winter coat like mine. I had seen him about in the East End on my visits there. I think he was one of the cousins.

'Down there,' he said, pointing at the stairs to the kitchen. We descended and he reached up and removed the lightbulb from its fitting with his gloved hands. We waited at the foot of the stairs in darkness. I had hardly slept in weeks. I had been drinking steadily for days. My world had spiralled into this. Above me, though I could hardly bear to think of it, were my children. I was electrified with panic.

'You wouldn't want us to have to take one of your

children, Lucky, would you? A nice little ransom note? Always messy, a kidnapping. No, I think we'll stick with the wife, don't you?'

This threat only a week ago when I had said it was impossible to know my wife's routine.

'Children are much easier, Lucky. They come and go at all sorts of regular hours.'

'Not my children,' I had said. 'Not them.'

'Then you tell us about your wife, eh? You tell us when she'll be alone in the house.'

'The news,' I said. 'She always has a cup of tea with the nine o'clock news.'

'But will she be on her own, Lucky?'

'Thursday night. The nanny has Thursday night off.'

'That's very good, Lucky.'

She flipped the light switch but nothing happened. Down the stairs she came and he was upon her. She dropped the tray, she started to scream but he knocked her hard on the head once, twice. She slumped to the floor with a groan. I knew it was not Veronica. I knew it was not my wife, but he handed me his weapon, a length of pipe, heavy, wrapped to make it easier to grip. 'There you go, Lucky, you finish her off. You do it nice and proper and they'll be very happy with you. You know what that means.'

I looked down at her still form on the floor. I held the pipe in my hand.

'Come on. Quick about it. Haven't got all night, you know. Go on now. Enjoy yourself.'

Did I lift the pipe? Oh, did I? Did I, in that dark hour, undertake such a terrible deed I have wiped it forever from my memory? I do not remember what happened. I remember awakening as if from a dream. I was back upstairs in the hall-way.

Veronica was swooning on the floor, her head bleeding. I lifted her up.

'John!' she said. 'Whatever's . . . help me.'

I carried her upstairs. Dear Frances was there watching tele-vision. 'Off to bed, sweetheart, Mummy is not well.'

She went without a word and I laid Veronica on the bed.

'John!' she said. 'Your face! It's covered in blood. Your pullover . . . '

I touched my cheek and looked at my hand. It was bright red with blood.

'Where is Sandra?' she whispered.

I will never know. Please God, never let me know. It is buried inside me. There is no doubt I was there that night. What did I do to her? Only Sandra Rivett knows. Only Sandra Rivett can tell. But Sandra Rivett plays with a boy in my house and puts music on to help me sleep. Sandra Rivett brushes her hair by the fire and it burns red gold in the light.

COMING HOME

UP THE ROAD PAST THE hairpin bend, council workers slowed us to a halt.

'Widening the road at last,' Lil said.

There was a digger at work and a dump truck. I turned and George was staring out the window.

'Look! It's a digger, it's a digger,' he said, 'and a huge enormous pile of sand. Can we stop, can we stop, can we?'

'We can't here, Charlie, not now. We'll go down later,' Sandra Rivett said.

'Okay,' he said. 'Will there be time when we get home? Can you come, Henry?'

Why doesn't he call me Father? He knows I like it.

Lili looked at me and said, 'We'll see. Henry's a bit tired, Charlie.'

'Are you, Henry? Is your head hurting?'

It felt very hard to nod my head. As if it was floating above my shoulders and had no weight at all.

'Maybe you could go in the morning. After Henry's woken up,' said Sandra Rivett.

George kept staring out the window. His eyes glazed and his lids fluttered. He said, 'I think I need a sleep too. That movie wore me out.'

George and Sandra had been to a movie together. Lili and I had gone to pick them up. I hardly went in the car any more. But I had wanted to go. I had wanted to feel the curves of the road again. To descend from the misty green, fern-banked mountain into the city where the river and the buildings lay side by side. I wanted to find the streets where I had walked and worked, to wind down the window and smell the fish crates and seagull lime and look up at the mountain with its mauve eucalypt robes shimmering slightly in the sea-breeze haze. I wanted to take the road from the city through South Hobart and up the long winding curve of Davey Street and onto Huon Road; the smooth steady corners with the mountain silent beside us as we climbed right up onto it with the sun flickering between the trees. I wanted to pass the tavern where Jimmy and I had leaned our elbows on the bar and washed the sawdust down our throats; and ease round the last four bends deep into the mountain with the river out to the left and the colours changing from dark to light, wet to dry, forest to sky. I wanted to drive in our gate and up the road and see the house with the paddock bright with daffodils. I wanted to know what it was to come home one more time.

In the kitchen, Lili began preparing food for a late lunch. I could hardly even summon the memory of the crispness of an apple or the soft rub of red wine on my tongue.

'Do you want to go outside?' George asked. 'I'll push you.'

'Suki can you . . . ' said Lili.

'I can do it,' said the boy.

'Damn wheelchair,' I said, attempting to move the wheels.

'Damn wheelchair,' the boy said as he came round behind me.

Pushing it awkwardly out of the room, he banged the wall and nearly collected the lamp on his way through.

'It's a nuisance chair, that's what it is,' he said, delivering me to the balcony with a frown.

Lili came out and sat beside me. She looked tired and I took her hand and rubbed my cheek with it.

'Are you not getting enough sleep, my love?'

'I'm okay,' she said.

'I'm coming,' she called out to George. She went down the path and held the reel while George ran through the grass, throwing the kite into the air. The sheep ran away to the far end of the paddock and George laughed and called out, 'Don't be afraid. I won't hurt you!'

I wondered if it was new, the circle in the grass. Who had made it? Looked like we were expecting aliens. Or was it to be a bonfire? I must ask Lili if it was Guy Fawkes Night.

'Up kite, up!' George yelled.

But it wouldn't go. Lil launched it for him and he held the reel and said, 'It makes my eyes go all shiny looking up like that right into the sky.'

When I woke I found a blanket about me. The kite lay abandoned on the table next to me. The sun was on the curve of the ridge behind. In the distance I heard the digger going back down the road. George and Sandra appeared from the house. He stopped, listening intently.

'The digger,' he said. 'We were going to go down to the digger.'

'Tomorrow,' said Sandra. 'Are you ready to come in?'

I nodded.

'Is it just a little way away?' asked George.

'Across the paddock, through the trees and a bit more,' she said.

'Will there be time tomorrow, Mum?'

'We'll make time,' she said.

DANCING LESSONS

IT WAS MORNING. LIL WAS sitting on the bed stroking my forehead.

'I think it's time we moved you back upstairs, my love. Suki has moved her things. The bed is made. I think it's time. Jimmy's coming soon to help.'

She sighed and said, 'I need you to know something, Henry. I need to tell it to you now, so it's over with.'

She settled her hands in her lap and stared out the window.

'When Aunt Lhien died in the fire, I did watch from the school. But I lit the fire, Henry. I always brought her lunch. That day I took a can of petrol from the convent. In the apartment I doused a bundle of my old clothes, the things I had worn for my work. I poured petrol on the gas bottle in the kitchen, tossed it over the walls. I could hear her calling out from the bedroom, 'Li-Le, what are you doing? Is that you Li-Le?'

'I took her in a jar of honey. I took it in with a spoon and I handed it to her. She was bed-ridden. She didn't understand. I closed all the windows and I lit the fire. I locked the door on my way out. Back at the convent, I picked up Suki and climbed the bell-tower and we watched the smoke billow into the sky.'

She looked at me with her dark, sad eyes.

'People assumed it was an act of war. It burned a warehouse down behind us that was filled with American supplies. It didn't make me happy, killing her. I didn't celebrate. I would do it again. I wished I could do it for thousands of women I saw all over the world. Women forced to do things no-one should be forced to do. I didn't hate that old woman. But I hated what I was. I think I did it to survive. So Suki and I could go on.'

She blinked back tears.

'But I don't want you to worry about me. I don't want you to be frightened. Sometimes you look at me and you look frightened.'

Not frightened. How sweet that would be. No fear. Like one of the boy's kites. Not victim of the breeze but captain of the elements. Admiral of the grand forces of nature. Admiral Lucan.

'Lili,' I said. 'Li-Le. You were the person I was happiest with. And I do not want to say goodbye.'

She squeezed my hand and bent to kiss me. Her lips brushed gently across my forehead and it was if she had electrified me.

She looked intently into my face. 'It's a cruel thing,' she said. 'To have learned to love. It is not something I ever realised took so much out of a person. The sun comes up and I think of you. I tend the garden, I drive my car and I think of you. This strange, empty, happy, fragile feeling as if I am dancing on soap bubbles. I want nothing but to feel the skin on your arms, to see your feet naked, to watch you undress, to have your hand in mine. Do you know,' she said, 'that you smell of the sea. Salty and there's this other thing, not ginger, maybe lime. A warm smell.'

'I love you,' I said.

'What will I do with my heart when you are gone? What will I do with all these memories, with the days when you are not here to smile at me? Who will know when it's time to cut back the raspberries? Who will know? How will I live without your voice on the phone? How will I sleep in the bed alone?'

Tears had escaped from the corners of her eyes and were running down her cheeks.

I felt a pain deep in my head and at the same time there was a pain right in the centre of my chest.

'We never took dancing lessons. Do you remember how we were going to do that? When I first came to Hobart. Why didn't we, why didn't we ever do it?'

'Would you like to dance, my love?' I said.

'Now?'

I took her hand.

'A waltz I think.'

She smiled tentatively and brushed the tears from her face.

'Close your eyes,' I said. 'We are in a great hall with a polished floor and the doors to the balcony are open. We are the only ones here. The air is fragrant with . . .'

'Lemongrass,' she said.

'Yes, lemongrass drifting into the room and Rachmaninoff . . .'

'Rachmaninoff . . . ' and she hummed a few bars.

I stroked her hand. 'It will be alright. I'll never really leave this place.'

I knew it was a lie. I knew I was going and I knew it was a very long way I had to go. I could not protect her nor spare her the coming months. The pain grew in my head and it was as if something very tiny, like a soap bubble, popped.

'Ah,' I said, suddenly weary. 'You dance beautifully.'

'You too.'

'Thank you,' I said, 'for teaching me how.'

'Henry,' said Lil. 'Can you hear me? Henry? Can you blink? Henry, just blink so I know you're okay.'

VENUS ON A CLEAR DAY

Sunlight was flooding into the room so bright I could hardly see. I could hear clapping, low and constant, outside. I shifted back the covers and put my feet on the floor. I went down the stairs from the bedroom. The living room was empty. The house was empty but the drift of gum leaves burning came to me and I went through the kitchen and onto the deck.

Jimmy had his fire going. He was near naked, dusted white all over. He was crouching by the fire and clapping slow and regular. I looked up at *Venus*. She was fully rigged, her sails furled. Her winch handles were glinting, every bit of brass on her was shining sunshine at me. I could see the sheets coiled on the deck. She was burning white and gold in the morning light and I climbed the ladder and stepped aboard her and stood upon the deck.

Slowly, with hardly a ripple, her genoa unfurled. 'I always liked that self-furling gear,' I said, and looked around for Jimmy, but he was standing there with Lili beside the fire. I looked for Charlie but the light was too bright in my eyes and

I couldn't see him. The mainsail was flapping. I sheeted it in. I could hear a breeze coming through the trees behind.

Suddenly, with barely a shiver, she eased out of the cradle and slipped gently onto the sea of moving grass. I took the tiller. She gathered speed across the snowdrops and daffodils. The tree line was coming up fast. The whole boat shuddered and surged forward. The breeze strengthened and we cleared the trees, lifting up, up.

Ah Lil, I didn't mean to go without you, but I'm going. I glanced back and saw her. She was standing there by the fire, my Lil. Charlie was standing beside her and Suki too.

Now the river was running to meet us like an eye waiting to swallow us up. We were diving for it as if *Venus* knew that was her home, the great river she had stared at every day as we built her. But the wind took us, the ocean blinked and missed us and the sky breathed us in.

I banked her to port. I eased out the main and brought her round in a jibe. My, she was a fine boat. We circled back over the field and passed right over them. Jimmy looked up from the fire, shading his eyes, and saluted me.

Lil lifted an earthenware jar into the air and a great rush of grey dust flew out and made a cloud that mingled with the smoke climbing up into the sky, drifting out over the house, the paddock. Charlie looked up and waved too. There were people all around him. Tall people in long blue robes. I waved again and this time all the tall people waved with him.

The grass and the trees were swaying and moving. Even the earth was breathing and sighing and getting smaller until I was way up, so far up I could see the curve of the horizon falling away and the dark of stars far beyond where this day was yet to be. It was beautiful, immense. I never wanted it to stop.

But it has stopped.

There are others now in the garden, though I can't make them out. Like a picnic there. They're wee specks. All my people are slipping away. Slipping far beyond my sight.

Strange, I thought it was only morning but the sun is dropping already. Great beams of burned orange and hot pink mark the sky behind them and the house shimmers there among the gums. The mountain lies like a purple beast slumbering and I must leave it. There is somewhere I am due. I take the tiller and steer *Venus* westward. I look back one more time and now there is just the pink and gold in a deep circle behind me.

Thank you, I want to say, but the words are all gone now. All the words that were ever mine, everything I had to say, has now been said.

AUTHOR'S NOTE

ANY REFERENCES TO PEOPLE LIVING or dead is entirely the imaginative work of the author and is not intended as fact.

The Butterfly Man is based upon the murder of Sandra Rivett at 46 Lower Belgrave Street, W1, London on the 7th of November, 1974. Henry Kennedy is a fictional character imagined from Richard John Bingham, the Earl of Lucan, who disappeared on 8th of November, 1974. On the 11th of December, 1992, eighteen years after his disappearance, the High Court in London declared Lord Lucan officially dead. They ruled that Richard John Bingham, Earl of Lucan, had died 'on or since the 8th day of November 1974.'

Probate was granted on the 11th of August, 1999 with the Countess of Lucan the sole beneficiary of her late husband's estate.

In early 1999 Lucan's only son, George Bingham, applied for a writ of summons to take his father's seat in the House of Lords, but this was not authorised by the Lord Chancellor. In 2005, Lord Bingham is still being denied permission to take his father's place in the House of Lords because the House has decreed there is no definitive proof that the Earl, his father, is dead.

On the 17th of October, 1995, the Tasmanian Premier, Ray Groom, announced the transfer of 3800 hectares of land of cultural significance to the Aboriginal Community of Tasmania including Risdon Cove and Oyster Cove.

The legislation for the transfer of land to the Aboriginal Council of Tasmania began under the Green Labor Accord, 1989–1992. It was blocked by conservative elements in government and the community. The events in this book have been drawn from those negotiations but have been fictionalised and are not intended as fact, nor to represent any persons involved in the process. No bodies were ever found at the site.

The character of Edward Collins was inspired by Stewart Gore-Brown, 1883–1967.

There is no certainty in writing such a book. It is a work of imagination. However at times the following material proved useful.

Patrick Marnham, *Trail of Havoc*, Guild Publishing, London

Rod Lucas, www.lucan.com

The *Sunday Times* and *The Times* for their coverage of the Sandra Rivett murder and inquest – 1974, 1975

Richard Deacon, *Escape*, British Broadcasting Commission

Linda Stratmann, web article – www.lordlucan.com

Lady Lucan website, www.ladylucan.co.uk

Christina Lamb, *The Africa House*, Viking

Jim Trefethen, *Wooden Boat Renovation*, Camden, International Marine

Le Ly Hayslip with Jay Wurts, *When Heaven and Earth Changed Places*, Doubleday

Henry's home on Mt Wellington was inspired by 'The House on Great Cranberry Island' by Peter Forbes published in the book *Ten Houses* by Peter Forbes and Assoc, edited by Oscar Ojeda and published by Rockport Publishers, Gloucestershire, Massachusetts, USA.

The book Charlie reads in the chapter 'Beetles and other Creatures of the Dark' titled *An Eye Full of Soot and an Ear Full of Steam* is written by Nan Hunt and illustrated by Craig Smith. *Thomas the Tank Engine* is written by Rev. W. Awdrey.

The letter in the chapter entitled 'Apology' is an original letter written to Michael Stoop by Lord Lucan.

The author acknowledges the assistance of Arts Tasmania in the first draft of this manuscript in 2000.

ACKNOWLEDGEMENTS

THESE WERE THE FRIENDS AND consultants who made this book possible. Thank you all.

Katherine Scholes, who lent me her film maker's eye; Lindsay Simpson and Rosie Dub, for fearless writing advice; Dr Ian Sale, FRANZCP and Mr John Chapman, clinical psychologist, for their understanding of human behaviour; Dr Dean Powell and Melinda Rose for extensive knowledge on the decline of the brain and palliative care; Dr Danielle Wood, John Godfrey, Xanthe Godfrey and Axel Rooney for being my mountain family; and all the Curry Girls for the medicinal effects of raucous laughter; Dr Richard Rossiter for generous writing support, a kettle and ugg boots; Peter Adams, spiritual and artistic advisor; Simon, I could never have understood Henry without you; Louise Thurtell, *every blade of grass has an angel who bends over it and whispers grow, grow* – you are that angel; Mike Fowler, opinionated proofreader, generous and salty man; Caroline Grubb and Susannah Slatter, for many a late dash to the post office; Cath Cave, for understanding through the juggle of art and business; Lucy Byrne for final proofing; Paul Kowalik for advice on the dying; Landmark Education for advice on living; Stuart Tanner, for wisdom on houses; Terry Lean and Graham Dudgeon at the Wooden Boat School, Franklin, Tasmania, for wisdom on boat building; Julia Stiles, my editor who brought her shining light to the book; Madonna Duffy, who took me under her wing at UQP; Ranald Allan, for indelible friendship; Delia Nicholls, Michael Roberts, Ali Roberts, for writing space; Tanglewood B & B, Sheffield, for a wonderful writing room; Kevin Rose, my beloved father, for a shared love of literature, and his brother Barry – together they kept the grass mown and the wood stacked on the mountain and the cookie jar filled at home; Alex Reeve, Byron Smith and Isabelle Smith who were there (lovingly, patiently) for the entire story – I am the luckiest mother in the world; and Rowan Smith, to whom this book is dedicated, maker of cauliflower cheese on Sunday nights, thank you for loving a writer.

Other fiction by UQP

THE GOSPEL OF GODS AND CROCODILES
Elizabeth Stead

Missionary Amen Morley arrives on a tropical island to find a community largely untouched by the modern world. The island soon becomes a magnet for colourful and eccentric characters. Its original inhabitants are bemused by the behaviour and customs of these strange intruders who are trying to civilise them. Instead of being the ones doing the converting, the foreigners end up being the ones who are the most transformed by life in this extraordinary place.

The Gospel of Gods and Crocodiles is both a clever parody of colonialism and religious imperialism and a compelling comic narrative. This bold and subversive novel is suffused with Elizabeth Stead's unique literary style, in which almost every sentence ends in a surprise or a twist of humour.

'Five stars . . . This is a thoroughly entertaining book, beautifully written, with a lightness of touch and a sense of humour reminiscent of Evelyn Waugh.'

Bookseller & Publisher

ISBN 978 0 7022 3602 0

UQP

THE PEPPER GATE
Genna de Bont

A novel about truth and denial – and who we choose to love.

Down the hallway we hobbled, moving as one, like an ant carrying a burden much larger than itself. Out through the exit, so we didn't have to return to the waiting room. A one-way circuit with people like me in mind: the difficult ones.

For successful artist Mallory Smith, painting has always been an escape – from his lonely childhood, his turbulent relationships with his three wives, and the birth of a daughter with a severe disability. But art is failing him now. Since being diagnosed with a terminal illness only two things matter: finishing the mudbrick house he started, and getting to know Em, the enigmatic young woman who must surely be the daughter he has not seen in twenty years.

As Mallory traces his colourful past, we see him through the eyes of the women in his life. His ex-wife Margaret challenges him to face his future, while his much younger wife Sueyen buries herself in her work to escape their failing marriage.

The Pepper Gate is a compelling and unpredictable novel about building relationships and deconstructing the past.

ISBN 978 0 7022 3584 9

UQP

SILENT PARTS
John Charalambous

Finding yourself can change the way you see the world.

Every family has its secrets – and its lies. The Lamberts have Uncle Harry, who fought in World War I but never came home from France.

Each Lambert relative now clings to a different story. Harry died a hero's death on the battlefield. Harry married a sweet French girl. Harry drowned in the mud at Gallipoli. Harry was a coward who ran from the enemy. As his great-niece Julie struggles to sift fact from fiction, she finds how easy it is to rewrite the past.

Gradually, Harry comes to life: the awkward boy in turn-of-the-century Australia, the obedient son caring for his ageing mother, the 40-year-old bachelor, the reluctant solider in France. Initially, placid Harry is posted out of harm's way – but then he's called up to the front, and makes a decision that not only changes the course of his life, but changes the way he sees himself.

Silent Parts is John Charalambous's second book. His first book, *Furies*, was shortlisted for the Commonwealth Writers' Prize Best First Book (South East Asia and South Pacific region).

'Charalambous has [Thea] Astley's ability to find the soft centre of a hard story. Like her, he is compassionate towards the trapped.'
Sydney Morning Herald

ISBN 978 0 7022 3562 7

UQP

AN ACCIDENTAL TERRORIST
Steven Lang

**Shortlisted for the Commonwealth Writers' Prize (South East
Asia and South Pacific region)
Longlisted for the Miles Franklin Literary Award
Winner of the Queensland Premier's Literary Award for Best
Emerging Author**

When Kelvin returns to his home town on the southern coast of New
South Wales he finds himself drawn to a community that lives back in
the hills. He meets Jessica, a would-be writer who has escaped the city,
and her enigmatic neighbour, Carl. Both are pursuing new lives
inspired by the extraordinary landscape around them.

As his relationship with Jessica intensifies, Kelvin is caught up by
some of the more radical elements in the community. No-one, however, is quite who they seem, and Kelvin makes a decision that will
have devastating consequences for all of them. Deep in the southern
forests, the story builds to a dramatic climax.

An Accidental Terrorist is thrilling to the final page. It's a compelling account of the everyday struggles of a man trying to come to
terms with the decisions he's made and the life he's built.

'Lang structures his story well, the tension and conflict building to
a dramatic climax. An impressive debut.'

Sydney Morning Herald

' . . . hypnotically written and engaging'

Australian Bookseller & Publisher

ISBN 978 0 7022 3520 7

SWALLOW THE AIR
Tara June Winch

**Winner of the David Unaipon Award for Indigenous Writers and
the Victorian Premier's Literary Award**

*'When Billy and me lost our mother, we lost ourselves. We stopped
swimming in the ocean, scared that we'd forget to breathe. Forget to
come up for mouthfuls of air.'*

When May's mother dies suddenly, she and her brother Billy are taken
in by Aunty. However, their loss leaves them both searching for their
place in a world that doesn't seem to want them. While Billy takes his
own destructive path, May sets off to find her father and her Aboriginal
identity.

Her journey leads her from the Australian east coast to the far north,
but it is the people she meets, not the destinations, that teach her what
it is to belong.

In this startling debut, Tara June Winch uses a fresh voice and
unforgettable imagery to share her vision of growing up on society's
fringes. *Swallow the Air* is the story of living in a torn world and finding the thread to help sew it back together.

ISBN 978 0 7022 3521 4